To Tom,

Stay focused—

Be safe—

write!

B...

6·06·

THE DEVIL OF SHAKESPEARE

THE DEVIL OF SHAKESPEARE

A NOVEL

Billy McCarthy

BENBELLA BOOKS
Dallas, Texas

BenBella Books
6440 N. Central Expressway
Suite 508
Dallas, TX 75206

Send feedback to feedback@benbellabooks.com
www.benbellabooks.com

BENBELLA

Printed in the United States of America
First BenBella Printing: June 2004

10 9 8 7 6 5 4 3 2 1

Cover design by Andy Carpenter   ·
Interior designed and composed by John Reinhardt Book Design

Distributed by Independent Publishers Group
To order call (800) 888-4741
www.ipgbook.com

For my father, Bill Sr., and Gordy "Hawkman" Hawkes.
The great really do die young. I miss you both.

ACKNOWLEDGMENTS

FOR YOUR SUPPORT AND ENCOURAGEMENT through friendship and professionalism, I am blessed to have the following people's support.

My beautiful mother Eleanor. The finest cook of Italian cuisine.

Karen, Ray Bixman & family. Catherine and Patrick McCarthy.

Professor Don Southard and Mary McCarthy.

Vince Manglardi and family: Thank you for your faith in me. I will never forget.

Susan Welter: For hanging in.

Barb Groshon: Fate works.

John Digles, Sarah Allen and The MWW Group.

Editor, Kent Carroll: Getting the job done–right.

Attorney Dale de la Torre: For your guidance and honesty.

Glenn Yeffeth and the entire staff at Benbella Books.

Cousin, Lisa Colangelo: For your brilliant advice.

Chip Z'Nuff, Bobby Zakhar, Justin Collet, Ron Flynt, Donny Paska, Rich Hazdra, Jani Lane and James "JY" Young.

Dave Muhr at Muhr Design.

Maggie: For your patience, intuition and love.

If I have missed anyone, please know you are certainly not forgotten.

AUTHOR'S NOTE

When I began this novel, I vowed to stay away from the remedy used in many thrillers, which consists of haunting spirits within the walls, and dead people that we all know will never walk.

For me, reality within fiction is why I've dubbed this story believable fiction.

I tried to write truthfully in the voice of blue-collar America and guess the whisperings of the inner Hollywood machine through my fortune of wandering within both communities.

Let's face it: television and movie screens paint a brighter, fortunate life at one time or another not only to the main character in this book, David Faulkner, but to all of us.

On Oscar night, I'm slightly enthralled, yet somewhat embarrassed over the many camped-out celebrity disciples screaming from those bleachers as they wait for hours, the star's arrival. Everyday laypeople abandoning integrity for a simple smile or nod from the celebrity they think they know.

Why is society obsessed with celebrity? Why do most buy into it? Occasionally, I buy. Not obsessively, but I am buying.

Hero is defined as distinguished, admired for brave deeds and noble qualities. These days, it's seemingly clear, interrogations, investigations, and ultimate sins are defining hero, because these days, after the smoke has cleared, we have again forgotten and forgave—much too easily. Unfortunately, sin and hypocrisy will never leave our world. It's too easy to purchase.

Within *The Devil of Shakespeare* are the voices of characters in ink from several walks of life. Voices I could feel cheering on my narrative as they fought for position. I could also feel them scorning my blatant take on their conscience.

In the end, as much as I despise some characters within this novel, or however hurtful or offensive their voices may appear to you (and me), to sugarcoat would be hypocrisy itself. About as believable as dead people who walk.

Is *The Devil of Shakespeare* painful honesty? It's your conscience, and, in the end, your definition of hero.

Yours,
Billy McCarthy

"We are all the greatest actors; it's just the lucky few who are grossly overpaid for it."

—Darian Fable

PART ONE

CHAPTER 1

THE SUN'S TWENTY MINUTES from waving goodbye to 12-year-old David Faulkner. He's finally finished his ordered chores on this scorching Friday in June. In nine slaving hours, he's clipped and bagged bundles of crab grass that checkerboard throughout the lawn of the brownstone bungalow he *vegetates* in. He's tugged out the dandelions *that never seem to fucking die* from the lumpy and cracked walkways of his cornered property. He's ripped up weeded shrubbery, which weaves the rusty cyclone fence that partitions neighboring territory. He's hosed down and stood in formation the many gimmick garden tools he's never had patience with in the paint-flaked two-car garage. The garage that obscures the spoked rims on Auntie Judy's brand-new '88 Mustang convertible, and abeds his father's '73 rusted-out Ford pickup that still starts in the blistering cold Midwestern months.

Now David whacks with a broom every corner of the home's basement, which he's coined "the Tomb." The sandy, concrete walls pant dust as he jabs, while mice hang on with their tiny frightened paws. Along the rotted 4x4s that run the entire length of the Tomb's ceiling, his bristled sword is now shrouded in a spider's web of cotton candy. But he continues to jab, showcasing his youthful quickness and fine precision of swordsmanship. It's the old Hollywood black-and-whites relived again; "Zorro the Great, that's who I am, come out, come out—wherever you are!"

He taunts the rodents, who scurry from their battlefield. But destruction means quicker desertion from the scary Tomb. He fears that the field mice and a lone "King Rat" will sprint and climb his flared pant leg to defend their buddies.

The dampness in the air was refreshingly cool today in the dusty Tomb. Maybe he'll revisit tomorrow, when he launders his few hand-me-downs of blue jeans, soiled socks, T-shirts, and other dead-people's wardrobes he garbs in from his yearly shopping spree at the Salvation Army store.

• • •

It's 8:35 P.M. and David's spun around the grounds one more time to assure no root shows life, no weed intends to blossom, and no web dreams of spinning. Toiled, exhausted, and dehydrated from the enemy sun, his limbs are in dire need of a *drop*. But not just any drop. Once inside his walls, David drags his way to the bathroom for a splash of cool water to his sauteed arms and neck. He fingers the flagrant scar above his left brow that has blended well with the burn he received today, compliments of Mother Nature.

Why am I so pretty?

Too pretty for a boy.

Go away Cindy Crawford mole above my top lip.

Fucking sissy.

Get zits.

Eat more chocolate.

Get ugly.

Drink more beer.

Fit in.

He twists his expression in the mirror, impersonating the King Rat's fangs. He's tried to be ugly and evil, but he's failed. His right ankle isn't as tender as yesterday, but he feels a stab when leaning his 103 pounds in a tilt. His temple pounds when he cocks open his jaw to peek at the molar, which stings daily now. He feels weak and dizzy. *Don't cry sissy—pick at that girly mole.*

The heat and humidity have caught up with him. But strength kicks in from the KFC wing from his father's fridge that was about as moist as the roof of his cottonmouth. That's not healthy feeding, he panics, but soon remembers the fried-egg sandwich with mayonnaise he scarfed at five. Since then, he hasn't had a dandelion to eat, and his flimsy bones at 5'6" are trembling as he tippy-toes forward to the mirror. He longs for a mother to make him a proper dinner; like the mothers he sees on a matinee movie screen or nightly television sitcom. He longs for a mother to ice his sore ankle, and deliver lemonade and praise for his splendid landscaping.

"All done?"

"Good boy!"

"You're so cute. I love you!"

Keep longing.

Why?

Because for ten years his mother is nowhere to be found. She went out for smokes on the evening that the '70s had six hours to live. David was two. She never returned. Ever since his house is not a home. He longs for a father to deliver him the love and guidance one desperately needs in this unforgiving world of man. But his father is all of the above, minus the guidance and love.

Hobbling to the kitchen, David snags a beer from the chilled formation of cans that dominate the refrigerator. Popping the seal, he chugs the chilled sedative to numb the sting of his rotten molar, soften the blow to his tender temple, and dizzy up his state of despair. Checking the stove clock at 8:45 P.M., he allows himself seven minutes to shower. Then he must get down to his homework—the one subject he faithfully studies before every sleepless night. So far this week, it's been Al, Robert, the dead Jimmy, and Marlon. Tonight, it will be his favorite teacher of all, Jack. *Jack Nicholson rules.* He scans the video boxtop while ignoring the deadline of his shower. His bully bastard father should arrive home around one or two from his nine-to-five workday; and it's anyone's guess if Auntie Judy scored a one-nighter some fifty miles north in the big city of downtown Chicago. Timing is crucial. Timing is everything. Timing is peace, for pain is king, in the walls of his father's chateau at 1933 Maple Avenue. Descending backward onto his natted mattress and soiled sheets, David glances at the box cover for a summary of the plot. The ceiling fan above seems to spin faster, as he stares in his comforting lay. Suddenly, the boy's instinct takes control, which, so far, has always played so right. He'll skip his shower for now and gulp more cans of his medicine. Then he'll sneak into his father's closet and snag that red crushed-velvet smoking jacket his mother left behind, and lounge in fear of Daddy's arrival, while tending to his scriptures.

CHAPTER 2

SHE'S KNOWN THROUGHOUT the work-drink-and-die-at-sixty town of Pleasant Park as the whore sister of Bustin' Bud Faulkner. At 38, she has only hours left to her looks, awakes in a different bed each sunrise, and has no desire of ever strolling the white runner toward an altar. She's a lust for the town's barfly men, an embarrassment to her only sibling, and a "trouble-making bitch" to the many women who lack the sexual steamings of loudmouth Judy Faulkner. At 5'9" and built for bed, the former volleyball spiker out of Old Main High holds up better than any woman her age in town. But her nightly juice and substance abuse are now cock-a-doodling crow's-feet under the tanning-bed tan she sports all four seasons.

Judy's down to her *final* hour.

You see, lately, times have been tough for Judy, or "Shudey," as she pronounces an hour before last call. In the past year, she's been scorned by both of her steadies. One was a "nigger" in the neighboring town of Roseland, who owned a carwash her nephew David worked at in June when brother Bud wasn't looking. The nigger bagged Judy and David's summer allowance. When Bustin' found out, he beat the "jungle bunny" silly. Then, there's the crooked Pleasant Park cop on a force of three. The cop was married part-time with two kids, but found full time to fuck Judy in his squad car, stalk her day and night, and continue to beg for more. He eventually gave up on her for a bubble-gum debutante, who worked the town's only video store—which is why Judy now flees nightly into downtown Chicago. Maybe there, she prays over her Absolut and cranberry, she can finagle a big-city lawyer or Board of Trade broker into a two- or three-day rendezvous. Then she can suck them dry, from cock to wallet, while bogarting her addictions far away from the soil of ugliness she was born to *rot* in.

• • •

OUTSIDERS UNFAMILIAR WITH PLEASANT PARK may be lured by the serenity of birds humming, neighbors chumming, and children swinging in the park. Sure birds do hum, and most neighbors chum, but only a handful of the cliquey 1,200 residents are swinging with innocence. Two miles of the three that stretch through town are dominated by trailer park homes. From a bird's-eye view it replicates a military base—outlined by dirt roads and filled in by stubby brick homes. Then there's the cemetery field, a mile wide to be exact, piled with the town's forefathers. The plumbing is weak and reeks of sewer along the walls of most homes and every small business on Main Street. The power is so weak, the electricity blows out below thirty in the winter months, and count on a weekly outage in the scorching summers. The sun may shine in California, but after August, it never shines on Pleasant Park. The only beauty in fall and winter is the dark blue sky that threatens downpours on the potholed roads, but for some strange reason always bluffs.

But not to worry, for the Lord is their light. Everyone prays in Pleasant Park, but they pray their own way, to their own God, and in their own homes. Prayer and religion are rituals to Pleasant Parkers. But it's a secret religion and it's a silent God. Not Catholic, Protestant, and don't you *dare* mention the word synagogue. Just pick a God, any God. *But don't tell nobody.* Just light your candle in your window to show you're practicing. Then ask your God for funds at Old Main High and Collins Grammar School. You see, the funds Pleasant Parkers pray for are not for books or computers—which are scarce and obsolete. They pray for football gear. That's right, football *is* God in Pleasant Park, and don't you ever forget that. Basketball is for those "jungle bunnies" next door in Roseland—baseball is for those "middle-class sissies" in Canary. Football is contact. Football breaks limbs.

At fifteen you can get your driver's license, and at eighteen you can taste your first legal drink—beer. The best beer in the world, microbrewed by Pleasant Park German immigrants, since 1896. Eighty percent of Pleasant Parkers are German and ten percent are spics. Five percent *dough spinners*, or *wops*, for the town's two pizza places that sit on the only major crossroad. And those "niggers, they'll never get in." Who cares if Illinois cuts the town from any financial aid.

Who needs a McDonald's or a Blockbuster Video? *Shit, ride the newly paved blacktop into Canary and pick one of 'em up.* And Illinois governor, Pete Hodgkins, couldn't agree more when it comes to Mayor Robel and his "Pleasant Park hypocrites." Together, they're both stubborn over the Parkers' refusal to admit any outsiders of a darker shade of pale. Hodgkins will never budge, ever since 13-year-old Tyrone Watkins was found beaten to death outside the cyclone gates of the East Street junkyard. Beaten, by five rounds from a cop's gun after suspicion of hubcap theft. But all's fine for Pleasant Parkers. They have just enough to get by.

In the morning, it's to Dunkin Donuts, the second major business chain in town behind Burger King. Then, on Fridays, for pizza at Marrolie's or Spazzeri's. Salami sandwiches on white bread for lunch. Bloody beef on their dinner plates, potatoes with butter floating, and sour cream layered on like a mud pie. More starches, more cholesterol, and more frustration after the first sip in the town's only pub, Swiggs Tap. Their lack of fluency, compliments of Mother Alcohol, has their founding fathers' dialect slanging "d'money," "d'Sox," "d'fuckin' niggers," and "d'oes fuckin' Bears." Most are hungover when they awake, crooked on their morning drive to work, drunk during work, drunk after work, and drunker than a wounded skunk when they close their bitter eyes at night to pray. *The people in Pleasant Park are angry.* You can smell the alcohol seeping from the townspeoples' pores in the summertime, when every day is hot and stickier than a wet lollipop littering one of its many dusty roads.

The people in Pleasant Park are filthy.

• • •

HER STRAWBERRY-BLOND HAIR whips across her hazel-brown eyes and sticks to her lip gloss, as she speeds southbound from the city of Big Shoulders.

• • •

AN HOUR INTO STUDYING, David drags on his twelfth Marlboro Red, as the sweet sounds of Pavarotti on his Walkman drown out the audio of his black-and-white TV. But who needs sound? This is the boy's favorite scene in the flick, where Jack's getting dressed and getting burnt out on his temp live-in girlfriend known as "Bobbie." By the bulge under little David's smoking robe, Bobbie's looking quite healthy as she lies miserably and bitches away to Jack in her black-lace bra and matching panties. David's eyes sneak a nipple shot as Bobbie snaps off her bra.

"Oh yeah, what a rack," he grins. "I like this older *broad,* Bobbie," he emulates Jack. "She *sure is* a real *ballbuster.*"

But it's an instant buzz kill when the telephone echoes down the hallway, outside his bedroom door. David jogs to the receiver and picks up before its second ring. *The medicine is working.*

"It must be Mom for the billionth time," he longs.

"Sorry I haven't called, but I still hate your father's guts. Could we meet somewhere tonight? Perhaps the airport and fly away for-ever?"

"Yeah, but why'd you wait so long?"

"I had to, sweetie, you wouldn't of understood, you were only two."

"Hey cutie!" Reality pierces his ear. "It's your auntie Judy!"

Keep longing.

"Whatcha doing?" she asks.

"Nothing, just watchin' the movie you rented me."

"Really? Good boy! Which one you watchin'?"

"Something Knowledge," he plays dumb.

"You mean, *Carnal Knowledge?*"

"Yep."

"Do you like it?"

"I like Jack," he grins.

"Jack! Jack! Jack! You're gonna be bigger than Jack one day aren't you?"

"Yep."

"Did ya do ya chores?"

"Yep."

"Light a candle?"

"Uh huh," he lies.

"Pray to God?"

"Uh huh," another lie.

"Whatcha pray for?"

"Things."

"So whatta ya think of Jack's ole' lady?"

"Kinda reminds me of you." Begging for a last fuck, he bites his tongue.

"Really. Now tell me Davie, in what way could *she* remind you of *moi*?"

"Don't know," he blows a smoke ring, "just does."

"You saw her pussy?"

David blushes. The clattering of freeway traffic clashes with the classic rock from Judy's car stereo.

"No … I just … "

"Just what?"

"Don't know," he blushes. "Maybe just the way she acts."

He searches for an out.

"And how does she act?" She won't let it go.

He searches again. Pause. Silence.

"Well, don't let your dad find out I gave you that movie. Shit, he'll just go off on me and all. You know what I mean, don't you?"

Whew! Relief.

"I'm not *stupid*, you know."

"I didn't say you were stupid! I'm just telling you the movies are—just between us! 'Member? It's our little secret."

More time. More thought. Finally, he gives in.

"Whatever," he mumbles.

"Whatever? Hey, you still like our little secret?"

Another long drag from his smoke and a longer pull of his liquid medicine. Judy fears the worst from his childlike stubbornness. Her cell batteries begin to fade as static invades their connection.

"Hello? Hey! Hellloooo?" Judy yells.

David hears a horn and manly laughter. *Probably spread her legs to a trucker. Better yet, stood up while steering and mooned the poor blacks along the El tracks.*

He finally speaks. "Yep."

"Yep what? Yep you like our little secret? What's that! Can't hear you!"

"I said yeah!"

"Shit, speak up boy!"

"I'm trying!"

"Okay, good! Hey, I think I'll pick you up another movie this week. How 'bout a nasty one?"

Here we go again.

"Nah, the acting's lame in those," he yawns.

Judy bursts into laughter so hard it falls to a hacking cough.

"You ain't supposed to study the acting! In those movies, you study body language. Body language sums up your *whole* personality darling. It's the kind of acting you'll thank your auntie for when you're all grown up. Listen to me. Practice makes perfect, and I'm the *best fuck* in this *whole city!*"

More horns. She laughs, then sneezes.

"Bless you."

"Thanks."

"Still have hay fever?"

"Yeah. Where's your dad at?"

"Don't know, probably down at Swiggs."

"Well, I'm on my way in, and I'll be staying over. You excited?"

David pauses. *Maybe. Drugs. Protection from the monster. His fingers in and out of her hairy bush. Wetter than a water slide at Great America.* Any love is good love, and he'll take what he can get.

"Yeah, whatever." He chugs his beer.

"Good, you want a hotdog and some french fries?"

"I ate already," he squashes the empty can in his hand.

"Well then, ya wanna taste me tonight?" *Something new, never been there, not too sure.*

"Answer me you little fucker!" she shouts, like a dominatrix.

"Hello? I can't hear you." He bluffs for an out.

Auntie finally lets it go. "Get back to your movie, I'll see ya soon."

He snags another can of chilled medicine then heads back to his room. He reaches under his four-inch foam mattress and pulls out a framed 8x10 glossy headshot of his mother. He studies her eyes. He asks himself, why do eyes follow you from a picture but never in real life?

Mother had passionate eyes, seductive eyes.

Eyes that smile, eyes that bitch.

Eyes that conquer, eyes of success.

She had…the eyes of a Star.

She may be gone, but her eyes are watching.

I know they are. They're the eyes that haunt around the coldness of my empty closet, while I sleep with one eye bewaring.

It's more than the field mice that nip their way throughout these plastered walls at night.

As he swigs his medicine, the boy studies his mother's eyes. "I know you're watching me, but why? See ya!"

He whips the photograph into the closet—glass, frame, and all. *Take that, you bitch! You poser, nobody, whore, selfish, stubborn bitch! Fuck you, Mom, motherfucker! Fucker Mom!*

The few swaying wire hangers *clang* to the linoleum floor similar to the church bell chimes that echo in Canary. But theirs is not as loud, beautiful, nor as hypocritical. He meant that violent toss a minute ago, but now regrets it. The boom causes the mice to scamper up and down the inside of the walls. Above, the ceiling wobbles from the spinning blades of the fan. *It sounds like the ruckus of a thirty-pound alley cat. Probably with eyes that match hers. But it's moving too fast and is too determined. It's that rat. It has to be. Dirty, ruthless and cold-hearted.* He releases the pause button on his VCR and cranks the operatic screamings on his Walkman till his head spins. He's vented, and now has the drop he's been longing for all day. The frame was only a buck down at Pic-A-Dollar, and there's many more glossies of his drama-queen mother stacked in the cluttered mess of his father's closet.

You like our little secret? Answer me, you little fucker.

CHAPTER 3

BUD FAULKNER SLUMPS BACK on his stool, crossing his dusty arms, while surveying his bloated face in the mirror across the bar at Swiggs Tap. At 6'6", 320 pounds, Bustin' Bud (as he's still sucked up to in town) was once an All-American middle linebacker at Old Main High. Early on, all bets were on Bustin' to turn pro after he was accepted into a Big Ten college. But only if he upped his poor 1.8 scholastic average. The only way to get there was if Bud cooled his after-game guzzling and hung on to his Swedish steady and high school drama queen, Elke. Now all bets are off on Bustin'. Now he's loaded on brewery suds, and is fatter than the alley cats that piss in the corners of his dungeon basement. Not to mention he's lost his drama-queen wife and the only tackling Bud's doing is for a measly $200 a week on the concrete floors of Pleasant Park's Auto Body Shop.

• • •

TONIGHT BEING PAYDAY, Swiggs Tap has mixed up its finest batch of filthy-fingernail name taggers with "Bob" and "John" sewn to their

14

greasy work shirts. Then there's the divorced women with nicotined chops and dirty toenails, who, over the jukebox overtones of Neil Young or Lynyrd Skynyrd, toss their Jell-O cleavages from one stool to another—hoping to score a rail of coke to retrieve behind the closed doors of the ladies room.

As the men flick caked grease from their fingernails, they pretend to pay homage to the WWF circus on three of the tubes suspended from the ceiling. The satellite weather channel is gathering clouds from the fourth corner. All this fine visual entertainment is free of charge from the tap's proprietor, Charlie Swiggs. Charlie loves pro wrestling, but is obsessed with weatherman Tom Turkskin's forecast of darkness five days a week. "Turk's the man" to Charlie, because the heat with no sun is profit-making at this neon-lit property, Swiggs Tap. The forecast is also important to the gambling patrons come college-game time on Saturday. Charlie never leaves his corner of the bar, because it's a perfect shot of the door—and of Pammy, the plump blond bartender, as she moves to the register, which sits some five feet away. As Charlie eyes Pammy's ringing and the swarming Doppler System, he appears to be quiet and calm, but underneath he's a sneak. He's a 6'4" closet worrier who barely smiles and rarely speaks a word. He just roams his eyeballs from corner to corner, following every move and shake of Pammy's chunky ass. His pasty baby face swells when leaning his massive potbelly into the rim of the bar. His three and a half chins are a gift of beauty from gulping twenty mugs of suds each night. Charlie makes decent money off his religious patrons, but, in turn, loses it all to his Irish bookie, Smitty, who frequents the tap never before Thursday and always on a Monday, after five.

Tonight, the men are mumbling parleys over tomorrow's opener between the Fighting Irish of Notre Dame and "The Fucking Hillbillies" of Texas A&M. The drunken McCallister sisters continue to lose on the poker machine, while mumbling to one another about the cost of feeding their rug rats at home. Everyone at Swiggs takes advantage of the public therapy sessions. The men moan across the bar about the lazy, flabby, bitchy wives they married out of Old Main High. Then they bitch about the money they'll need to fork over to the "ex-bitches" for the kids' public schooling in September.

The people in Pleasant Park are ugly.

• • •

BUSTIN' BUD STARES AT THE TOP SHELF of 100-proof desserts. He needs to level his blood sugar out after the four dogs with onions, ketchup, and relish he's just devoured for dinner. So far, he's had five shots of Crown Royal, and an unknown number of 50-cent mugs of draft. But now his *buzz* has been interrupted from the dogs, and he needs to fire it back up.

Bud feels a friendly squeeze to the back of his beefy neck.

"Oh, Bustin', how the hell are ya?"

"Whoow, goddamit!" Bud swings his stool around. "If it ain't the fuckin' Germmy!" He looks over his former high school teammate from his steel-toed boots to the M on his MACK TRUCK baseball cap. Herman Robel is the only person in town nicknamed "The German." Everyone likes Herman, and why not? His dad, Stedman, has been mayor for twenty-one years, so it's a given ole "Hermmy" will die in the political job he holds as the Park's streets and sanitation supervisor.

Bud reaches to pull an empty stool in closer. Hermmy opts to stand and leans his truckish frame into the bar. He wiggles a toothpick between his teeth nodding "heys," while tipping his brim to all who tip back.

"How's work going at the shop?" the German asks his paint-splattered captain.

"It fucking sucks—just like life. Pammy!" Bud hollers across.

"What now, Bud?" Pammy hollers back.

"Get a round for me and the German."

"Oh, *hell no*, Buddy! Just stopped by for a quick look, that's it," Hermmy panics.

"Oh, what the fuck, Hermmy, you a married pussy now? Loosen the fuck up and have a shot with the Buster Boy." Bud nearly pleads.

The German also blew his chance at the pros, but at a smaller Big Eight school. But Hermmy isn't frowning, since his job as supervisor pays more than most in town, at $290 take-home per week. Not bad to raise two kids on, not to mention the payoffs from small business owners in Canary or "those bunnies in Roseland" who may need a load of blacktop to cover their weeded lawns for basketball courts. Pammy strolls over.

"Hey Hermmy," she smiles.

"Hey Pammy," he blushes.

"So what's it gonna be now, Buddy?" she tosses a fresh coaster. "How 'bout a bite of your ass?" Bud cracks.

Hermmy laughs. Everyone joins in. Pammy smiles. Charlie *frowns.*

"If you wrestled I might," she points to a corner tube.

"Shit, I'll kick anyone of those sissy asses," Bud smirks. "Hit me with a Goldschlager."

Hermmy backs off from his lean. "Goldschlager? I don't want *no* part of that stuff," he tugs his cap's white beak. "Just get me a draft, okay, Pammy?"

Bud ignores Hermmy as his eyes follow Pammy's stretching reach to the top shelf. Pammy has her meat distributed in all the right places. She's not solid, not fat; just healthy. She's got an ounce or two of *steam* in her look. Sometimes Bud teases, calling her "Pepper," because she resembles Angie Dickinson of *Police Woman.*

Bud slaps Hermmy's arm. "I'd like to poke her wouldn't you?"

"Shit, Bud, *you're* ..." Hermmy catches himself almost saying the married word.

Bud misses it as he concentrates on the bottle Pammy holds.

"Did you know those are real 14-carat gold specks floating around in that bottle?" he says to Hermmy as Pammy sets up and pours.

"Get outta here!" Hermmy doesn't buy.

"Not joking!"

"He's right!" Pammy adds.

"Here's something else I bet you don't know," Bud adds.

"What's that?"

"There's real 24-carat gold on Notre Dame's fucking football helmets!"

Hermmy thinks a moment and strokes his beard. *This could be a rare moment of* Final Jeopardy *at Swiggs.*

"Now that I knew!" He slaps Bud's arm proudly.

"Yeah, no wonder it's a goddamn fortune to go there!" Bud blares to all.

Everyone laughs.

Hermmy grabs his mug. Pammy snatches a five from the soggy singles on Bud's side. Charlie eyeballs her move to the register. *$2.00 better pop up.* It does. No wonder she's on her twelfth year. Bud salutes to Hermmy and raises his 14-carat specks.

"Well Robel, here's to the blue and gold I never got to wear, and

God dammit, I should've." Then down his hatch the gold specks of Bustin's dreams vanish.

Hermmy tries to calm his old captain. "Come on now Buddy with this *should of* shit. Live in the future, not the past."

"Oh yeah, the future. Easy for you to say," Bud stares into his empty shot glass. Herman senses it's time to baby-sit.

He and Bud rarely see each other because Hermmy rarely gets out. The German pretends to focus his attention on the WWF that's drowned out by the jukebox and his eavesdropping on the conversation a few stools down. Hermmy may act concerned for his former team captain, but underneath his premature gray beard, he's a seasoned town gossip. He fronts as a motherly listener and stores every word in his tiny brain. Just gather the leaves and the German will strike the match. Especially every word from this distraught *buddy* he may only run into once a month. If Hermmy Robel can't tell you how much you owe Smitty from last week, your marital problems at home, or when your family last ordered a pizza from Marrolie's, his wife, Jane, can. She's editor for the *Pleasant Post Newsletter.* It's a ten-page newspaper delivered free once a month to every villager's doorstep. It sets out to be a typical small-town paper, but screams more like a rap sheet about the month's DUIs and spousal abusers. Then there's the missing-person section "that wants to know" any information regarding the eight-year-old disappearance of Pleasant Park's former goddess, Elke Faulkner. The German smells a story and closes in. "Heard anything on Elke yet?" He leans closely to Bud. *A word that kills.* Elke.

Bud reaches to the pockets of his work trousers and rips his asthma piece out. His blood pressure jolts upward to 220. Sweat beads his forehead. He's sucking that asthma piece hard, wrestling with anger, while gasping for air. Sure it may be nobody's business, but he's in Pleasant Park.

"Pammy, another shot!" Bud orders angrily. He wipes his forehead. *The nerve of this fucker.*

"Now Hermmy, what kind of question is that? I mean it's been eight fuckin' years!"

Hermmy throws his arms in the air.

"Now don't go acting stupid," Bud's eyes flare up, "and as long as we're on the subject, do me a favor and tell your wife to take Elke's picture outta the goddamn paper! She wasn't fuckin' kidnapped, and let me set the record straight right now, okay, Hermmy?"

Hermmy's all ears.

"She wiped out her fucking closet!" Bud spills.

"What do you mean?"

"Don't you get it? She was just an unhappy whore like all the women in this fucked-up town. There, print that!"

Bud swings around and faces the mirror. Pammy returns with another shot and draft.

Hermmy turns away. Bud's general comment on women couldn't have applied to his wife, Jane? She's a good wife and he's a decent husband. They have a son, Josh, who's well balanced and going to be a pro quarterback one day. Their daughter, Betty, is the swim-team captain at Old Main. He's not like Bud, who's lost his piece-of-ass wife every man's eyes undressed at the annual Fourth of July parade. And what about that weird kid of his, who's too bony to play high school ball, has a chick's face, and is one of three faggots in some drama class out of a school of 250. Hermmy redeems takes a healthy gulp of his draft. He is now faced with a two-minute warning before his good buddy explodes. *Gotta keep plowing. Jane would be proud.*

"Just got back from Old Main and d'team looks good this year Buddy," he starts up.

"Oh yeah," Bud could give two shits. *Hurry up with another shot, Pammy.*

"Yeah!" Hermmy lights up. "Looks like Josh will jump to the varsity squad a year ahead."

"Well, good for you, German. Here's to your boy, Josh," Bud toasts.

Hermmy babbles on. "Yeah, hoping the kid sticks hard to it. Don't want him to fuck up like his old man did."

"Shit, you didn't fuck up, German—and besides, whatta ya' complaining about? For Christ sake, ya got a good job," *a nosy fat-ass wife, and a daughter uglier than sin,* Bud bites his tongue and swallows his beer.

"Yeah, I guess I can't complain," Hermmy sips, dazed and confused.

"You know, Bud," he leans in closely, "speaking of Josh, he says your boy didn't register for ball last month."

Bud plays deaf.

More shots arrive and disappear. His buzz is now refired. *Seven's always a charm.* But Hermmy's mouth has caused the captain to enter the danger zone.

"Let me tell you something, Germmy," he plops his hand on Hermmy's shoulder. "If you're tryin' to push my buttons, it ain't gonna happen. My kid's a sissy. He doesn't wanna play football. What can I say? He's got his mother's blood, not mine! He just looks pretty and watches movies all fuckin' day. He's a fuckin' *waste!* Whattya want?"

"Hey man, I'm not trying to push any of your buttons! I just think the kid was a lean and quick quarterback two years ago with Josh in junior league," Hermmy lies. "It's just a damned shame he's not moving on."

"Oh, yeah! Bullshit and more bullshit my man! Well guess what, *Herman*? Everything's a fucking shame! It's a shame I've got to get up every morning and sweat my ass off in the body shop spraying crippled cars. A hundred and ten fucking degrees in there today! It's a shame that *some* people never have to work an honest work because of politics, and it's a shame I could have been somebody in life, but I had to fuck up and have a kid right out of high school.

He slams his mug on the bar.

Nobody laughs ... not even a smile. They all know Bustin' Bud too well. He's either gonna turn on his buddy from Old Main or pick on someone his own size. Hermmy's bladder quickly summons him to the boys room. Bud gets a cold stare from Charlie.

"What the hell you looking at, Swiggs?" Bud stands and pulls his trousers high.

Charlie looks away to the radar screen. He knows better. He played on Bud and Hermmy's squad but the only dirt on his jersey was from the Hershey bars he smuggled to the bench he sat on. Bud salutes Charlie with his middle finger, and blasts out the side door—beer mug in hand. He climbs into his rusted-out pickup. It's only a four-block ride to 1933 Maple Avenue, where he can get tough and pick on someone his own size.

CHAPTER 4

THE FINAL CREDITS ARE ROLLING as little David opens his ninth can. It's time to close shop on his studies, but only after one more final take for the evening. He plays to the Farrah Fawcett poster above his bed.

(Bobbie) "So what's it gonna be?"

(Jack) "You sure know how to screw things up."

(Bobbie) "So where does that leave us?"

(Jack) "You giving me an ultimatum? Is this an ultimatum! Is this an ultimatum! Answer me you ballbustin,' castrating son of a cunt bitch! Because if it is, I'm gonna tell you what you can do with your ultimatum! I'm gonna tell you what you can do with it! You can make this goddamn bed! That's what you can do with it! Try and clean up this filthy pigsty! That's what you can do with it!"

He's nailed it. Jack is down. His vocal infliction, his attitude, and his movements. He's even got Bobbie perfectly. It's good to hit those high notes of a woman, David smiles. Never know, it might come in handy one day. I'm good. Oh, am I gonna be big. I'm gonna be outta *this* shithole town. It's a wrap, when suddenly the bedroom door is booted open Western-style. There sways the meanest cowboy in suburbia Illinois.

It's midnight, and Dad is early.

The surprise arrival of the *monster* causes panic even in the candle's innocent flame that sits kindling atop the window ledge. David's been caught off guard. He was just about to fire up another smoke and return the robe to the *monster's* closet. The boy freezes in shock. The tub-of-lard *monster,* pumping with asthmatic anger, is now *ready to rumble* the slender, lanky one; the frightened one who must now muster his youthful quickness to escape the grasp of this slow *has-been.* But the tubbo blocks every crevice of space the doorway has to offer. There is *no* escape.

"Whatcha' say to me?" the *monster* announces.

David's eyes freeze as does his tongue.

"Say what?" the *monster* speaks.

"Nothing, I ... "

"What d'fuck ya' doin with that robe on?"

"Sorry, I ..."

"Say what?" His boots move a step. "You been using that talk again?"

"No sir."

"Don't lie to me, I just heard!"

"Uh uh," he shivers.

"What were ya' screaming a minute ago, something 'bout making a bed?"

"Nothing, I ... "

"Where's your fuckin' aunt?"

"I don't know, sir."

"Why not?" He moves a step closer.

"I think she's out ... she's been out all day."

He starts to shiver as the *monster* takes another step forward.

He repeats himself for the record. "I said I don't know, *sir.*"

The *monster* pulls his dusty green trousers up above his bloated potbelly, then swats a mosquito that buzzes about his hairy ear. The backlighting that bleeds from the kitchen through the hallway paints Bud's expression as that of a circus clown who's finally gone *mad.*

"Did ya mow the lawn today?"

"Yes, sir."

"Clean d'basement?"

"Uh huh."

"Say what?"

"Yes, sir."

"Scrub d'garage floor?"

"Yes!" He trembles.

"Did ya' pray?"

"Yes I did, *sir*!"

"Mow d' lawn?" He tries to trip him up.

"Yes sir."

"Register for football last week?"

Silence.

David thinks, pauses.

"I don't ... "

Bad choice.

"You don't what?"

The clown towers over his enemy.

"You don't wanna play football? Is that what you're tryin' to say? Do you know who d'fuck I am?"

He kicks the boy's TV off the pedestal stand.

"Hah? Do—you—know—who the fuck I am!"

"No!" The boy begs.

He yanks him by the robe collar and slams him to the floor. Nothing to it, just like a feather pillow. The *monster's* ears ring with the roars and sounds of a high school marching band. The boy's fragile bones bounce hard off the floor, like the *monster's* did on Astroturf twelve years ago. At 5'7", 103 pounds, old Bustin's finally met his match.

He screams like a varsity coach—"Get up and get tough!"

The boy crawls to the closet just inches from an icicle of glass from that shattered picture frame.

The *monster* squats low—his forefinger and thumb around David's neck.

"I can kill you now you little bastard! Don't you ever lie to me you little fucker. Ya' hear me?"

The clown's mad. Maybe he'll throw David through the screened window? Why not? That'll wake him up. This is fun. The *monster* scoops him up and pins the boy against the wall.

"I was with that asshole Robel tonight, you little bastard! And he told me his boy didn't see you last month at football registration. And now word's around of how Bud Faulkner's kid's a loser and a faggot! He ain't *mean* enough to follow in his daddy's footsteps! Are you listening to me, you little pain-in-my-ass bastard?"

The glow of fright in David's eyes has to mean a *yes*, since there's nowhere to nod in the *monster's* clamp.

"I kept thinking what a mistake you were in my life and what a mistake your whore mother was! And then I thought how stupid I was to let her kill my only shot in life! Do you know what shot that was?"

He squeezes tighter.

David prays. *Take me now, God.*

"It was when she spit you out!" he says into his son's face.

He lets go and David slides to the floor, like a picture frame slipping off its hook.

Now, he's down to eye level of the *monster's* steel toe. That scruffy toe terrifies the boy. His sore temple begs for God's mercy. *I won't drink or smoke again; won't watch any movies that show bush; won't throw Mom's picture; won't use the f-word when killing spiders, tugging dandelions, or taunting "King Rat".* He expects that any second, the perfect petite nose he inherited from his mother will be crooked and pudgy for life. Although his perfectly straight teeth have escaped many blasts to his skull, it's suddenly a 2-to-1 bet that tonight they'll go like popcorn kernel. *Where are you, God?!*

Suddenly through the screened window rock music blares from a car that has pulled aside the house. The boy recognizes it, and so does the *monster*. It's the classic rock of that "sissy" band, Cheap Trick and their familiar haunting summer-hit melody, "Heaven Tonight." A whore has saved the day. *Mary Magdalene has risen.* The engine and music cut. The car door slams. The *monster* realizes his other bad half has arrived. He kicks the boy in the ribcage for a final goodnight. The *monster* then sways from the bedroom into the kitchen to greet his precious sister. *She'd better be goddamn holding a gram or two.*

CHAPTER 5

THE CANDLE STILL KINDLES as David peeks through the doorway and down the hallway into the brightly lit kitchen. Judy flings her keys, which jangle to the butcher-block table, and makes her way to the bathroom.

What perfect timing. Thank you, Lord. Now she can cool down the steamed beast. Auntie Judy loves me. Maybe too much. Maybe not? Who cares? She does love me.

"What the fuck are you looking at!" Judy snarls while strolling to David's doorway and zipping up her black Levi's.

"Where the fuck were you? This ain't no fucking flophouse!" says the *monster*.

"Don't start, asshole!" She stops in stride.

David plays asleep.

"Don't tell me where to start in my house, bitch!" the *monster* growls.

"Hey, baby, whatcha' doin?" Auntie lowers her voice upon entering David's room. With one eye, David can see she hasn't zipped all the way up. She plops aside him on the mattress. Her elbow pinches into his thigh.

"Ouch!" He suddenly awakes.

"Ooh! Sorry honey, ya' okay? What's going on in here, is he picking on you again? Did you miss me?"

She strokes his rosy cheeks with her fingers.

"He just got home," David whispers.

"What's this mark around your neck? Is that from your bandanna?"

"Poison ivy in the alley." *Three lies.*

She cradles the boy's head forward into her deep cleavage. With one free hand, she begins to rub slowly from his knees up—never stopping.

"Oooh yeah, happy boy," she whispers. "You're almost there aren't you?" She rubs firmer.

"You're gettin' hair down there?" she enters his briefs. "Don't worry, you're gonna be okay now. I'm here, I'll take care of you."

"What the fuck's going on in there?" Bud's voice blares down the hallway, through the bedroom and into the silent street.

"I'm gonna talk to your dad and maybe have a beer, then I'll check on you before I sleep, okay?"

David nods, knowing "before" means "never."

She pulls him close and captures his pudgy lips in hers, sneaking a tongue in, before waving her way into the kitchen.

The cleats on her boots resonate as she struts to the kitchen to greet her brother.

"Can't you just mind your own business? I was downtown fucking niggers. There ya' happy?"

"Wouldn't put it past ya. And that fucker in there's been in my beer!" he pants away.

"What did you say?" Judy's hands rest to her hips.

Bud ignores her.

"Let me tell you something, I'd rather fuck ghetto niggers than loser slobs who live in this town."

Let the games begin. David spies and cheers from the crack of his door. Go tell him, Auntie Judy. Kick him now. Right in the face with your steel-toed cowboy boot!

Bud's bloodshot blue eyes look into Judy's straight and cold.

"You know what you are?" he taunts.

"No, tell me!"

"You know."

"I know?"

"That's right."

"That's right?"

"Yeah, that's right."

"*Yeah! That-is-right!* Just like your *ex*-wife, a fucking slut! Is that what you're tryin' to say?"

Bud's watery eyes freeze wide. *The clown is back.*

Suddenly it's silent. So silent you can hear a freight train whistle two miles away.

Bud begins to choke up. First that robe, now *her* again. Embarrassment blemishes his bloated face.

Judy watches.

He'd like to punch the lip gloss off those nigger-cock-sucking lips, but he can't. His father taught him not to hit women. Just break them down verbally. He's obliged well. His mother was never hit, just smacked with enough Valium to put her in the grave after losing her husband of twenty years to a heart attack at 42. Bud was 10, Judy was 18. At the time some neighbors took over the reigns, but let 'em loose when Bud hooked up with the town's wealthiest family. They owned a bakery on Main Street named Seedin's, and had an only child. She was shy, blond, and her name was Elke.

Judy knows it's time to make amends.

"Don't just sit there, get me a beer," she orders while searching her purse. Bud turns his anger around, because "big sis" scored the white stuff, probably from a well-to-do downtowner. David returns to his foam mattress but continues listening in the dark.

"She ain't coming back is she?"

"Oh, get over it, Bud. Are you pathetic or what? I mean, what are you, a titty baby?"

Judy unwraps a folded white packet. She speaks softly, barely breathing over the fragile dust.

"Maybe one day, I don't know. Move on, there's plenty of women out there. Go out with one of the McCallister girls," she half smiles to his hurtful stare. "She never loved you anyway."

She chops away with a razor.

"Now why you sayin' that?" Bud is close to tears.

"Because she loved herself, Bud! Besides, she never fit in Pleasant Park; she was too fucking snooty; thought she was too good for everyone!"

"Well, where could she be?" He moans on.

"Who knows? She's probably living in L.A. with all the queers and weirdoes."

David's eyes awake. *That's where Jack lives! He ain't queer. I saw him on the Academy Awards. He dates that famous director's daughter who's as tall as the Sears Building... Anjelica Houston!*

The snorting and sniffling begins. The tension has eased. David sighs deep and his sore ribcage aches.

It's gonna be another long night of drinking, snorting, and carrying on. Soon, Auntie will make her way to my room. She'll soothe her fingers on my sore face. Then she'll tell me how handsome I'm gonna be when I'm older and how many women I'll have at my feet. But what does she know? She'll never settle down. She's Bobbie and Jack in *Carnal Knowledge*. Where can I run?

The answer is nowhere. He has no friends 'cause he's not into hanging out at the Burger King parking lot and being hit on by every laborer's pudgy daughter or beaten up by every corn-fed jealous jock. He's not into busting out windows in the sleeping homes of *niggers,* just minutes away in Roseland. Quietly, he leans into his door. Unfortunately, it won't shut all the way. He's forced to listen to the miserable overtones of two drunks. They'll taunt each other about their regrets in life the entire night, and do their twenty or so rails of coke on the family kitchen table. But David's brighter than most kids his age. He does say his prayers nightly and faithfully before he sleeps. He prays for little things to make him happy. Like finding a winning lottery ticket in that weeded alley and fleeing to the sunny hills of "Queers and Weirdoes."

He prays he'll marry a wife as beautiful as his lost mother, but stronger and patient, *till death do they part.* He prays to become a movie star and pay poor blacks and Mexicans triple minimum wage to cut his green acres of grass while he enjoys an afternoon drink and smoke with Jack. He prays for himself dying one day, and his father suffering in guilt over the loss of his only child. Then he prays for the *monster* himself to die. Die in pain. Set fire in his rusty pickup truck. Burn in hell you bastard! He then stops his dark dream and apologizes to God.

"I'm sorry," he whispers to the ceiling fan. "Take me God, I'll go. Either take me now, or give me the strength to bottle my suffering. Strength is all I need. Let me hold onto the pain for days, weeks and years to come, and I will put it to good use, my Lord. Just promise to keep me sane long enough to break free of this trap I fear to die in."

CHAPTER 6

THE JUKEBOX IS ON ITS THIRD REPEAT of Neil Young's "Rocking in the Free World," and little David Faulkner at seventeen has finally graduated. He's gone from stolen beer to a Coca-Cola laced with Crown Royal from his legal guardian's purse, who herself tees off on Long Island Iced Teas, as all four tubes showcase the World Wrestling Federation's Championship of the year at Swiggs Tap.

Young David has good reason to celebrate. His faith in God and nightly prayers paid off some six months before this night. No, he didn't win the lottery. Nor did God kill him off, like he does so many of the good that die young.

Instead, on New Year's day, at 2:31 in a cold, sub-zero, early morning, God chose the *monster*. Driving 60 in a 25 zone down icy Main Street after the town's annual New Year's Eve bash at the VFW hall, Bustin' kissed a crater-size pothole and slid right on into Seedin's Bakery front window. How ironic, and how *so sweet*. Elke's dead parents were probably applauding from the sky they rest in. The *monster* was killed instantly. The glass from the old windshield sliced right through his beefy linebacker neck. His decapitated head was held in place by the thick suede collar of his hunting jacket.

So now, the boy can finally rest. One of his prayers came true. But the prayer and dream he wishes for most lies some two thousand miles from home—in the land of *Queers* and *Weirdoes*.

• • •

OVER TWO DOZEN OF THE TOWN'S pro drinkers are gathered at Swiggs on a breezy early evening in June, to enjoy their Friday gulpings of 50-cent tap beer. There's Petey, the weathered, 100-pound "idiot" to the regulars, employed by Charlie to run the wooden basement stairs fetching cases of cans and bottled beer every hour. Between takes, Petey mops up the men's stall, whose slimy floor saturates hourly with urine from a broken toilet seal that's been leaking now for almost a year. Then there's Jose, the shy Mexican who used to run for parts at the body shop where Bud Faulkner once worked. Now, since Bud's death, Jose has climbed the ladder of opportunity and been promoted to the chief sprayer. Then there's Tony Fernandez, half Italian, half Mexican, a.k.a. "Bananas" for his love of banana daiquiris. No one ever heard of a daiquiri in Pleasant Park, let alone alcohol mixed with fruit. "Must be a queer drink," they all tease Tony who drives for C.J.'s Towing. He pulled Bud's limp carcass from the shattered glass of Seedin's.

Then there's Herman the German, who's talking in the corner with Charlie Swiggs himself. Ole Hermmy seems to be taking a turn for the worst, ever since his son, Josh, was rejected at the University of Illinois, his daughter, Betty, ballooned to 170 pounds, and in his guilty mind, it couldn't have been a pothole that caused his "good buddy Bustin'" to lose control of the wheel that night.

"Look at these fucking eyes!" Judy squeezes her nephew's cheeks.

"Have you ever seen fucking eyes like this before?!" she announces to everyone, who pities the kid's embarrassment.

The two McCallister sisters, still at the poker machine, turn, look, and then ignore Judy and dig in their purses for another twenty to burn.

Drunken Petey howls to anyone listening. "Boy's a little too pretty for 'round here."

Bananas breaks into a laugh.

"Bud's boy," Pammy nods a smile to the tiny Jose, who points to his mug of Budweiser, confused.

"No," Pammy shakes her head. "You know, Bud?—your old boss?"

Jose nods, but still doesn't get it. And never will, because the only English he comprehends is "boss."

"Isn't that Bud's kid over there?" Hermmy asks. He pulls a stool tighter to Charlie, who stares at the weather channel's Doppler screen.

"Yeah, and that's Bud's sister," Pammy answers for Charlie.

"That's Bud's sister?" Hermmy says.

"You're correct sir," she nods.

"Is that right. So that's the one that ran with that nigger from Roseland couple years ago?"

"And more," Pammy says as she sets a fresh coaster down.

"Got that right, big Hermmy!" chimes Petey two stools away.

"She's watching the kid now?" Hermmy stares their way.

"Yep, every night," Pammy answers. "After Bud died she sold the house. $17,000 cash," she whispers. "I don't get it though. She's living in a two-room dump a block away, with the kid, for 250 a month."

Hermmy's jaw drops. "You're kidding."

"Nope, figure that one out." She wipes the bar.

"Now wait a minute, Pammy. I knew Bud," Hermmy leans in, "and he couldn't of had home insurance that paid off at death. I mean come on."

"Who says it was home insurance?" Pammy smirks.

"Whatta ya mean?"

"Rumor 'round town has it she took out *life* on him."

"Life?"

"Yep. She's no dummy," Pammy smiles.

Charlie pretends to be glued to the tube. He hates the *punk* Faulkner kid. His dad was a drunk who beat anyone silly and stole at least a good dozen beer mugs on his way out. He only takes to the punk's aunt because she takes to Charlie. Since Bud's death, Judy's been secretly chumming him with nightly delights in the back office adjacent to the bar. That buys her a free pass to drag the kid in and blast her mouth off to anyone and not be blackballed.

"What about the kid?" Hermmy fakes a concern. "Shouldn't that be his money?"

Pammy shakes her head no. "Come on, Hermmy, she came in here 'bout a month ago bragging about how she bought him a new $200-mattress from Sears. Poor kid sleeps on the floor."

"Yeah, and what about that damn dirt bike," Charlie finally speaks.

"Oh yeah, I forgot," Pammy says. "He's got a Kawasaki dirt bike. 'Bout 1500 bucks. Fastest one around. Cops still trying to catch him to give warning to keep off Main Street."

"What? He can't drive no dirt bike on Main Street! What's wrong with that punk?" Hermmy looks serious at Charlie.

"Well, he does," Charlie says.

"Kid's a punk anyway," Petey speaks for Charlie. "She's probably fucking him, too. Shit, why not, she's fucked everyone else in town!" he adds.

Bananas shakes his head and grins. Hermmy's dumbfounded. The German's just seen a ghost. Sure Petey's an idiot, but to Hermmy, idiots have high IQs when it comes to gossip. And he should know. Charlie glares at Petey.

"Shut up, Petey. Get the mop and hit the john! When's that damn seal for the toilet coming in, Pammy?"

"Charlie, how many times have I said, we *don't* have to order it, Canary Hardware has one. It's a lousy two bucks. I told you over a month ago."

"Man is that kid gonna be fucked up." Hermmy wishes David the best.

"Already is!" Petey drains his mug and flees downstairs.

"His aunt looks *too* cozy next to him. And he looks different than most boys 'round here, doesn't he, Charlie?"

Charlie looks, then tugs his pants.

"He's got that oily shit in his hair, like Elvis," Hermmy smirks.

Bananas fills in for Petey. "Looks like Elvis. Probably needs a smack upside his head, too."

"Hey, Charlie," Hermmy says. "You let the punk in here to drink alcohol and smoke stogies?"

"He drinks Coke," Charlie mumbles.

"Oh yeah," Pammy covers. "Only Coca-Cola."

The German's now obsessed with the Faulkner boy. So bad, he can't, and won't, let go. David has more than a hunch he's being whispered about from across the ugly room.

"He's got those eyes you can see a mile away, like his mother had," Hermmy dreams and wishes.

"Good-lookin' kid, I'll give him that," Pammy dreams with him.

Charlie tugs his pants. "Kid's a bastard," he mumbles.

"Pammy, get me another draft. And hit me with another shot of that Goldschlager." Hermmy orders.

He then makes his way to the middle of the bar, to pay homage to the *cool* kid Betty's friends have a crush on. He hasn't seen little David since Junior League Football, and the kid's filled out pretty well. He's taller now, with the broadness of a Varsity basketball forward. This is a perfect opportunity for Hermmy to report to Jane on the orphan's well-being. He approaches the couple that's seated *strangely* close to each other.

"Hey, aren't you Bud's sister?" he asks.

Judy's long drag and bitchy smirk say "get lost," as she looks to David to answer. The punk eyes a James Dean smirk through the same mirror his father stared into nightly. He fiddles with his shades atop his head and plays deaf.

"Who wants to know?" Judy swings around and eyes the giant.

"Do you know who I am?" He extends his hand and smiles. "I'm Herman Robel. I played football with his daddy," he points to David, "in high school."

David blows a giggle of smoke. But nothing's funny, just dark. He begins to shiver his leg up and down from those five words that still haunt; *do you know who I am?*

"Football, ha," he mumbles to Hermmy via the mirror.

"Yeah, you're David, aren't you? Josh's friend!"

Two more haunting words. *Josh Robel*. The fucking snitch.

"Yeah, I guess I was," he lies.

"What do you mean—you guess you was?" Hermmy cocks his head, confused. "You and Josh were tight at one time."

The punk looks to his aunt, who intercepts for him.

"Ahh, excuse me ... Mr. ... Hermmy? He has a new name now, and it's not David."

"What do you mean it's not David?"

Judy swings around. "His new name is Darian Fable. He's not David Faulkner anymore. And while we're on the subject," she slurs, "guess what? He's going to be a big fuckin' movie star one day, so *you* look out!" she jabs her partner, Darian, with a friendly elbow.

Hermmy's stumped. *What's with this Darian shit? And what does Fabe-something mean? People in Pleasant Park are named Bob, John, Betty, and Sally. What kind of name is fucking Dario Fabis? Poor Bud's rolling six feet under.* The kid and her have secret sign language going on, and Hermmy wants in. David can tell his new ID is irritating the German. What more does this idiot want? "Get lost" the punk wants to yell. Hermmy's patience with the couple's game has now expired.

"You gonna play football at Old Main?" He leans in closer to intimidate. The punk doesn't budge. Instead, he blows another round of smoke, which clouds in Pammy's and Charlie's direction, who recognize the humiliation Hermmy is undergoing.

David senses it's time for "Darian" to take over.

"I don't go to school anymore," he says.

Hermmy frowns. "No? How 'bout sports? Don't ya' play sports?"

"Look, I have no desire to play football. I don't plan on ending up like every other *loser* in Pleasant Park. Like she said," he points to his aunt with his lit smoke, "I'm gonna be an actor."

"Oh now... an actor, huh?" Hermmy smiles to Bananas, who's stirring his daiquiri, keeping score.

"That's right," David nods. "You won't find me filling potholes in this shithole town when I'm forty."

The one-liner gets a chuckle from a stranger, a stool down.

Bananas looks away to save Hermmy from further humiliation. Judy gleams with pride at the quick verbal slicings from her boy. He's been trained well and Auntie's taking full credit. She licks her lip gloss and beams. He's turning her on.

Hermmy wants to crawl away from this booby trap, but needs to save his popular ego. *Jane will be highly disappointed.*

"Oh well," he finally gives up. "I just wanted to pay my respects to you, 'cause your daddy and I were good friends in high school." He extends his hand for a farewell shake.

But David sees only his father's brawny cold hand.

"My daddy was an asshole!"

And, with those five words, Hermmy grabs the punk by his silky mane, shoving him off the stool to the floor. Judy instantly lunges at the giant and pounds away with her fists.

"Hey, you big fucking asshole!" she screams.

The giant bends down to David, with Judy, the wild monkey, still punching.

"Your daddy raised you and don't you forget that!" He spits through his beard into David's frightened face.

Judy screams, "Charlie! Charlie! Get this fucker out of here!"

Pammy tries to look over the bar but can't see below to the patrons' side. She boosts herself over. "You okay, kid?"

"No, he's not okay!" Judy hollers. "Charlie, you fucker! Do something!"

Charlie tugs his pants then walks downstairs. Hermmy exits the bar at his own sluggish pace as if nothing had happened. The punk rises and swipes his crooked shades up from the floor. Judy notices a cut next to his left eye. Blood trickles down the punk's face. Judy slams her drink on the bar. Cubes jump. Juice splatters. She turns to Sally McCallister, who slips her a sixty-buck package. The boy named David, the punk turned Darian, and his aunt Judy then return to a mattress on the floor just around the corner from the tap.

CHAPTER 7

DAVID PACES THE ROOM with an ice cube wrapped in a paper towel he holds just above his eye. "I want out of here; I hate this fucking town."

"Just hold on, I have to show you something. You'll like it," Judy tells him.

She leaves and retreats to her bedroom, and returns with a Folgers coffee can. She pops the lid and dumps a wad of folded money in rubber bands, which bounce off the toe of his Doc Martens boots.

"I have a plan for us." Her eyes glow.

David's eyes widen at the many rolls that showcase Franklin's mug.

"What do ya' think?" She puffs her smoke with a sassy grin.

"Where did you get this?" He bends down and snatches a roll.

"Where do ya' think? Your aunt's no dummy, honey. I sold the house and was saving it till you were 21," she lies.

"God, how much is here?" He drops to his knees.

"'Bout nine or ten grand." She drags her smoke.

"Nine or ten grand? You mean that shithole was worth that much?"

"Well it was worth a little more. I mean, I've got some in the bank.

He bounces a roll on the orange shag carpet.

"So, what's your plan?" He catches his breath.

"Well, you're always dreaming of going to Hollywood and becoming a big movie star like your fucked-up mother wanted to do."

David doesn't smile.

"Hey, I'm just teasing!" she says.

"Whatever," he pampers the paper towel back to his eye.

"I was thinking, we could just make a split."

"Split?"

"Yeah, you know, you and I."

"You and I?"

"Yeah, me and you, the two of us! It's crazy out there in L.A., David," she slips. "Sorry, *Darian*. Anyway, I could take care of you. I could watch over you like I have been, and hell, who knows—maybe even be your manager! Whatta ya think? I know we could do it! You and fucking me! Ladies and gentlemen, I give you Mr. Darian Fable!" she bows.

David thinks. Slowly a smile comes to his face.

He's two for two. He's won the lottery. But with the newfound jackpot comes excess baggage. As he thinks, Judy snorts the celebration powder on her glass-top table. He knows he doesn't want to run around L.A. with a big mouth like her. Jack would run at the sound of her horn. But maybe he can deal with it. Anything to escape Pleasant Park.

"Sounds like a plan; when do we leave?" He heads to the kitchen for a cold beer and fresh paper towel.

"Well, first we'll have to book some airline tickets," she yells over the stereo. "It's cheaper if we wait a week, besides I'm gonna be busy getting things together this week, so why don't you look into it."

He returns and snaps off his bottle cap, slightly confused.

"I thought we were a team?"

"We are!"

"Then let's just split now—I mean what do we have here?"

"Come sit over here," Judy pats the sofa. He takes her invite.

"You were good today." She strokes his hair. "I'm proud of you. You know, I can pay someone to kick that German's ass. Do you want me to?"

"Let's forget about him. I want to talk about L.A."

"Just hold on now, okay? Just relax, get high, and then maybe we'll play a little bit. Whatta ya say? You wanna play a little with your auntie *Shudey* now, don't you?"

CHAPTER 8

THE MORNING AFTER SEES THE USUAL of cigarette butts overflowing a tiny aluminum ashtray. Twelve or more beer
bottles clutter with two empty, red Marlboro boxes.
A razor blade and powdered mirror rest, beaten, on an oak table,
the only piece of furniture aside from his mattress on the living-
room floor. David senses something went wrong again last night.
He senses, but *just can't remember*, because, for all the Faulkners,
it's common to have memory loss after a few too many, and he's no
exception. Naked, he gathers his clothes and checks his watch at
11 something A.M. He makes his way into Judy's room. He looks to
her bed, where the sheets are tangled, but she is gone. Did she say
something about going into the city, something about being busy
all week? In the darkened room he sees a clutter of clothes in the
corner, clothes over her opened dresser drawers, and clothes piling
out of the closet. Right now he'd like to search for that magic can
and count that cash. Maybe he'll get enough nerve to split town by
himself. *No, I can't*, his conscious dictates.

He makes his way into the kitchen for some water to get rid of his
dehydrated mouth and brush his teeth over the dirty plates that pile
the sink. He spots the coffee can lying under the kitchen card table.

Has she lost it?

He bends down to rescue the pot of getaway loot that sports the look of an abandoned child. He pops open the lid, where he discovers many green minibundles gone, replaced by some yellow notepaper. Sadly, the can only holds a thin stack of a frowning Jackson. He slips the cash out and reads the scribbled note.

> *My loving David, my loving Darian.*
> *I know I made a promise to you last night. And I know you know how much you mean to me.*
> *It's been painful for both of us to live here in a town where we're not meant to be. So after thinking long and hard last night I had to leave this morning. There's someone after a freind of mine. I can't talk about it now. Please take this $1,500 I'm giving you. You can stay in the apartment, if you choose, and pay rent. Or you can leave and fly to L.A. I hope you leave. Please don't be mad. I'm sorry but I'm sick. This whole family's sick. Please forgive me and persue your acting dream. I will come for you one day, I promise. Call when you get settled.*
> *I love you, Auntie Judy*
> *P.S. I'll send you more money when you call me*

He sits in disbelief on the kitchen chair.

"I look weird, I know it. I'm too fucking weird," he evaluates himself.

He runs to the bathroom. *Why does everyone run from me?* Anger gives him strength as hope flares through his blood. He begins counting his cash inheritance.

There're a few hidden Grants, many Jacksons, many less Lincolns, and far too many Washingtons. $1,503, to be exact. He does the math. Two or three hundred for a one-way ticket, then enough to get by on for three months. I'm rich, he smiles. This is good. She would have gotten in the way. I'll make it! I just need a ride to the airport. But what about the bike? Paved hills in L.A. and no dusty alleyways. Shit, I'll buy a thousand bikes after I make it huge in three months. Down to Swiggs he runs.

CHAPTER 9

HEY! COME HERE!" David motions to the confused Jose, who's about to have a Sunday afternoon caper.

"You going in there?" He points to the side entrance of Swiggs. Jose recognizes him and smiles.

"Bud?"

"Yeah, I'm Bud's son," he smiles proudly. "You go in there?" David asks again.

Jose mimes downing a shot.

David speaks slowly.

"Listen, I got to ask ... *por favor*."

"Por favor?" Jose frowns.

"I need ride to airport." He points to the overcast sky.

"Plane?" Jose looks up.

"*Shh*," David whispers, "it's a secret."

Suddenly, the side door opens, and it's Petey dragging a plastic tub overfilled with empties from the night before.

"Hey kid, how's your face doin'?" he teases.

David ignores him. Jose stands still as the skinny weakling drags his way to the Dumpster in the back alleyway.

40

"Heard your aunt took off this morning," Petey says.

"Oh yeah?" David plays dumb, "took off to where?"

"You really wanna know?"

David shrugs. Petey volunteers.

"Took off on a plane with Charlie to Vegas. Rumor has it they ain't coming back till Swiggs pays up. He owes too much to Smitty. He's given Charlie two weeks to come up with the dough—or else."

Petey drags two more feet, then pauses. "Wanna know what *else* means?" He grins.

David shrugs.

"It means Smitty's gonna lease the tap to someone else."

David looks away like he couldn't care less. Jose's getting thirstier, eyeing the empties.

The idiot babbles on. "Not to mention old Charlie got busted last night from his wife about his sessions with some woman in town. You know what I mean dontcha kid," he laughs.

I hope Swiggs burns in hell. The kid interrupts his wish and pulls to the curb. Petey gets the hint and drags on. David reaches to his jeans and peels a twenty.

He rests his hand on Jose's shoulders. "Could you *please* give me ride, now?"

Jose's eyes light up at the sight of the twenty. Drinking can wait. Twenty is four hours' pay down at that dusty shop. He can buy groceries for his wife and four kids at home, not to mention a bottle of tequila. Jose hesitates no further.

"Okay," his English kicks in.

"Good, I'll be back in a half hour," David taps his wristwatch.

"Yes sir," Jose salutes.

David sprints back to the apartment to fetch his one duffel bag of personal belongings—his soiled laundry. When he returns, he finally gets some loyalty from this complete stranger.

At Midway Airport, Jose refuses to accept the twenty. Jose has a tough life, as do all of his Mexican brothers and sisters in Pleasant Park. But unlike others in town, his prayer takes place in the house of the Lord in Canary on Saturday nights. On the way back to dusty Pleasant Park, Jose starts to worry about the boy. The boy's father was mean and crabby from booze all the time, and most at Swiggs made fun of his good-looking kid. But Jose has a feeling the outcast will get the final laugh. *Wonder if the kid will write? It was nice of him to take my address. Just in case.*

Finishing prayer to the Lord, he kisses his rosary for luck then makes the sign of the cross, but, instead of kissing his thumb, opts for biting his nail.

Run pretty boy, run.

PART TWO

CHAPTER 10

A T 7:20 A.M., THE AIR'S UNSEASONABLY COLD, and the sky is charcoal gray, as heavy rains inch along a 21st century screen idol and his heavy-hitting other half. The two are headed to a surprise press conference at World Artists Agency building, which towers over the three-to-five-story showbiz boutiques, agencies, and motion-picture barracks along little Santa Monica Boulevard, in Beverly Hills, California.

Just sixteen hours earlier, as luck'd *better* have it, the 87th Annual Academy Awards were held. Then, it was a typical day of polluted sunshine and thousands of fashion nightmares, all gathered in the bunkers of downtown Los Angeles. Hordes of disciples screamed in bloody tones to solicit a nod from a box-office messiah who proudly marched the red carpet. It was one huge playground of dreamers, known to all as "celebrities." There, the achievers walked off with an Oscar, while the dreamers departed with little more than their souvenir programs, thoughts of adultery, and ceremonial substance vials, tucked secretly into their tuxedos and cleavages, during the four and a half hours of reality bites.

But last night, reality did not bite for one man, who snagged his third straight Oscar for Best Performance by a Leading Male Actor in a Motion Picture. Add to that his millions of annual paying box-office disciples, and you have *the* leading man in motion-picture history. Ladies and gentlemen—I give you Mr. Darian Fable.

Just refer to the many magazines and early morning editions that refer to the ceremony watched across the globe by over 500 million people. Like the headline on the *Vanity Fair* cover, which has the 39-year-old god of Hollywood frocked in a red, crushed-velvet smoking jacket and grinning with a Cuban cigar, posing to the question on everyone's mind, "What Planet Did This Guy Fall From?"

Or the *Hollywood Reporter's* runoff that blares, "*3 for 3.*" Or *Variety,* which quotes, "He swings a brass knuckle of magic and sex appeal to every man, woman and child in the box office world."

Or the *L.A. Times,* which prints, "He has a presence unlike anyone on the silver screen. In a field where talent is slim and longevity even slimmer, the world has chosen him the king of motion pictures."

"Too much power for anyone, too much power," replays the looped fear in Darian's head.

It's no secret, the adulations and glory that lie below the legend doesn't move the star the slightest, and hasn't in several years. For the Hollywood game of fame has made him sick. The posers, flavors of the year, and junk promotions have shut Darian Fable's true love of the art *off.*

To him, the real talents of the big screen were alive when he was pissing his pants for mercy at 1933 Maple Avenue. Which is why today David Faulkner is very tired, and Darian Fable is very weak. Somewhat uncanny for a man with fame beyond Elvis, and more monumental than his childhood hero Jack. But Darian's a bright man. He knows to bite his tongue, say his prayers, and let the Lord watch over him while he's still breathing and still sane.

But this morning, the pelting rains and the cold chill play as a dress rehearsal for his soon-to-be shocked millions of fans across the globe. So now he must run and beat the Hollywood Machine. Though many may ask how anyone with billions in assets, millions of fans, and a devoted wife can still be unfulfilled in life?

Perhaps an evil *mist* is smothering his success. A mist of guilt that has haunted the actor. A mist not even he, the Messiah, can shake, no matter what mystical talents he posseses. A mist playing dirty little tricks in the mind of poor David Faulkner, for the callous plan

Darian Fable's team served up on his rise to Hollywood's Mountain. The one cloud which has been lingering but never acknowledged. And perhaps never will, as long as he and his team are still winning at the box office. The mist that's pleading for Darian to trade in his present wealth and health for a daily dose of that secret recipe from childhood that's made him currently elected above all in his field as "The Chosen One."

The Chosen One, whose life is now a fable of its own. For he is untouchable in box-office returns, unspottable in public life, and stubbornly unavailable to all. His every move and every breath is meticulously choreographed and monitored by his faithful manager and wife, Faith, per the hoodlum-controlled Summerville Studios, that also own him.

The studio that has propelled orphaned David to not only becoming the legend he is today but the profits he will bank tomorrow.

And so today, the working class, the middle class, and the few of class that "couldn't give a damn," will not only hear a 5:00 P.M. news blurb on the "post-Oscar hoopla," "rain by the buckets," or "miles of backed up traffic" on the 101 or 405 freeway.

What compels this gloomy day is the final chapter of frightened-boy-turned-frightened man. For today, the disciples and the rulers of Summerville must prep for the biggest Armageddon since the invasion of Godzilla. Because as of today, March 28, 2015, Hollywood dies. But Darian Fable lives. Yet to live happily ever after is the question. Which is why this Fabled King is just as terrified this morning as he was in his Maple Avenue chateau. But so right is the man's natural intuition and perfect timing. For terrified he should be. *The Devil of Shakespeare* is in the air.

CHAPTER 11

OVER THREE HUNDRED GALLONS of salt water, coral, and pigmented barracudas, blue tangs, yellow tangs, and others, flop to a slow death on the oriental rug that sprawls across the office of Summerville Studios' CEO, Seymore Testa. There, he sits in a daze, hunched in his leather throne in the barrack he rules.

The ruler is buying time for a guess as to why his client unalerted him to the invite at the press mania down at WAA, which starts in an hour via satellite across the entire globe.

Seymore's eyes are tired as he gazes at the powdered breakfast that forms scribbly lines atop his marble-top desk. His Louisville Slugger bat, beaded with saltwater from his recent sluggings, now rests in his clammy palms. He pokes around the rails of powder, with his rolled up Jefferson straw.

He gets a vision of Darian's wife.

He snarls at the 18x24 framed poster promo hanging in sterling silver on his east office wall.

Seymore sweats profusely from his receding hairline, which is slick with a dab of olive oil. His tuxedo shirt is tightly tucked under his cummerbund. His fingers graze his nose. He whiffs the aroma of the Lagerfeld cologne (available exclusively on Rodeo Drive) he was dousing from ears to wrists fourteen hours earlier. *Then* Seymore was happy, but sensed something was amiss.

A safe distance away lies his $5,000 rent-a-girl known only as Ginger, who seductively stretches aboard his black leather sofa in just a black evening slip. Ginger watches Seymore behind her Chanel shades while snapping her Beechum gum and twirling her silky black hair.

Seymore Testa bears the resemblance to a New Jersey club bouncer, and with his Italian-Jewish bloodline, he emulates the mannerism when it comes to running Summerville's 200-billion-dollar empire. To many seasoned veterans in showbiz he's nothing more than a lucky clown. Right time, right place, but that's Hollywood. He has little-boy whining pipes when he speaks, which mimic the deceased Hustler Publications chief, Larry Flynt. His public persona fakes out any negative media. Many take a cartoon liking to the "clone of Al Capone," who has ruled a year since the passing of Summerville's founder, and father-in-law to Darian Fable, Frank Barsolla.

Those who whisper Seymore's never paid his dues are silenced by fear of Summerville's thug shareholders, who hold court in Las Vegas.

All are aware of Seymore's barbiturate use and fraudulent screen tests to hopeful starlets. All are aware of his appetite for Ginger and her teenage friends of 90210.

Many whisper. Many despise. But only one has no fear of "The King of Sleaze" who snuck in from Summerville's parent company Platinum Records to oust Frank Barsolla.

"Candace!" Seymore yells to his assistant, who stiffens a door away.

"Yes!"

"Get me Sid Greenspan! Now!"

Sid's the heavyweight attorney for the Fables when it comes to the bottom dollar. Like the 200 mil he snagged Darian for his last picture, which returned Summerville their billions in profits, and brought home another gold statue for the legend.

Sid was lifetime friends with Frank Barsolla. But now, at 73, Sid's too old, too slow, and is losing the authority a heavyweight contender in showbiz needs. Sid's client, Darian, has been stalling contract renewal for months, which has Seymore enraged while Sid's biding time to sneak off with his Jewish clannys to retire in South Beach.

"Line one Seymore!" Candace's voice crackles.

"Siddy?"

"Speaking!"

"It's Seymore Testa."

"Seymore, how are you? What's on your mind?" Sid plays as though nothing is happening.

"What's on my mind? Well Sid, I'll tell you. Do you know what the hell is going on at WAA this morning?"

"I have no idea, Seymore," he lies.

"Don't give me your cock-a-deenee *bullshit*, Sid," Seymore whines. "Next, you're gonna tell me Darian wants more points than we gave him on his last picture. Then we'll sign his contract this week!"

Sid the old shark thinks fast.

"Technically he's a free agent, Seymore. And what are you yelling at me for? I just got in the door and the whole place is up for grabs!" he laughs. Sid's a good schmoozer, but a bad liar. It's almost eight, and few in the barracks of Hollywood sip their coffee before nine. Let alone the day after Oscar.

"Hell, I haven't been able to even get a hold of Faith!" Sid adds.

"Fuck that bitch!" Seymore's voice slips an octave lower. Sid, the shark, won't hang you, but he'll gladly sell you the rope.

"You *know* she's a pain in my ass, Sid!"

"Now hold on a minute, Seymore."

"No, you hold on a fucking minute, Greeenspamm! If this is some kind of power move it's gonna be fucking war!"

Sid jots on his legal pad. The half-breed's just shown no respect for his dead friend Frank. He's going to have to swat down the hot-tempered "*Wop.*"

"Now listen to me, Seymore. Your temper will get you nowhere with me, nor Faith, nor Darian. Just relax and everything will work its way out," he consoles.

Seymore snorts a blast up his nose and loses Sid's rare free advice.

"Well, I got news for you, Mr. Siddy, the kid, and her."

Seymore refers to Darian, three years younger, as the kid. He tolerates the kid. But hates the kid's wife.

"I'm going over to World, and then I'm gonna call Vegas—who won't be amused. And then we're gonna just see, Sid. You got that?"

Silence.

"Look, whatever you feel you need to do, *my son*, then do it! And good luck to you," Sid politely clicks off.

Seymore throws the phone at the already battered fish tank.

"My son? Fuck you! My son? Fuck you! You old fucking Jew! Candace!"

"Yes, sir."

"Get me the car, and get someone in here to clean this mess up!"

Seymore circles his desk with bat in hand. He unloads a swing that explodes the head of his W. C. Fields porcelain statue that sat minding its own business on his desk for years.

"Ooh!" Ginger lowers her shades, impressed.

Seymore looks at her like she's next. But with her thighs spread and tongue that licks her lips, she sells him into simmering down.

"You know, you've got some fucking balls, woman," he says.

"Hey, can I come with you?" she rises as the strap to her slip slips from her shoulder.

"What are you, on smack? No, you can't fucking come! This is the big leagues, now get the fuck outta here!" He drops his bat and peels from his money roll. "Here," he tosses her, "have Candace call you a car—we'll be in touch."

Ginger gathers her evening dress, purse, and heels in under ten seconds. "Fuck off asshole, I have my own car!" She stampedes for the exit and salutes him with her middle finger.

Seymore giggles. "Some fucking balls, woman."

His patent-leather shoes pop the eyes of a dead barracuda, as the sound of coral and broken glass crunch louder than a bowl of breakfast cereal.

Meanwhile,—a mile away, Sid proceeds as planned. He hurries Sylvia to put a call in to Faith Barsolla, who's moving quick as a snail in Los Angeles rush-hour traffic.

CHAPTER 12

DRIVER, SANTOS LUPE, HAS JUST CAUGHT his third red light on little Santa Monica Boulevard and Benedict Canyon, but the jolly Mexican chauffeur doesn't mind. He's enjoying the morning gabbing of DJs, who poke fun at the acting *flavors of the year* his boss stole from, in front of billions, last night on national television. The volume is shallow enough not to embarrass the humble star, and relaxing enough to drown out the orders shooting from the star's other half. Santos revels in his convenient title of protecting and driving the star, morning, day, and night. "If you could only see through these tinted windows." He hums his homemade melody in Spanish to his *little* trafficking neighbors.

• • •

As SHE INHALES her cell phone voice and exhales her tenth non-filtered Camel of the hour, Faith Barsolla spews orders to chief spokeswoman Sheila Deblin's 18-year-old intern known as Gigi. Poor Gigi's fum-

52

bling every duty, from fear of the 51-year-old former-beauty-queen-turned-venom-biting-manager, confidante, and wife to Darian Fable for thirteen years.

"Just make sure we have a silent entrance through the north doors! Got it? North doors!" Faith walks Gigi through.

"Heard from Testa?" she adds.

Poor Gigi fumbles.

"Come on! Don't fuck me now honey! Seymore Testa? You know … Summerville?"

"I'm sorry it's loud, I can't … " Gigi panics.

"Good enough," Faith cuts her off. "We'll call when we're thirty seconds away, you fucking bimb," she snarls after disconnecting.

Faith Barsolla scorns all women in the business, and "blond bimbo" Gigi's spared no mercy.

But Gigi shouldn't take it personally. Miss Barsolla's snappy to all in the morning before her three chilled lattes, as slushy as a milkshake. "Miss Barsolla," as most address her, adds her own *twist* on the morning pick-me-up, with a shot of gin. Then, it's on to her lunchtime chilled martinis. Finally, it's capped off by her bedtime sippings of a brandy snifter. Or maybe "just one more." Her husband, Darian, frowns and bears it. And he should. For, without her, he'd still be in a loft in West Hollywood.

He married Faith for her three Bs—beauty, brains, and breeding. And, at 51, she still possesses them all. An immaculate complexion, a seductive frame, and a tongue that could have made Muhammad Ali forfeit before a fight. Many male execs in the barracks of Hollywood fantasize of fucking out the secrets that make the *bitch* #2 in Forbes Magazine wealthiest in the world of entertainment—tightly behind her husband who ranks … as you guessed it … #1.

"Just what the hell are you thinking of now, Dare, and what's with those white socks? We don't wear white socks!" Faith releases a sigh of smoke like a dragon.

Darian uncrosses his legs to pick at nothings on his navy wool sports jacket.

"I *like* white socks," he tosses fuel to her fire.

"Well, you look like a fucking Pollock!"

"Well, I don't give a damn, they're comfortable."

"Well I … "

"Faith! Drop it, all right?"

"What the fuck time is it around here?" She checks her wrist.

"I think I have more on my mind then white socks right now." He doesn't let it go.

"Like?"

"Like, I hope this is a good idea." He cracks his window a half-inch.

"A good Idea? Give me a fucking break will you? This is a great idea! Trust me lover," she pats his knee.

Santos ups the volume to downplay eavesdropping.

"Now listen to me, honey," smoke blows with her words. "We've been planning for months, and you've been unhappy for years, so let's just do it! It's as easy as one, two, three. We don't need the power, the fame, or..." she hesitates a moment, "the money. We're going to start a family like everyone else. A *normal* family. See? Simple. Hurray for Hollywood!"

Darian smiles slightly and picks at more nothings on his leg.

"What's that smirk for?"

"Nothing."

"You *do* want to give me a baby, don't you lover?" She moves close to him, stroking his hair.

He grabs her hand and begins to caress it, half uncomfortable, half passionate. He then touches her shoulder-length blond hair that weaves brown roots and is ponytailed tightly. "I'll give you whatever you wish once we leave this world." He eyes the foggy view through his rain-pebbled window.

Faith kisses his cheek, but the brief, passionate moment is short-lived by a ring. The ring of Sid Greenspan.

"What is it!" Faith answers.

"Faith, it's Sid!" the voice yells.

"Hey, Sid, how did you find me?"

"Faith, thank God we connected! It's Testa, he knows."

"Oh well, tough shit! So do fifty million other people around the world. I just got off the phone at WAA and they're feeding live coverage as we speak. There's nothing to say! The whole nation is watching!" she laughs.

Darian senses they're talking about Seymore.

"He's pissed, Faith!" Sid's blood pressure panics.

"So the fat pig's angry, who cares! Is that all Sid? I mean *really*!" she winks at Darian.

"Is that all? Faith, be reasonable!"

"You just relax Uncle Siddy, 'cuz in two weeks you'll be in the sun and this will all be history. Love ya—gotta go!"

"Wait!" Sid yells.

"What?"

"Can I speak to Darian?"

"You sure? He has white socks on," she smiles.

"He what?"

"Here," she hands her phone over.

"Hey Sid," Darian opens flat.

"Darian, I spoke with Drysdale today."

Tom Drysdale is Darian's personal accountant who handles his, and only his, portion of the power-couple's assets: the billions. "Yeah, what's up?" Darian smiles to decoy Faith, who's buzzing like a bee through her daily planner.

"Darian, this is getting out of hand. We're almost up to a fucking billion and counting! Who are you, the Goodwill ambassador?" Sid babbles.

Darian looks to Faith, "Like I always say, just do it, Sid."

"But why?" Sid argues. "I mean first, this, this Pleasant Park. Come on, they were in worse shape than Kosovo after the bombing in '99. And where the hell is this new town of yours called Roseland?"

"Well, like I said, Sid—keep going."

"Keep going Darian, Tom's getting nervous. You don't have to feed the homeless and build a new schoolhouse on every block. And what's this all for? I mean you're not getting any medals or rewards."

"Darian frowns. "Just keep going."

"Tom wants out!" Sid snaps.

"But why?"

"Because if Faith finds out, we're all going to get shot!"

"Maybe, but you know … my portion is mine."

"Sure but … "

Darian cuts him off. "Well Sid. Like I said, that's fine. Just do it!" He disconnects.

"God, he's going to have a stroke, like my father." Faith sips her latte.

Darian begins to pick at more nothings on his jeans.

"Let's see, flight leaves at 10:30 sharp," she conveys for all onboard to hear.

"Darian?" she looks up.

"Yes."

"What was that about?"

"Oh, nothing. I'll tell you later," he looks away.

"Oh Lord, please take me outta this shithole traffic," she sighs. Through the rearview mirror, Santos observes while he nervously, two-finger-strokes his handlebar mustache. His loyal boss has a troubled look, and Santos is concerned. But not to worry, he reassures himself, for he's in good hands as always, next to his wife of satin legs and *steel* balls.

"Santos?" Darian politely summons.

"Yes boss."

"Please don't call me boss, and shoot some more air back here, please."

"10-4, boss."

"Yeah, and please step on it!" Faith chimes in. She then flips the phone to her ear and punches those irritating melodies of numbers, which disturb the operatic choir blaring silently in her husband's brain.

CHAPTER 13

SANTOS LUPE WAS BORN IN SAN DIEGO, California, back in 1992. He's a giant bluff of 6'5", 300-something pounds, with a potbelly he conceals well in his pleated white button-downs and trademark tanned-leather suspenders, handmade by family members who still reside back in Mexico. Santos has a .38-caliber pistol tucked somewhere under his black double-breasted sports jacket, which is large enough to pup-tent a child. He thanks the good Lord every night before he sleeps for not calling on him to use this *unloaded* firearm. For underneath the bodyguard's domineering stature lies a man of disarray, similar to a retarded cocker spaniel. Santos is grateful for his ten years with the Fables, which pays silly amounts more than his native buddies who valet cars and sweat in the kitchens of posh L.A. restaurants.

He and Darian share a brotherly bond. Both came from nowhere and landed in Hollywood with nothing more than a dream and desire. But one almost got beaten to death by a jealous biker who claimed pretty boy David (at the time) was smirking dirty thoughts to his troublemaking *angel*. And so what if he was? The biker was Hulk Hogan in size to the discouraged rebel whose only performance back then were flops into the beds of countless women.

That evening in Barney's Beanery, what rescued the wiry boy from a crooked nose, jaw, and tooth popping, was the monster bricklayer, who sat quietly at the end of the bar sipping his Coronas and eating his platter of seven-steak tacos. Santos loves tacos five days and five nights a week. He eats chicken tacos for breakfast with eggs and salsa, steak tacos for lunch with guacamole and beans, and shrimp tacos in between to up the protein spill for his nonexistent sex life. He may socialize for a quick beer at a local pub in the Valley around Sherman Oaks. There, he chats with other security chiefs who protect Hollywood's elite.

But Santos is "king muscle" in the security world. He protects the biggest *and* the best, and will only take so much prying from his colleagues about the personal lives of his clients. He's well aware of come-and-go security guards, sprinting to a TV gossip show or magazine, that would kill his brother-like loyalty he's held to his boss and friend for years.

He, like others in the circle of maids, butlers, and personal assistants, tolerates the verbal scornings of "Miss B" (short for bitch) because like most who cross her path, he's shit scared of her. Darian understands that Santos's bluff of the English language is an innocent facade to avoid orders, like pulling over to fetch more gin at the store for a last-minute quenching. Faith insists to her husband that Santos is gay, because he's never been seen with a woman on his arm or caught sneaking one into his private cottage on their Bel Air estate. But Darian knows their code when an attractive female is present. Santos clears his throat, then caresses his mustache, followed quickly with a smirk. The smirk, if broken to a smile, reveals the tender panderings of a gentle Mexican cubby bear.

• • •

OVER HER LACED SIPPING and smoke inhalings, Faith connects on the wire with Sheila Deblin. Sheila's Faith's right-hand woman, as well as the only spokesperson for Darian through his last hot five years.

"Is it packed yet?" Faith excites to Sheila.

"Of course it's packed! It's crowded, loud, and no one has a clue why they're here. Most have a hangover, so it could get brutal. Tell Darian to be on his toes," Sheila warns.

Faith winks to Darian.

"Sheila, he has white socks on, can you fucking believe it?" Faith teases.

"Oh, leave him be, what's he gonna get, fired?" Sheila laughs.

Darian smiles. He can hear Sheila's laugh over the wire. Hoarse and coarse.

"Well, I just love teasing him, what can I say." Faith pats his knee.

"Listen, this is going to work out just fine, Sheila dear. Who's all there?"

"Barlow," Sheila answers.

There's cold silence. Faith's head spins, and it's not from morning sickness.

"Barlow?" she repeats. "Now, Sheila, why in the fuck would you let him in?"

Faith fears the worst. Clyve Barlow's been a pain in the Fables' ass for years. He owns an online trash mag. Its address is www.falsefable.com. The Oklahoman big mouth hates Darian Fable and his bitch wife, "Fate." He's been a pest from day one, since arriving in Tinseltown from his humble hay farming six years ago, earning his title as "Clyve The Fly." He's out for more than just a speck of dirt on the power couple. Clyve's building a mountain. He doesn't buy into the "star who fell from the sky," which states Darian was born in Sweden, bred in Vermont, and landed in L.A. an orphan, after his parents died in a plane crash when he was twelve. How Darian Fable became an orphaned superstar through sheer determination and natural-borne pain is a "pile of wet horse manure," according to The Fly. After countless hours of investigations and not a shred of documentation, Clyve still wants to know what plane, what crash, and who really has a last name of Fable in rural Vermont? Nor does he buy into the couple's perfect Hollywood marriage and how, according to their *few* close insiders, "inseparable and faithful" they are to one another. No one's good in Hollywood to Clyve. Everyone's evil, and the Fables are no exception. They have a dark secret, and through his Southern knack for the Gospel truth, Clyve's going to find out, even if it kills him. But when he does, anyone with credibility will still continue to ignore him, because Barlow's roaring mouth is an ongoing joke to the serious, hipster journalists in La-La Land. Clyve screams with a story that's already pressed for edition well past midnight. He'd scoop to the world a nuclear bomb was striking, three seconds before impact. And still no one would listen.

Sheila's back to Faith's ear. The car is now about three blocks away. In L.A.'s rush hour, that's a good thirteen minutes.

"It's getting mad in here, Faith!" Shiela yells over the commotion.

"Okay! But where is the fucking bug going to be!" Faith yells back.

Sheila tells her it's out of her control. Freedom of first come, first seated, "it's an open forum today."

"Oh great!" Faith snaps.

"Don't worry Faith, it'll be fine!"

"We'll call you when we're close," she disconnects. "Fuck me!"

"Ah, Faith?" Darian calmly calls.

"What!" she snarls.

"It's the mouth, can we clean it up just a little?"

"Oh please. I'm not a fucking child. *Don't* tell me how to speak."

Faith knows this last dance could be a rough one. Clyve's seeking revenge for Faith turning down his actress girlfriend for a bit part in Darian's movie that propelled him into a household name. After months of Southern Comfort ass-kissing, Faith finally gave in to The Fly for an audition, but ten minutes into it, laughed the girl from the room after her opening line. Being the sensitive pro that Miss Barsolla is, she offered constructive criticism suggesting to her to "rent a chicken suit and stand in front of Popeye's."

The girl was angry and coldly dumped The Fly. Now she wins the last laugh up everyone's ass in Hollywood, as the number one female in movie rentals—in the *adult section* of your favorite video store.

CHAPTER 14

I'S BEEN A GOOD FORTY-PLUS MINUTES of inching traffic, and Darian decides to shift his secondhand-smoky brain to the view on the streets.

He follows the moving targets of Rodeo Drive tourists and celebrity hunters, who flee into nearby neon-lit croissant shops and perfumed boutiques, to escape the downpour that's washed away the usual smile of this heat-lamp city.

Watching people rushing for shelter, his view is suddenly and rudely blocked by a bulky sea-green Range Rover that inches aside his black corporate buggy. He observes with pleasure the brunette inside, who appears to be one of *them*. *Them*, meaning someone in the industry. He now wants to sum her up. He's good at that. Knows every kind, every mind, and every good and evil that lurks this earth. Is she an assistant (Hollywood's term for secretary) or is she an up-and-comer? Or maybe a "bubbling under," meaning someone who's climbing their way up the ladder of success, demonstrated by the way she's glued intensely to her cell phone, searching for nothings in her briefcase while applying her eyeliner without caution. Whatever she is, he admires her *Cosmopolitan*-cover beauty and self-confidence.

He hides his interest from his woman-hater-shadow, who's all too busy puffing away like a dragon and devouring another somebody's ear at $1.50 a minute.

The legend's new subject doesn't care to acknowledge her neighbors, or the drops that pounce the hood of her shiny waxed Rover. She has a seductive aura about her. A beautiful shell on the surface, a hard shell, but I bet a mountain of frustration under that black leather jacket. Or so it looks from his view. She has a perfect front. A controlling front. Because of her striking dark beauty, she *has* to be single. Why waste it on one man? But so wrong are probably the many men who haven't the nerve.

Darian looks to his wife and smiles. Faith smiles back.

Santos clears his throat, adjusts his rearview mirror, and strokes his stash.

This neighbor plays the traffic game well, Darian admires.

She's queen of her lane now, but he bets once she's sequestered at her thirty-day temporary parking space, her front as queen will vanish. For then, she'll have to play a secondary part to a more polished slave-driving heavyweight. Perhaps bastard or even bitch. He looks to his wife again.

"What?" Faith looks at him like he's weird. Darian doesn't smile, for he knows the unfairness the press has penned about her throughout their years. "The string of the fabled puppet, Box-office Hero and the Beast, Cat Woman and Wonder Boy, Yoko and John," the list goes on.

"Amazing," he mumbles.

"Amazing what?" Faith covers the receiver from his annoying interruption.

"Some of the greatest actors in Hollywood are driving themselves to work," he smiles.

• • •

A DISMAL RESIDENTIAL SIDE STREET is ruled by an enormous cornerstone building known publicly as WAA, World Artists Agency. Its bright-white block letters flash brighter than the Times Square countdown clock on this overcast morning. There sits a chaotic clutter of news vans, satellite trucks, police barricades, and reporters who flee from the rain through the front glass lobby doors of the agency. This innocent residential side street on which call girls loiter for lunchtime snacking is now being taped off by a dozen of LAPD's finest cadets. Curious onlookers, mostly disciples, who've heard the morning scoop from network and radio cut-ins, begin to gather by the dozens with umbrellas in hand, there to search for *the man.*

The Fables' town car, followed by three rent-a-cop sedans, swings a left turn to a gray steel door in the cement alleyway, which reads in bold black-and-white: **Deliveries Only**.

The alleyway is incognito. Faith whips open her cell phone and fires up that ugly melody. Who should be so lucky on the other end but the unfortunate Gigi.

"We're 35 away," Faith announces.

Poor Gigi fumbles again. Faith patiently walks her through.

"Seconds! Let's go!" the viper rips.

CHAPTER 15

THE MINGLING SOUNDS OF MUFFLED CHATTER, suspense in the main dome of the WAA lobby, bears resemblance to a courtroom awaiting the verdict on an accused nigger rapist. Faith peeks a quick look from a small holding room at the fidgety sea of cameramen and reporters. There, she smiles with her glow of bliss for the few who spot her, as Darian depicts the couples' image of adolescent love for the agency bystanders, who are enticed by this last-minute announcement. Now, at show time, Faith Barsolla, with her immaculate poise on the 5'9" frame, could easily pass for a former New York supermodel rather than the Russian-Italian chess player who mends her husband's career. Her breezy demeanor *in public* reveals not a hint of stress in the lazy eyelids that contour her subtle brown eyes.

Quite the opposite image for a woman of her power. So should be the perks of the time-bombed, prescriptive-popping allies many in her business of show are rewarded with.

There, the Queen Bee smiles and peers, in and out, as she dangles around her peach-scented neck the favorite piece of silver she uses in times of hidden worry. It's the silver heart-shaped locket, which inside conceals the dime-size image of her second true love, her husband—behind her love of number one. *The love of power.*

The silver locket never deserts her cleavage and draws more attention than needed to her perfectly proportioned *au naturel* chest. She's a workaholic/alcoholic manager, with beauty and brass that serves as a weapon for her only client. Together it's a perfect combination and a winning front. Welcome to Hollywood.

"Remember darling," she whispers to Darian, "family, it works every time."

Darian nods yes, as he spies the room and waits for the countdown from Sheila. Then he'll hit the platform podium and give what will go down in history as the State of Hollywood Address. He clears his throat from nervousness while fidgeting with his tinted Hilfiger specs that reveal just a tease of his eyes. Sheila weaves her way through the chaos towards the pair. Sheila's more than a key figure in the life and rise of Darian Fable. She's a major strategic force behind the planning process that propelled the actor into his current-day phenomenon.

"Well, look who's here!" Faith smiles at Sheila, who bear-hugs the couple together.

"Can you believe this shit!" Sheila snaps off in her Boston accent. "Darian, be calm," she warns. "The sleaze may be sneaking in."

"Oh fuck him," Faith slashes her feelings on Seymore. "It's no sweat, we'll handle him, won't we Sheila?"

The two women giggle, and have a good right to. Sheila's hard-nosed. Just ask Darian, who barged through the doors of a rival agency early on, when she was the house publicist. He made that entrance only to be grabbed by Sheila and humiliated by her echoing cries of "No walk-ins!" "Here's a stamp, asshole—mail your resume! Better yet, forget it!" Now, many years after that first encounter, Sheila hasn't had a day's rest or a romantic social life, because she sports only one B, and it isn't beauty. She has a head bigger than Charlie Swiggs, a pudgy nose like dead Bud, and spreads forty pounds over her 4'9" frame. She has potholes on her face from her childhood worry of going nowhere in a profession where beauty buys you a pitch, then pitch buys you print.

But tough Thomas C. Deblin changed that for his little girl Sheila. He made sure that his power bases in New York listened to his little girl and printed any story she burped. He could do this because of his stockholding shares in the *New York Times*, *Vanity Fair*, and that toilet tissue known as the *New York Post*.

With Faith's beauty, the two brilliantly planted the seeds of Darian Fable, then watched them blossom. Together, the couple make up a force of Hell's Angels frightening a group of preschool toddlers for rights to a swing set. Their successful recipe is simple. While other "flavors of the month" come and go by way of personal scandal and overexposed photo-ops in every fashion-bashing Hollywood magazine, Darian Fable has bit his tongue. Not a word spoken from him on his personal life. Not one interview, not one opinion. Just a wave, a smile, and press releases that keep Mr. Mysterious forever the legend he is.

"I see Nikki's here," Darian comments on his loyal friend of many years.

"Oh Jesus," Sheila speaks. "She's been on me all morning. 'What's the scoop, Sheila? Come on, fill me in!'"

"Well, we did promise her a scoop and I think we may throw her the final when this is over," Faith says as she eyes down the room.

"Well, we might as well, I mean it's either her or Barlow," Darian jokes, at which Faith's gazing stops.

"Over my dead body." Suddenly Faith spots The Fly. "Look at him, he's pathetic."

Clyve's busy trying to interpret with a Japanese journalist.

"He makes me puke. Santos!"

"Yes, Miss Faith."

"Don't call me Miss Faith! Do I look Japanese? Go somewhere and fetch me another latte."

"Yes, Ma'am."

But Santos doesn't sprint off so quickly.

"And what are you waiting for? Do you want five bucks?"

"No, ma'am." He splits. *Miss Faith is getting warmed up.*

Darian turns to the dozen or so polite-looking teenage interns lined against the back wall of the lobby. But one of them isn't so polite and, rumor has it, innocent. It's the little troublemaker, Missy Steinberger. Missy's breasts are too full and her thighs are too firm for a runner who fetches coffee and faxes, according to Miss Faith's eye. There are eight girls, all dressed in pleated thigh-high gray mini skirts with white bobby socks and ties, like they've just stepped out of a London boarding school. The few handsome Beverly Hills boys are in their gray sports jackets, black pants, white shirts, and black silk ties, mostly clip-ons. This is to identify the *gofers* for any quick chore someone in the agency should need. They're all related to so-and-so, or friends of so-and-so, and so on and so on. In short, they're the line that never stops growing in the nepotistic world known as Hollywood. It's 2015, and interns are now earning more than minimum wage, for scholastic credits, thanks to their role model Monica, who earned more than hers, in Washington back in '98.

As Darian watches last-minute preps being made by news reporters and network cameramen, he has a flinch of guilt over the ludicrous hype of a small blue-collar nobody. What better timing he reassures himself, than to go out at the peak of his finest performance.

"Gigi!" Faith snags the frightened intern over.

"Yes ma'am."

"Tell Sheila let's get it on, and call upstairs to Lucy Helms. Tell her to get rid of the fucking ball girls." She refers to Missy and the boys.

Gigi looks to Missy, who cracks a hello sneer back.

Whatever you say you insecure bitch, poor Gigi wishes she could say, but can't.

"Yes ma'am." She bolts up the marble stairway.

CHAPTER 16

IT'S 8:15 A.M. PACIFIC TIME, and the many who glance at early morning news shows before their daily dressings have suddenly volumed their sets to ten while parading half-dressed from one room to another. A later arrival at work is a good excuse to listen to what this century's king of the silver screen is about to launch to a nation from the WAA barracks in Beverly Hills.

Women have fallen back to their beds for a vision, as they fondle their tidy pressed curves to orgasms beyond any that their loyal partners yearn to achieve.

Dressed in a navy wool sports jacket with faded blue jeans, Darian Fable projects an Oxford symbol of safe, but cleverly contradicts any conservatism with his five-o'clock scruffy face, which plays as a perfect combination to the imperfect ones of his large loyal following. Innocent but rough. In actuality, he could dress as a bagman and get away with it because of the gift he holds that is essential to any legend's legacy. His eyes. The eyes that speak before spoken to. They're not the typical blue, brown, or hazel. They're a kaleidoscope sprinkle of every color, which changes like the weather forecast. There's something compelling about the way Darian Fable's eyes look one over. For women they lure, for men they hold, but for *all* they possess. And when captured on Panavision film, they lure you into his story and times of pain, passion, and trust. They're the eyes that reflect another messiah, who comforts souls, forgives all, and soothes the daily turmoil of his loyal billions who forever will always follow. The Son of God and forgiver of man.

CHAPTER 17

THE PRESSROOM JABBERING SETTLES to a simmer as Sheila wobbles her way to a podium of twenty-eight microphones.

"Your attention, please, listen up people," she holds court.

She then waves her few pages of *power* for all to see. The room soon deadpans to near silence.

Sheila begins.

"Okay, on behalf of Darian Fable, WAA, Barsolla Management, and myself, of course, I'd like to thank you all for attending on this very wet and ugly morning."

Some chuckle.

"We anticipate this will be brief, and with your cooperation," she eyes Nikki Hopkins with a smile, "painless."

A few groan.

"As expected, Darian will make a brief statement, then will answer a few, and I stress a few, followup questions." She eyes Clyve, who's mounted for attack.

"So without further adieu, people, I give you the three-time Oscar winner for Best Actor, Mr. Darian Fable!"

The room explodes with applause. The blushing star slips into his wife's loving grasp and proudly makes his way to the podium, quickly, determined and confident.

Whistles blow throughout the room, bulbs blind the air, and traffic halts on Wilshire Boulevard. Curiosity invites a few stuck in traffic to desert their vehicles and pinch a closer peek before red lights turn green.

Clyve surveys from his tippy-toes, but doesn't join the respectable homage. *What perfect timing for some crazy ass to shotgun Fable's skull off* is his silent applause.

Darian absorbs the reaction in humble fashion, as he fiddles with a microphone in the bunch of many. He nods, smiles, and thumbs-ups his good friend Nikki, who beams at him proudly. The applause doesn't simmer, but only rises to new heights, as he acknowledges the balcony one floor above. Agents and assistants of WAA, with their headsets on, lean over five floors of brass railings, cheering Darian on in merriment. WAA is the agency that locates the C-movie scripts, fires the D-writers who submitted them, and contracts the B+ rewriters that Hollywood's been accustomed to since the word "idea." But not to worry. Mr. Fable has bailed many out with his talent for delivering a simple line. Whereas most heavyweight agencies take a standard cut of 10 percent on their top performers and more on their screenwriters or rock stars, WAA takes only 3 percent from their top client and Fabled King. But who's complaining? After all, 3 percent of billions far beats 100 percent of nothing. Darian Fable and his team need no agency to fetch down the next big script. McDonald's, Burger King, and other junk promotions always will continue to shove B-talent hype down starving moviegoers' throats. And as of now, we're all still swallowing. Is that the art of entertainment? Maybe not, but it's the art of Hollyw$$d.

The applause has finally tamed.

"Ah, once again we meet!" Darian opens to a choir of laughter and smiles.

Missy and her intern friends are escorted out in perfect file. Santos returns with Faith's latte. All is well.

Darian proceeds.

"But really I want to thank all of you for being here today. I want to begin by telling you all here and you up there," he points to the sea of agents, "and the public out there," he points to the cameras, "how grateful I am to all of you. For you have granted me something I never dreamed would be so rewarding since I first landed in Hollywood sixteen years ago."

Seymore barrels through a side door, just yards from Faith.

"What's this, the second half of his thirty-second Oscar speech?" he whispers to an Italian cameraman, who recognizes the general of Summerville and fakes a nodded smile.

"I cherish," Darian continues, "all the success the public has blessed me with and all my years of making pictures. However, I am here to announce that as of this moment, I will be taking an indefinite leave of absence from Hollywood and the motion-picture industry."

The room gasps, as cameras snap over the exploding commotion. *The verdict is in.* Agents and assistants above flee from the railings to their offices, like ants to a hill under the shadow of a human's foot.

Seymore's stunned jaw drops his unlit Cuban cigar. "What the fuck?"

Darian tries to nurse the commotion down. He looks to Faith, who deserts his eyes and stares at the floor nibbling her bottom lip.

"Please. Please, everyone. This is not a sudden decision. This is a decision that I have struggled with over the last few months. Because of my wife's undying support, I now feel I can carry this through. I know that this is the right timing to exit this business of Hollywood"

A reporter from the *L.A. Times* shouts, "Darian, why now, at this stage of your career? I mean after last night, aren't you just getting started?"

The star blushes. It buys him time. He then chooses his words slowly.

"Well, success differs for each person. Success is never certain to continue. But more importantly, life itself is uncertain to continue. So, I would like to live an everyday life with my wife and perhaps a family, far away from Hollywood and out of scrutiny from the public eye."

The Fly buzzes in. "Is there maybe more to this, Mr. Fable, than you're revealing? Like perhaps some health problems?"

Darian wishes to be deaf, but plays fair. "Ooh, *Mr.* Fable," Darian mimics. "I'm getting old," he plays to a few reporters in the front row. "No, I mean, look, I can assure all of you *today,* I have no health problems. But of course I'm probably not all that sane since arriving in Hollywood."

The lobby breaks in laughter.

"This decision is what I want for myself, for my wife, *and* for my life. I mean, success is great, the money is … *okay*, don't get me wrong." Laughter bursts the room again. "Look, I just want a simple, normal, everyday life from here on out. And that can only be made possible by not making movies."

He then offers more than perhaps he should.

"Besides, I'm just burnt out and don't have the passion to act anymore."

"Sheila, it's time." Faith pokes her.

"Hold on, don't worry," Sheila says.

Nikki Hopkins drawls in, "Darian, how do you think your fans will take to your sudden departure, and what about Summerville Studios? Don't you owe them another film or two? And what about your production company—Fortune Pictures? Will that still be running?"

Darian smiles her way. *Leave it to a friend to pull you out of a mess.*

"Boy, you sure get your money's worth, Nikki," he jokes.

Laughter.

"I believe the public will understand and respect my desire for change. You today in this room all realize the constant pressures of being a celebrity. Being hunted day and night. It's overwhelming, overintrusive, and overbearing to live the pressures of fame in the public eye. As for Summerville," he pauses, "I can't comment now. Fortune Productions, we'll see."

"Get him off now, Sheila," Faith growls in her ear.

Clyve launches again.

"Is that a put down of Hollywood? I mean, after all, you haven't promoted your films in the last ten years, not to mention spoken so candidly until today, *Darian.*"

"I know, and it's killed me, Clyve." The room roars again in laughter, but The Fly doesn't smirk at the legend's quick-witted humor.

"No, of course not, *Mr.* Barlow," Darian repays.

"I'm extremely grateful to Hollywood for my success. But at the same time I don't feel an obligation to the world, or Hollywood for that matter, to bare any more of my soul than I already have. I mean, Hollywood will be just fine without me. There are plenty of people to fill my shoes."

Nikki frowns to another reporter next to her.

Darian spots it and lightens the mood for her with playful conceit.

"Okay maybe not...But!"

Another sea of laughter. The party is in full swing, and the legend's feeling good. He hasn't had this much fun in years since he walloped big Hermmy down at Swiggs.

"Okay, Sheila, that's it," Faith orders.

Sheila starts ahead, but not before Clyve stings all by bullhorning one final question.

"Darian! Who's David?" Suddenly, it's dead silence. So silent you can hear extensions ring from five railings above.

Darian looks to Sheila, who speeds to the podium faster than a groupie attacking Bruce Springsteen on stage. Sheila knows David, Faith knows David, and Darian knows David. But two of the three don't know *the* David from Pleasant Park.

"Okay!" Sheila wraps up the party. A loud sigh overcomes the lobby at the sound of her.

A reporter from *Variety* taunts Clyve. "Where the hell did that come from?" "Who the fuck is David?" "Just what conference are you at, *Barlow*?"

"Thank you all once again," Sheila patronizes. "The reason this was short is because there will be statements released in the days ahead. But as of now, we will have no further comments. So once again, thank you all for your cooperation, and like they say in L.A., have a nice day!"

Classical music blares over the lobby from the PA system. Darian scampers off to a holding room, clinging to Faith's waiting hand. As Sheila escorts the couple, she tugs Darian closely and gives him a pat of approval. "Way to go, politician," she leans to his ear.

CHAPTER 18

SHEILA, DARIAN, AND FAITH COLLECT THEMSELVES to flee to the waiting motorcade. But the door of their private room flings open; they're met face to face with the presence of a distraught and bewildered Seymore Testa.

"Darian," he offers his clammy hand out for a somber shake, "would you mind telling me what the fuck is going on here?"

The star looks to his wife for an answer.

"Well," Faith intercepts, "maybe we should discuss this at your office behind closed doors? Now isn't that a splendid idea, Seymore?"

"Oh, yes, certainly, Miss Barsolla!" He eyes her up and down in disgust. "Maybe we *should* discuss this behind closed doors. In fact how about like right now?" He taps his watch. "Shall we say in twenty minutes?"

"No problem, see you in thirty," Faith coldly accepts.

Seymore holds his stance. He stares despicably at the three who round up their nothings as he lights his Cuban. Santos's posture isn't jolly anymore. Seymore opts for someone his own size to pick on and goes for Sheila.

"And you, young lady," he scolds, "the next time a statement's made on behalf of Summerville, you'd better have the fucking decency to approve it through us first."

Sheila drops her bag.

"Ah, if you were listening, Seymore, I never mentioned Summerville Studios, thank you! And like my client, I am not under contract or obligation to you at this moment," she says, tapping her watch.

Seymore's face flushes a red that comes close to matching Sheila's cracked lipstick. He kicks open the steel delivery door. It knocks the snooping Clyve into a pothole of muddy water, deep enough to bathe a baby farm pig.

A minute later, through the same doors, Santos mean-faces the barricaded crowd on his way to the town car. One last bone will be tossed for a final photo-op to the vulture press and paparazzi. Now, through sprinklings of a misty rain, Faith struts to the town car as Sheila wobbles on beside her. The camera crews push and shove against the yellow plastic police tapings as reporters fire off in last-minute desperation. Their questions go unnoticed and unanswered as they bounce off the glass and marble monument and echo through the residential side street that's suddenly Loiterville, USA.

Hundreds of gathered well-wishers behind the barricades scream farewells to the fleeing entourage.

"You son of a bitch," baritones a male voice loud and clear. Women voice farewell offerings of "You fucking whore," meant for his wife. Many angry and more than *few* contradict the Messiah's prophecy of understanding, patience, and good luck fortune from his loyal followers.

Faith and Sheila reach the car first and quickly duck into the back seat. An unmarked LAPD car is notified by Santos to reroute the trio to the back lot of Summerville Studios some three and a half miles away. Darian is now last to emerge from the building. He strides with panicked eyes, as he notices the hateful chaos that tosses about the misty air. Suddenly, in all the chaotic anger, he spots a vision of a young woman, late teens perhaps, who appears to be shivering under a bare oak tree far away from the flock of frenzy. The girl's presence leaps from the chaos of angry madness that closes in and surrounds the motorcade.

From afar, Darian can sense her serious dark stare. Her long dark mane falls across her olive-toned complexion. Her attitude sends a pity of enormous magnitude to Darian's eyes. But he reads it as a selfish pity, meant for her and not the poor fleeing actor and his two-woman sideshow that awaits his arrival. He is stunned at the girl's projected energy, so much so that he stops dead still. Maybe, he sums up; she is a saint of sorts. A saint who has appeared to him, for his eyes only, to comfort and soothe his mind, through this difficult time.

Nevertheless, it's a strange attraction for a man, who rarely acknowledges public fascination or curiosity towards him. He holds his one-on-one eye contact with her, as she freezes her pitied look for him. Her numb reaction punches home a mountain of more and more curiosity to him.

"Darian, get in the fucking car now!" Faith screams.

He finally ducks in, and they whisk away, but he turns and looks through his back window to acknowledge this angel dressed in a long black coat.

Maybe this vision of her will never desert his mind. Or maybe he'll get lucky and it will vanish in minutes, like the face of a stranger in a car next to you at a stoplight. All these flashes come and go, as the entourage slushes its way from the misty jungle of Beverly Hills into the angrier barracks of Summerville Studios.

CHAPTER 19

THERE SITS SEYMORE IN HIS MAHOGANY high-back leather throne in his office. He basks in childlike amusement, his rising cigar smoke swarming the ceiling like giant cloudy saucers. The silent tension and troubled air play like a high school dean and a trio of bad-seed, troublemaking teens. Seymore notices Faith eyeing her watch and swaying her nylon calves from the chair. He takes it as his cue for her lost patience and senses it's time to begin *thy scolding*.

"So!" he swings around his throne straight on, "you're giving up show business to...did I hear correctly, start a family?" He follows with a giggle that falls into several coughs. That giggle irritates Faith to the highest, and Sheila just enough. It's like the Penguin in *Batman*. But Darian's silently taken. He's always found that giggle amusing and nonthreatening.

"That's what I heard, right, Darian?" he speaks in a father-to-son tone.

"You know, it's more than that, Seymore." Darian straightens in his seat.

"More than that? Explain how. I mean, you're giving up fame? 150

fucking million dollars a picture? The expectation of fans who count on you, the financial expectations of Summerville Studios, to … did I hear you right?—start a fucking family?"

"Well, with all due respect," Darian tries.

"With all due respect?" Seymore cuts him off. "What fucking respect?" he spits from his mouth. "The respect of leading us on? The respect of pulling our own cocks, believing you're going to pick up your option and make more pictures for us! Only to turn and deliberately *disrespect* the one studio that made you who you are? Now where did you learn the word *respect* from, son?"

Faith takes over.

"Okay, now just hold on a fucking minute! You did not *make* Darian Fable! Because you know, Testa," she pokes her finger on the briefcase resting her knee, "my father's blood, along with my domino theory and my husband's natural-born talent, arrived long before you did from fucking Platinum Records—so fuck you!"

"Really, Faith? Fuck me? Is that so?" He wipes his forehead. "I think you should get over it," he smiles calmly.

"Now hold on a minute," Darian tries to referee. "I don't like where all this is going."

Seymore has a look of surprise. "Oh you don't, do you kid? Well, I'll tell you where it came from. Ever since Frank Barsolla kicked the bucket, we're considered a fucking playhouse! Well, I don't think so!" He rises from his throne, but stays behind his desk. "You see we're not *IBM*, we're not *Paramount,* and we sure the fuck aren't *DreamWorks!* We are the top dog in the world of financial and media power, Miss Barsolla! We are the fucking biggest! And you, my friend," he points to Darian, "cannot just waltz away with a wave and a smile. You must show respect! And so must you, my dear friend," he barely airs out the final sentence to Faith.

Darian spills his words but avoids Seymore's eyes. "Look, Seymore, I'm going to be honest with you. I'm sorry, but I have no desire to ever act again. I'm burnt out."

Seymore giggles and gags. "Oh shit, now I've heard it all! You're burnt out! At 39 fucking years old, you're burnt out? Darian Burnout! Who you trying to shit? You ain't burnt out, Darian, your wife is burnt out, and this is her payback to *all* at Summerville, from the grudge she still holds over her dead father and the changes this company desperately needed. Now isn't that right, Faith?"

"Wrong, wrong, wrong! Testa!" she rises. "You know what though? You're close. Let's face it, I don't feel like sticking a feather in your cap and why should I? I've had my time and, God knows, drank my fucking wine."

"That you have," Seymore smiles.

"Yeah, well it was different when it was all in the family. Now we just don't feel like playing with your slimeball friends."

"Faith listen to me, we're all going to lose a lot of money here! Stocks are down forty points as of an hour ago. Come on! Don't be stupid," Seymore begins begging.

"Who said anything about being stupid?" She checks her watch.

Seymore looks to the giant clock on the wall.

"That's right," she smirks. "It's 9:38 in L.A.; 12:38 in New York. And guess who got out of bed early?"

"You can't do that and get away with it," he warns, "they'll throw your ass in the slammer."

"Well, who said I did it today, yesterday, or even a day after my father's death? Now, you still wanna play ball with us, Seymore?"

"You fuckin' bitch, think you're so fucking clever, don't you?"

"No, I think not you or anyone in this office will any longer dictate my reasoning or my husband's after today. And furthermore, we made this studio billions. You see, the way I look at it, we don't owe you or anyone around this fucked-up town another goddamn thing. So why don't you show your real talents as chairman and go find yourself another piece of meat? This meeting's over." She motions to Darian and Sheila, who follow her lead to the door.

Seymore remains remarkably calm, but gets in a last word of good farewell.

"Good luck to you, kid!"

Darian stops and turns, as if to say thanks, but moves on after feeling the heat of his wife's eyes.

"Oh, and, Faith?" Seymore tempts her for a listen. "Your secret, and I'm not talking about *shares,* won't hide long in this giant little town."

CHAPTER 20

DARIAN REQUESTS THE LONG ROUTE to Santos, as the unmarked vehicles proceeed through the gloomy dampened streets that once red-carpeted his journey to fame. Then he, Faith, and Santos will board their way onto a private jet at LAX. Darian knows it will be some time, if ever, before he returns to Smogsville, USA, so a reminisce of where it all started doesn't seem like a bad idea before they are secluded in peace in the confines of their cozy castle in Westport, Connecticut.

It's a verbal wrap. In just twenty-one days, he's to give his final performance, an exclusive interview to *Prime Star Magazine*. Darian's doing the interview to carve in stone his mythical life and future solidarity. And, on whom would the man of mystical silence bestow this blessed privilege to? None other than his longtime trusted friend Nikki Hopkins. Although he expects Nikki will ask some tough and personal questions, he's prepared to make some surprising revelations.

But in the still-creeping traffic, the reality of his departure from the business is now sinking in. Suddenly, there's a swirling in his stomach. He starts questioning his quick split and disloyalty at not turning out maybe a film or two for the hoodlums of Summerville. And what about his millions of followers who yearly flocked to his box office?

Darian spots out his side window a bohemian girl with her vaga-bond musician boyfriend, whose guitar case swings over his lanky shoulders. They slack their way into the newly refaced 9000 building on Sunset Boulevard, which was recently crippled by a shaky quake one year prior.

Faith follows her husband's interest to the flowered couple.

"Darian?"

"Yes," he answers in a blank stare.

"What, may I ask, picqued your interest so much when we were leaving WAA this morning?" She's referring to the angel he saw, for his eyes only. Now, two hours later, her presence still not only has an effect on him, but also has moved on to his wife. The light turns green as Santos drives on.

"Oh, nothing. I just couldn't believe the rage and anger from ev-eryone," he bluffs for an out.

"I'm telling you it's those fucking white socks," she tries for hu-mor.

He smiles.

"Well, listen, Dare, I wouldn't worry about anything honey. Like David Geffen used to say, if everyone loves you in *this town*, you ain't shit."

Darian eyes the cubes that float about the cup holder on her side. "Did you eat?" he asks.

"I'll eat on the plane," she sips in a daze.

He rolls his eyes.

"Faith, you do plan on slowing down once we get back East, don't you?"

"Oh, Jesus, *please*, darling! A deal's a deal. Of course I do! Here's to you and I, and family," she toasts and he doesn't smile.

"Excuse me, but it's almost noon and this is the first and *only* real drink I shall have today, thank you!"

"What about this morning?" he stares.

"What, a latte?"

She takes a deep breath, then reaches for her husband's hand.

"I know what your thinking, Dare. *They* have a connection."

"Who?"

"*That* couple. You know … the musician and his girl back there."

Darian looks at her, dumbfounded. "What's this about?"

"Just don't worry," she replies.

Darian would like to be optimistic, but he only sees the problem that jingles along her cup holder. It's a familiar flashback of the bumpy shaky turns he silenced many years ago on his own.

"I don't think you and Seymore get along too well," he lightens in fun to escape his dark thought.

Faith's hand leaves Darian's as she frantically gathers up her personals, hustling them into a shoulder bag. She lowers her window and tips her drink out. The wind empties the liquid quickly from her plastic cup. "Darian," she looks to him nervously, "I've been seriously thinking about something for a long time. I don't know if this is good timing, but we've … "

"What is it darling?" he looks to her.

She looks away, suggesting to *forget it*. Darian notices her eyes are getting emotional.

"I don't know … this seems like bad timing," Faith looks up front to Santos, who's focused on the road.

"Tell me," Darian insists.

"I will not cry, I will *not* cry. It's just *today* … has taught me how I've never gotten along with not only Seymore, but with *anyone*—including myself. Darian, I'm a little frightened of what lies ahead for me, for us, but please do not misconstrue this moment for weakness." She then lays her head to his chest, as she begins sniffling.

"Faith, calm down. You're being too hard on yourself. This is good. Let it go—it's all over now. I love you for who you are, Faith—no matter how. Have patience."

She wipes the few tears from her eyes and breaths a deepest sigh of relief.

"You make everything sound so simple, Darian. What gives?"

"Exactly my point, Faith. It *sounds* simple. If one mantains to work on simple, all will be sound."

CHAPTER 21

A T 58 YEARS OLD, Mary Newman is the mother of all trades. For fifteen years, the cook, the keeper, and the watchful eye of the Fables' summer castle in Westport, Connecticut. Mary's energy is an addictive one of spiritual peace and comfort, which loiters the sprawling green summer grounds Faith and Darian rarely visit. But now the two plan to settle in for many years of safe habitation, far away from the threatening temptations of the big-city life.

You'll most likely spot Mary, dressed in her daily leisure of baggy blue jeans and a bandanna, sporting a water bucket or garden tool, scampering from the main house to her living quarters. Always a beat behind Mary is Spark, the golden retriever she tends to, like the child she never had. She's, for handier terms, the Martha Stewart of the Fables' castle, who, we're told, resides a little more than a mile down the road from 16 Mulberry Drive. Mary oversees every detail, to assure the grounds have *Home and Garden* stature. From cooking healthy meals for her employers, whose yearly drop-ins are for measly hours at a time, to dotting the performance of the grounds-keepers and construction designers who continuously reinforce the 19th-century Victorian mansion.

Laid out for a monarch prince in modern time, the castle of 68 rooms is spread amongst plush green hills that recede into tamed forests. It has several mini-lakes, waterfalls by the dozens, and floral gardens inside the twelve-foot sculptured brick walls, which ensure privacy from high atop its private hill. Two indoor Olympics swimming pools, a state-of-the-art workout facility, a tennis court, and a riding stable stocked with prized thoroughbreds year round make a luxurious excuse for anyone to rarely leave the grounds.

A city-block distance away resides "the shed." It's an aluminum garage big enough to reassemble a 757 jet, which stores Darian's sixteen foreign and American classic cars. There are also several Harley Davidsons, from Sportsters to Fatboys. But not to forget the twenty-one Kawasaki dirt bikes. Twenty-one exactly. Darian loves to burn on his half-mile, customized dusty trail surrounded by tumbleweeds and grassy knolls. There, he can relive his childhood rampages, up and down hilly slopes, in speeds of 60 with no crooked cops in sight.

Just across from the shed lies the most treasured part of the entire twenty acres. Forget about the interior stained-glass Tiffany windows that adorn every room of the couple's home, or the hand-painted artwork on the game room's ceiling, or the flowers carved in stone in the balconies of the three-level "cottage."

The main attraction, to Darian Fable, is the old, paint-flaked, wooden barn. The barn that probably slept the many peasant servants back in the late 1800s, when it was first built by a tycoon department-store founder. At Darian's will, the original paint remains scarred on its exterior, to replicate that garage of tired bones on Maple Avenue. Inside, the barn is a masterful conversion to a modern-day performing playhouse. The star thought it would be a good venture, after he made some earnings off his early pictures, to retire and open his door to underprivileged dreamers from the poor outskirts of New York. There, he would direct, while they crafted their anger within a safe, fairy-tale surrounding. Unlike the cesspool of fear and doom that frowned at his desire and aspirations growing up. But with his sudden rocketing to fame, paranoia took over his plan. He guessed at the curious and not serious sneaking through the cracks of his precious playhouse. So for now, and perhaps forever, his plan will have to rest.

The barn's interior is a duplicate of his Old Main High School drama stage. Black velvet curtains snuggle the sandblasted brick of the inner wall of the stage. A sign dangles by a piece of thin wire above the outside entrance, reading in red paint, *Shakespeare's Cub*. This room would also be a perfect screening theater for the star's latest masterpiece. It's equipped with state-of-the-art film gizmos. There, the privileged few could relax in an original Mann's Chinese Theater chair. The master himself, Darian, can just flick an electronic remote, and the giant movie screen rises from out of nowhere, just like the state-of-the-art Dolby movie theater, which now hosts his latest box-office smash, minus, of course, the $12.50 admission price. All this could be relaxing and life would be normal. But there's a problem with the theater, the flourishing grounds, and the home itself that sits high above Mulberry Drive. Its every doorway lacks a customary welcome mat. You see, this "home" is different, because this house is the Fables'. And sadly, but truly, the Fables have no friends.

CHAPTER 22

HE MORNING AFTER HIS BIG COLD SPLIT, Darian is into his
daily routine of an 8 A.M. jog along the quiet rural roads
of Westport. Spark leads the way, with Santos a good
two blocks behind. Darian inhales with pleasure every crisp scent
the Long Island Sound has to blow his way. The smell of this early-
morning dew substitutes just finely for the toxins that linger far
away in Los Angeles.

Finally he is free of star gawkers and the curious who roamed his
L.A. canyon roads day and night. Anyone who does notice him respects his privacy in one of the richest and most conservative communities in the nation. There's old money in Westport, and older showbiz
pensioners for neighbors. From a few retired talk-show hosts right
into the music business, where one or two burnt-out mega pop stars
now rest in peace, to the envy of a few alcoholic novelists.

Though Darian complies with the passing smiles of "I know you,
and you know me" from his heavyweight colleagues in the snuggled
community, he can't help but feel he'll never win his private life back.
Nor fall into a normal one. Something will always lure him back to
the spotlight. Maybe not suddenly, but surely it's destined to happen.

It just has to be, for a man of 39 years who has achieved such success at such speed. He can sense that inside his next-door neighbors' million-dollar cottages, the news is out. *That couple is back, but don't make it obvious.* For underneath their scholared and creative shells of old money, they are well too familiar with the presence, name, and face of their mysterious neighbor, who visits rarely in June, but, we're now told, is here to stay forever.

CHAPTER 23

"ELL, HELLO, AND GOOD MORNING TO YOU ALL," Mary smiles to the sweaty Darian, the exhausted Santos and the sluggish Faith, who just rolled into their spacious country-style kitchen.

"Okay, I've got some scrambled eggs, some sausage, some fruit laid over there and . . . "

"Mary, where's the morning papers?" Faith cuts her off.

"Now, can't you please eat first?" Mary mothers.

"Come on, Mary, give 'em up." She snaps her fingers and fakes a lazy smile. Mary leaves the room while Darian continues horsing around with Spark.

"Did you sleep well?" Darian asks.

"Not bad," Faith answers with a yawn. "How 'bout you?"

"So-so."

"Only so?"

"Those damn raccoons, they're everywhere," he looks to Santos. "All night I heard them pouncing on the rooftop above my room. It reminds me of when I was a kid in Vermont. Santos, can you get rid of them?"

"Oh, yes boss," Santos nods, preparing for his assault on the breakfast buffet.

"You had raccoons in Vermont?" Faith asks.

"Yeah we *had* raccoons in Vermont."

Santos digs into the buffet. Mary remembered the tortillas and guacamole. *Mmm ... life's gonna be good around here.*

Darian makes his way from the devouring bear to sneak in on Faith's ear. "Is there a chance we could really get normal and sleep in the same room like most married couples do?" he whispers. Faith pulls her head from inside the fridge.

"You know I've been consumed in nothing but papers, politics, and numbers for how many years?"

Santos chows, but is all ears.

"Please Dare, give me some time; it's not easy shutting my mind off at night. You think the raccoons are trouble? Try me tossing and turning. Besides, you know I love you, don't you? Whatcha nibbling on?" She rubs his back.

"A sausage."

"That's fucking disgusting, since when do you eat red meat?"

"Since I stopped that veggie diet two years ago."

Mary returns with a stack of papers.

"Mary?" Faith calls.

"Yes, dear."

"I want you to do me a *huge* favor today."

"And that is?"

"I want you to go to the game-room bar and take every unsealed bottle of alcohol and dump it out."

Santos stops his woofing. Spark licks his chops. Darian thinks he's sleepwalking.

"Okay," Mary pours Darian's coffee, "but can I ask why?"

"No, just listen. Then I want you to replace them all with sealed bottles."

Mary looks confused. Is this a contest or a trick? Darian has a suggestion.

"Why don't we just get rid of all the alcohol?"

"Darian, it's downright rude not to offer your guests a drink when they're entering your home. Not everyone is sober in this world, like you dear."

"Yeah, we do have a lot of guests coming and going from here, huh, Santos?" he mocks.

Santos bounces with a full mouth of eggs and guacamole.

"Very funny Darian. Maybe it's *you* they don't like," Faith jabs.

"Ain't shit in this town if everyone does," he refers to the David Geffen quote.

"Also, Mary, call around today, I would like to have a chilled latte machine for my mornings."

"Ooh, chilled latte," Mary smiles, "I just love those."

Santos bounces from his silent giggle. *If naive Mary only knew.*

"Santos?"

"Yes, ma'am."

"What's so funny?"

"Oh, nothing, ma'am."

"Good, 'cause when you're finished eating do something about the raccoons. This isn't going to be a vacation now that we're out of L.A. There are no free rides around here."

"Yes ma'am."

Faith summons Darian.

"Is this going to be an every-morning ritual? Breakfast with Padre' and the Fables?" She speaks through her cigarette smoke.

"Oh, just leave him be for this morning, Faith—we're all tired," he defends his hungry cub.

"Now," she turns away, "get ready for some not-so-pleasant news. Darian, pour me a cup of coffee, *please*."

"I'll get it," Mary covers.

CHAPTER 24

THE HEADLINES LAUNCH INK BOMBS across the nation as *Variety* shouts, "Hollywood Is Stunned!" Its rival, the *Hollywood Reporter*, one-twos, "Darian Dumps His Career," while the *L.A. Times* seems to ridicule "Start A Family."

The tabloid papers run with the star's joking account of poor health. Darian might have been clowning, but The Fly managed to convince some that "here lies a pushy bitch wife whose shadow is close to the verge of an emotional breakdown."

Then there's the quote from the ever-bold top-brass Seymore, who sounds like a scorned woman left on the streets with ten children to feed. "Darian Fable was family to us, the fueler of the motion-picture industry we all depended on. We put out, he took, then ditched."

Darian's leaving the business has also been commented on by the nation's first female president, who knows the pressures of a scandalous split, being the divorced leader of the nation, whose ex-husband let it be known he couldn't care less about the magic kingdom that lay between her legs. In a firm accent of confidence, Hillary predicts to a baffled nation and Hollywood that the star "will one day return."

"I've had enough bad news today," Darian pushes away from the rubbish print. "I'm hitting the bike trail."

"Wait, Check this out, Dare—you have to see this," Faith lures him over.

It's a picture on the cover of the New York Post of Darian's lost buddy and film producer, Nick Nichols. Nick was the star's partner when the rebel first hit the streets of Hollywood. He's an Englishman who occasionally falls off the wagon. According to the ink that's barely dry, Nick's going to be on national television tonight to discuss the ethics of Hollywood and the sudden bail of Darian Fable.

"Well, look at this," Faith scorns, "Nick Nichols, Hollywood's biggest loser."

"Oh, come on, Faith. He did produce a good movie or two."

"No, no, no! His dead father was a legend, he's a looossser! Your buddy, old St. Nick, lost his ass on that last script he tried to steal."

"Nick never stole anything," Darian defends his buddy.

"Yeah, and I'm the Virgin Mary. You, my dear, are so naïve sometimes." She throws her arms up in disbelief.

Darian pities his old pal while glancing at his mug shot in black-and-white. What happened to the two of them? He and Nick were so tight back when. Wish the doorbell would ring, especially before Mary dumps the bottles dry. Nick's funnier than Dudley Moore when he's had a few.

"You may think I'm crazy, Faith, but I really could use a dose of him right now," he stares to his picture.

"A dose of who?" she looks up stunned.

"I don't know. Just to talk," he shrugs.

"Talk? Absolutely not! Are you retarded? He's a drunk, a big mouth, and, next to Seymore, the biggest sleazebag in the business! You want to know what he's doing, Dare? He's producing car commercials for GM."

"Is not."

"Is so!"

"It's just another rumor."

"I don't think so!" She draws her cell phone from her robe pocket.

"Here, call Sheila."

He balks at the ugly tone of that phone.

"Listen to what this English idiot has to say, and I quote from print," she snaps the paper and recites: "'In the back of many peoples' minds in Hollywood is the notion that the man who shyed from the media throughout his entire career is now playing a hoax on everyone. And that he will return after a brief rest, to carve his legacy in stone. But I know Darian Fable, and that rumor is a complete fable.'

"Oh, such profound savvy," she pokes.

"Well, I don't care, I still want to see him," Darian says.

"Now, don't start," she warns.

Darian sends her a stare.

"Don't!" she warns again.

"Don't what?"

Santos skates out. Mary follows. Darian joins. As does Spark. Faith doesn't realize she's alone, as she speed-reads along. But the verdict doesn't get any brighter. This whole idea, this whole surprise. Darian Fable's loyal followers have declared blood over his premature retirement.

Few are willing to understand his plea for serenity in a mad world that funded his rise to stardom. The majority now declare—in fact, demand—that he owes a more defined reason. Threats demand that the star continue working or they'll blow up a theater his current box-office smash, *The Sun's Darkness*, is playing in. And "that bitch Faith Barsolla," to quote one deranged fan from a tabloid, "maybe *she* needs to bite a bullet or two—unlike that lucky *Jap* bitch of a *Beatle* outside The Dakota in 1980."

The Fables could sure use that welcome mat right now.

CHAPTER 25

LATER THAT DAY, THE SUN HAS SET. Darian is in his study, sulking 28 minutes into the verbal debate between his friend Nick Nichols and the Southern flamethrower Clyve Barlow. Faith is lounging comfortably on the sofa in gray leggings and a white button-down cotton shirt big enough for Santos, while stirring her cubes of mystery liquid and stroking Spark's head. Mary is in the kitchen, helping a maid from a neighboring bungalow load pots and dishes from dinner. She occasionally glances at the kitchen's mini-monitor, while Santos sneaks a leftover. An estimated 22 million viewers are glued to their sets for the hearsay from a dumped boyfriend of a porn star and the has-been son of a legend, who defends his buddy with British arrogance.

Night Chat is hosted by Dominick McBride, an ex-attorney turned talk-show host after being disbarred while representing the widow of a CEO, who was tried for her husband's murder. Dominick tried to prove she didn't have a motive to "hire for kill," but it was revealed through her eldest son that she paid the handsome bachelor lawyer more than just a retainer fee to defend her.

Dominick lost the case, but America embraced his boyish motive.

That's America. Night Chat is ranked 7th in newsmagazine shows of 18 a night on 750 channels. Number one is Nikki Hopkin's, *Prime Star Magazine.* McBride mixes his courtroom interrogations with his Italian suavity and Irish bullying, to force his guests to 'fess up or get out when they're in his courtroom.

"We're back, and it's been a hell of a half hour," says the *Dom,* as he fiddles with his pen Johnny Carson-style. "This has been a battle of the old and the new in Hollywood. Nick, let me ask you," the Dom leans in, "you and Clyve here have different opinions on Darian's leaving. But tell me, why is the nation and Hollywood reacting like the man has just died?"

"Well, it's quite obvious, *Dom,* the film community are the ones dead here. I mean, listen—here you have a good, decent guy from good old Vermont ... "

"Not so!" Clyve cuts him off.

"Now, just hold on a minute, lad! You've had your say."

"Oh, I don't believe this buck." Clyve slumps back in his chair.

"Well, believe!" Nick speaks. "He's got a beautiful wife and now he just wants to go home and mow his lawn like the man next door. Is this really a sin? I ask."

"Well, there's one brownie point for Nick," Faith mumbles as her eyebrow arches.

Darian smiles. *Keep baking, buddy.*

"Oh, come on, Nichols!" Clyve piles on. "I mean, first of all, the Fables are very far from June and Ward Cleaver."

"I didn't say they were perfect, Barlow!" Nick fires up a smoke.

"Not at all, Mr. Nichols! You haven't seen your good buddy since when, the opening of your only hit some ten years ago?"

Faith smiles to the tube. "Well, Clyve does have a point."

"Now, that's false." Nick messes his scraggly curls of gray as he reaches for his coffee mug. "As long as we're on the subject, *Barlow!* What hit do you have?"

"What hit?"

"Yeah! Besides your online *trash* that rips Darian Fable twenty-four hours a day and charges by the bloody minute?"

"Well, at least they get their money's worth."

McBride's roaming eyes are amused, but he must end this badgering circus. "Okay, gentlemen, let's not get out of hand here," he tries to referee. "I mean, he's only an actor."

"Damn right, the greatest actor!" Nick snarls.

Clyve laughs.

"Dominick," Nick almost begs. "All I'm trying to say is we have a living legend who didn't need sex and violence to sell tickets. And, with all due respect, he's not just another *actor*. It's as simple as one, two, three! The Beatles landed, we went to the Moon, and Darian Fable was born! I rest my case."

"Oh, now I've heard it all!" Clyve roars.

"Well, now hold on—that may be true," Dominick defends Nick. "Is *he*, without question, the biggest force of influence since, let's say, John Lennon and the Beatles?"

Clyve snatches his Oklahoma Sooners cap off, without realizing his 28-year-old fuzzy baldness is panning to a camera of millions. "Well, let's just say there's more to Darian Fable than meets his sparkling eyes, and ... "

"Oh bloody hell!" Nick bleeds the background. "That's all you got?" he barrels in laughter.

"And ... " Clyve holds a finger, "hold on Nichols, you've had your say."

"It's yours; go on, continue, lad." Nick reaches for his mug.

"And, when all this is all exposed, Darian Fable will be screamin' for help."

"When *what* is exposed?" Nick belts.

"You'll see," Clyve smiles.

Dominick swings his chair to cross-examine Nick.

"Isn't it true, the actor *once* had a drinking problem?"

Spark barks.

"Well, I don't know 'bout that one, Dom. I mean, don't we all have a drinking problem at one time or another now." He reaches again for his coffee mug.

"Yeah, don't we all," Faith reaches to the floor for her glass.

Dominick swings on. "The *Global Film Magazine* is reporting tonight that his wife, Faith, has had a serious problem with the bottle on more than one occasion. True?"

"Oh, bring *me* fucking into it!" Faith blurts out.

"Ah, that I wouldn't know," Nick says.

"When's the last time you spoke to Darian, Nick?"

"Oh, I'd say," he scratches his head, "'bout three weeks ago."

"One lie!" Faith chalks from the gallery.

"Did he tell you he was leaving?"

"Nope. Absolutely nothing."

"And you yourself, Nick, you had a drinking problem at one time, correct?"

"Ah … yeah," he shrugs, "but not bad."

"Not bad?" Dominick questions.

"Not too bad. I mean, I haven't touched a drop in 'bout, hmm … let's say ten years."

"How 'bout ten seconds," Faith springs up from her comfy lay. "What a bunch of bullshitters! Do we have to watch this?"

Darian is more than amused. He's enjoying this. It's a legitimate circus. Suddenly the phone rings, and Faith answers.

"Hello?"

Silence.

"Helllloo?"

"Are you happy now … you fucking whore?" a voice whispers.

"Who is this?" Faith snaps back.

The other end disconnects.

"Who was that?" Darian breaks his amusing trance.

"Wrong number, and what *is* this *shit* we're watching? Why doesn't everyone just get a fucking life!"

Darian isn't content with her answer. She nibbles her fingernail. It's a giveaway of emotional confusion in her head to his observing eyes. The fingernail-nibbling doesn't mean hungry or thirsty to Faith Barsolla; it means worry.

Her husband plays dumb. "Faith?"

She ignores him.

He now plays lawyer.

"Who would call our unpublished number at this time of night, Faith? We just had it changed, didn't we?"

She looks at him like she's seen a ghost.

"Darian, it was the wrong number! What do you want from me?"

She plops her drink down, grabs her cell phone and stamps the study like a Beverly Hills brat.

Darian ignores. Spark stays put.

He then heads over to her glass, which now rests on the oak coffee table. He picks it up, and before sniffing in caution for the aroma he was born into, swallows it till the cubes slam into his pearly whites.

The verdict is in.

Not guilty. His instinct was right, and he knew it.

The "Faith" in his marriage may be renewed. Life may be normal after all. It wasn't that she had a serious addiction. It was the lunches and numbers that turned her everyday schmoozing into a full day and endless night of boozing. But that's to be expected. He looks at the tube.

Finally back from the seven-minute break of commercials, Darian laughs at old St. Nick's humor. He's torn up the southern-fried Clyve with his English wit. Flashbacks of his old friend bring a hunger to the good fellow in his peaceful study. Back then, David was poor and Darian was starving, but for some strange reason *both* were happier in life. No pressures, no answering to anyone. Just nonstop drinking, sleeping, and sexual escapades with the many starlets who revolved the doors of his buddy's Laurel Canyon house.

Nick looks tired and lonesome. He looks beaten and hurt, like he needs a friend. But so does the legend he's been defending. Tired, sad, lonesome, and no one to trust. The man they now speak of round the clock on several-hundred-plus stations has everything in life a legend could dream of. A few dozen houses, money for thirty lifetimes, and a queen-bee beauty he's been waiting on for years to sting him into normal living. Darian makes a vow to himself and then clicks off the circus. He and Nick will meet again, and again his timing will be perfect. The man, Darian Fable, will no longer hide behind the shadow of the boy named David Faulkner.

CHAPTER 26

I'S BEEN SIX WEEKS IN WESTPORT, and things are moving as planned. The new bottles in the game room have remained sealed, and Darian's wife is now sleeping side by side with him nightly in his master bedroom on the third floor. Their passion is blooming as well. So well, it's three times a day behind closed doors. Too much time on their hands is now being consumed in bed, and the fear of a dysfunctional offspring has them both playing with suspicious pleasure. But Faith, as always, has a plan of a more productive work schedule towards their imminent future. She toys with opening Shakespeare's Cub to a select group of independent producers who pass her screening test of "artistic legitimacy."

Faith also reminds her husband of his scriptwriting and urges him to pursue some "shorts" for the groups, should they launch the plan sometime early fall. Darian thinks it's an okay suggestion, but bargains her into a little time to travel to Europe. He even throws in a bid to greet some of those passing strangers they see along the jog she now shares with him since her five weeks of sobriety. Faith agrees, but warns him to "beware of old sleeping dogs that wander Westport's rural roads of right-wingers."

• • •

"WELL, I'VE GOT GOOD NEWS and bad news, honey," Faith says, smiling, as the two putter in the kitchen before their daily jog.

"I'll take the good news first." Darian heads to the fridge.

"Well, our house is sold," she refers to the Bel Air estate.

"Oh yeah? Well that *is* good news." He really couldn't care less. "Who bought it?"

"Some Iranian. But the bad news is I'm headed for La-La Land and you're not coming." She pours some grapefruit juice.

"I'm not coming? Whatta you mean? Why are *you* even going?"

"You knew I had to go!"

"Faith, you never told me."

"I didn't? … Oh," she thinks. "Oh, well, I'm sorry."

"Wait a minute. If you want, we'll just postpone the interview with Nikki for another week and I'll give you a hand," Darian offers.

"Not to worry. There's not much to do with the house. And you're in no state to face L.A. right now. I mean, you're just getting settled here with peace and quiet, so enjoy. Besides, we've made it straight with Prime Star; you can say whatever your little heart desires. We have the final edit. You'll be fine."

She moves in close to him.

He embraces her and grazes his hand over her glowing cheekbones.

"The question is, can you bear to live without me, my dear?"

Faith nibbles his ear. But as they heat up, she pushes away and dashes out the swinging screened door to the yard, in a little-girl fashion, on this perfect, sunny day in July. Life is good and almost normal with the true friend David Faulkner's never had.

CHAPTER 27

LATER THAT NIGHT, THE TWO CONFER over halibut, sautéed potatoes, and asparagus, prepared by Mary. They touch on Faith's list of plans, from her last-minute landing tomorrow in L.A. to a skimpy daily regime when she returns.

"Which guard is Santos putting on you?" Darian asks.

"Which guard?" She looks around, "Did I hear you right?"

"Well, he's going with you, right?"

"Like hell he is! What are you thinking, Dare, he's already on my nerves. And he's *not* living here forever, so don't get any ideas."

"Okay, but are you crazy, Faith? You can't go to L.A. without personal protection. I mean, come on, isn't now the perfect time to make another psycho infamous?"

"Oh, listen to you! Just what are you trying to say?"

"The days of Hinkley and Chapman are *long gone*. We need another star killer, and guess who we can get?" He tries to shake her.

"Hey, you, first of all, don't try to freak me out, and secondly ... did you forget?"

"Forget what?"

"Forget this is part of the reason *you* wanted out. To live a normal life. Remember. *You're* what the world craves. Me, I'm just your bitch wife. Besides, we have a big enough staff here, and I don't feel like adding another stranger to the payroll to follow my every move."

"Wait a minute. Is this about money?"

"*Yes* and *no.*"

"What? What do you mean yes and no?"

"Darian, if you want to sustain this lifestyle, we have to be careful."

"Faith, we have enough money to house an entire world."

"Well, my world is different than yours now isn't it?" Her eyebrow arches.

"Yeah, but, *you're* the reason."

"What do you mean, *I'm* the reason?" She drops her fork.

"Nothing." He picks fish with his.

"No! What in the hell did you mean by that comment?"

"Well, okay, you want to know?" he drops his fork. "It's quite obvious to everyone that you make all the decisions and you're the force behind my entering hot and leaving so cold. And, hey, I don't fault you, Faith…we all know stars need someone to do their dirty work for them. But, honey, in this one, managers count to a crazed world of mad people."

"Well, I don't care what the fucking people say, Darian. I'm my own person, always have been, and no security for me, thank you!"

He sighs, "It doesn't sound good. I'm going to put a trailer on you."

"Oh no, you're not, and you're pissing me off! Listen, who's going to know I'm in L.A.?"

He thinks for seconds.

"Hello?" she snaps her fingers. "See! No one! End of discussion. As always, I'm right!"

Darian remains silent. Faith feels a tiny guilt over her stubbornness. She realizes her husband is just concerned for her. After all, he is *a man.* But guess who wears the pants? She reaches across for his hand and clutches it.

"Darian, honey, I'm a big girl now, remember? Remember the decisions I've made throughout our years? The decision that got us both here? I'll be fine, don't worry honey, okay?"

Once again Faith has won. She has persuaded him with her will in a matter of minutes; and once again, he has backed down like the good husband he's been trained to be. He's trusted her instinct, and an asset that sits deep inside her stubborn but breezy shell. The asset that has kept his fire kindling for years. The professional years. Her decision to take the ball and run with it no matter what he may think. Like how she shoved him down the throats of a starving world. Starting with the big setup and closing with the big deal, after bigger deal.

I love my wife, he reminds himself.

She interrupts his thought, "As long as we're on the subject of stalkers," she fires up one of the seven she's now down to a day, "I don't have to remind you of Nikki's teenage crush when I'm gone, now do I?"

"Oh, I *knew* this was coming," he blushes.

"Darian, it's not funny."

"Faith, have you ever caught me with another woman?"

"Have we ever been apart?" she asks.

"God, you're right. We haven't ever been apart, have we?"

"Maybe a room away, but never apart, lover," she refreshes his memory.

"Well, Nikki's harmless."

"No. Nikki's single, Nikki's from Texas, I *do not* trust Texas women."

"Faith, not to worry. Mary's here, and my heart is here," he places a hand to his chest.

"Who cares, I'd kill that bitch if she even thought," she stabs her cigarette out.

"Come on, Faith, why don't you let it go?"

"No! Why don't *you* let it go?"

CHAPTER 28

THE FOLLOWING MORNING IN THE KITCHEN FOYER, Mary and Darian wait for Faith, who is on the phone confirming with Sheila their noon meeting at Barsolla Management complex in Studio City, California. She clicks off and turns to Darian, who looks lost.

"Oh come on, loosen up honey. Are you gonna miss me?" she softly teases him.

"I don't know Faith if this a good idea..."

"Oh Dare, let's not get into it, I'm a big girl now. Besides, you've got Spark Plug to play with!" she says, kneeling to smother the dog.

Spark tugs from Faith's grip and sticks to Darian's pant leg.

"See, the little bastard hates me," she smiles.

The two then exit arm in arm to the idling town car, as Santos patiently waits.

"Hey there!" Darian lights up to Santos, "where've ya been, ol' buddy?"

"Oh, you know, just hanging inside a little," Santos shrugs. "I'm just getting organized."

Darian senses a lonely look in Santos's eyes.

"Hey, you okay, little brother? You look different."

"Oh, yeah, I fine, yeah, I okay boss!"

"Hey, Santos?" Darian whispers, "want to hang out while the wife is away?"

The cubby bear breaks a smile.

Faith is busy with her shoulder bag, which she packs away in the trunk.

"Now, listen to me, Faith," Darian attempts to wear the pants, "I want you to be careful and stay close by Sheila."

"Oh, Dare?"

"Yes, my dear."

"Before I leave, I just want you to know."

"Know what?" He leans into the back window.

"Know that I love you, more than life itself."

Mary throws a ball to Spark, who chases it while she wanders steps away to respect their privacy. Santos hits the driver's side.

Faith lays a lengthy wet one on her husband's lips.

"I know you love me, and I'll continue to love only you. Just do me one small favor?"

"Anything," she surprises him.

"Call me constantly. I don't care what time it is, just call me."

He then moves to the front of the vehicle where Santos sits ready for takeoff.

"Santos?"

"Yes, boss."

"Will you stop calling me boss and drive carefully?"

Santos strokes his mustache. "Of course, boss," he smiles.

"Santos, don't listen to him," Faith yells, "step on it!"

And so, with that pleasantry of departing done, Darian watches his lover and closest friend process around the cobblestone driveway and down the sloped hill. As its shiny bumper exits the iron gates and onto the asphalt road, he realizes it's not going to be easy, a few days apart from his born-again wife. Lately, the two have been inseparable for most of a day and all of the night. Now he's on his own for three long days. Now, paranoia sets into the star. He fears the worst. Auntie Judy enters his thoughts. Maybe she'll run off with another man? Mom enters. Perhaps a producer in the business. But not to worry, he reassures himself. That was long ago, when David was a little person—a nobody. Now everyone rushes to Darian Fable with open arms. Everyone, like his longtime friend Nikki Hopkins, who's preparing to launch into his kingly estate any moment now for the views of a never-before spoken *LEGEND*.

CHAPTER 29

UPON DARIAN'S RETREAT INSIDE, he plucks from the steps of his kitchen an *L.A. Times*, which, as always, was delivered to him by Teddy the watchguard, who mans the main entrance gate of the estate. The star, who's all smiles, fumbles his fingers to the Arts & Entertainment section. It's been over two months, and though God himself would probably lie and tell you differently, Mr. Fable's ego is more than a little low by the absence of his name in a front-page headline. With nothing new, like the closing of his production company or record sales on video rentals of his ten former releases, the "fabled one" is slowly but surely slipping to page 40-something. As he skims for his *ego*, a headline leaps out of nowhere in the Real Estate section that screams of tycoons posing in hard hats with dirt plows in the foreground.

"**Fables Sell Bel Air Estate For 32 Million**," it reads in black boldface.

Darian Fable can't believe his sparkling eyes.

"Who will know I'm in L.A?" the words so wrongly spoken from his wife. He begins to feel shaky about the tip-off. The Fables' agent, Dolly Hinsdale, sports a proud face at the gateway of his Bel Air castle. *Oh happy Dolly, your big commission was not enough. Oh Dolly, you halogen-lipped big mouth,* Darian freezes.

"Oh well, what can we do?" he speaks to Spark, who fakes panting for more ice in his bowl.

"We sold the house, right? But that doesn't mean we've returned to town now, does it?" he pets him.

But now for the biggest question the man of the house is faced with. Should he alert his wife of the meager but lethal blurb in the *Times*, or is he just being paranoid? After all, Sheila will be at her side, and that's enough to mildly soothe his concern. Santos and his pistol have never been called upon. Surely there must be a reason. There must be someone looking over their shoulder. Or is it his wife's iron fists that has kept Darian Fable safe after all these crazy years? Or is life like the movies? A place where the good die young, but the bad live on.

He blows off his worry and proceeds with his ritual of cereal, muffins, and grapefruit juice. Suddenly, through the iron gates rumbles an army of white midsize semis with a blue-trimmed-in-black *Prime Star* logo on their campered fronts and sides. The semis rumble tightly in a long caravan as a flow of wardrobe trailers follow. They're striving up the deep slope, similar to IRS agents paying a surprise visit to a tax-evading Vegas performer. The rumble gets louder, while the exhaust that puffs the sky gets cloudier. Spark is now barking spastically, demanding they pull over and show their press credentials.

"Mary!" Darian screams through the bay windows that view the ruckus.

Mary hurries in out of nowhere.

"Oh my God, so many," she says, staring.

"Welcome to show business, Mary. You're up to bat, darling, and I'm outta here."

Darian zooms around the corner and double steps the thirty flights of stairs to his master chambers. There he'll prep, hide, and spy for hours on the vultures, who will unload, set for fire, and await the Queen Bee of TV *journalism* to arrive.

CHAPTER 30

THE HOURS HAVE PASSED LIKE MINUTES, and already it's noon. The production crew of a hundred or so techs, have turned the peaceful plush surroundings of a king and his ruling queen wife into a *studio back lot carnival of clutter.* There are people dodging scaffolds, poles, tarps, and cardboard drops; mini sub rack lights; giant spotter lights; cables, more cables, and the ever delightful munchie perks, known as *craft service.* There are soda cans, or "pop," as it's called in the Midwest. There are peanuts, fresh fruits, chips and dips, deli-style finger sandwiches (mostly tuna and roast beef) along with crumbs from all of the above for the thankful birds who descend, peck, snatch, and resnatch, to store in their nests what looks to be feeding for decades on. Darian peeks occasionally from his bedroom balcony. The pacing of brawny, bearded grips reminds him of Swiggs, back in his dirty hometown. Maybe some are from Pleasant Park. He fears dirty men like this don't sprout so mean and angry in the streets of Hollywood. Or maybe they hail as far north as Bakersfield, California. The Doc Marten's walkie-talkers with buzz cuts and boyish complexions prance amid the musclebound brawny ones in flannels. In Darian's mind, the Docs are no doubt bred and right out of West Hollywood, close to the latte machines and that infamous hangout Mother Lode, on Santa Monica Boulevard. Whatever the case, this crew is a scare to the star, who fears it looks more like a preparation for a four-part miniseries shot on location than the contracted 120-minute "unedited" reel of tape his wife and Sheila will chop to 38.

Mother Mary's frantic running from main house to guest house, to the backyard's outdoor terrace that overshadows the crystal-blue pool, the minilake of gliding white geese, and the tall green elm trees that taper off into the tamed forest. Santos has returned from JFK and is marching the front grounds with his walkie-talkie in hand. He pauses to declare, with his newfound role of authority (and Miss Faith 50,000 feet in the sky), that his brothers from Mexico needn't worry about the lawn and shrubbery... they've just won a free day's pay. He sends them back to their five one-bedroom bungalows that weave throughout Darian's dusty bike trail.

Flown from France is director of photography, Jacques Lamar. DPs make or break you in front of the camera. No script can capture beauty to the eye, and Jacques's eye is the best. Just ask Sheila Deblin. "Shock," as it's pronounced, in his CK baseball cap, ugly horn-rimmed shades, and short shorts that are tighter than Fruit of the Loom briefs on his boyish derriere, dramatically mimes with gay hand rhythms to the wardrobe girl.

"Darian must wear something light, maybe something soft blue, like your *eyes*. How 'bout a blue button-down?"

It's smart lawyering that a witness wear shades of blue to project honesty and win sympathy from prospective jurors. Jacques will use the blue-garb gimmick to bring forth the serenity of gliding white geese in the distance. The massive green elm trees will push *peace* to the billion plus jurors who will tune in. Then will all unconsciously and sympathetically fall into a world of baby-blue innocence, heavenly whites from the geese's gliding feathers, and a breeze of calm understanding from the elm trees—a heartfelt honesty. Just like the breeze of heartfelt honesty that *lies* in Darian's hometown in rural Vermont.

• • •

At 12:30 p.m., the queen of journalism, Nikki Hopkins, finally arrives in her stretch white limo. Darian greets the Dallas cosmo beauty who's decked in her *Chanel* cream suit which showcases her mile-long, tanned legs.

Nikki's a sex bomb, around 5'8", and with her cover-girl essence, she's not only the best but the sultriest at getting the famous to 'fess up when cameras roll. She's number one in Emmy winnings and holds the rumor lead of rolling her way into the beds of most leading men she's interviewed.

Like in the exciting anticipation of a childish slumber party, Darian greets her with a friendly hug. "My man, you are looking *so* good!" Nikki looks him top to middle.

"And likewise," he smiles.

"Well, *you still are my man* and don't you *ever* forget it! So Faith's out of town?"

Darian isn't fazed at her quick scoop. She's a longtime friend of his and a tolerant acquaintance to his other half. He and Nikki met when he was swaying from David to Darian after landing from Vermont (she's told). She ran with him and Nick for a couple of summers. Back then the trio were an inseparable, perfect combination for nightly sin in the City of Angels. Nikki would learn the ropes about stars' double lives and secret lies, per Nick, then repay her jottings by baiting beautiful club women back to the home of his father, who was always away on location. She was the person who stayed friend and knew Darian "when." And still is, some fifteen years later. That's a rare stroke of fate and credit for anyone who swings the friendship tree in the jungle of *hangers-on*. Before the interview takes place, the two play a friendly game of tennis, in which Darian shows no mercy on his home turf, trouncing her five games to love. He's always been good at tennis, better at basketball, and number one on the dirt trails. The Faulkner stubborn genes that rule his blood mandate winning—*at anyone's cost*.

They then settle down for a bit of lunch and small talk about their early years before success, not to mention a tease or two about their fixations on one another before he and Faith became the ever-faithful combination.

Darian tells his buddy-girlfriend how she needs to settle down and find a good man to hold on to. She tells him how lucky he is to still have Faith after many years in the playground of temptation. Nikki then slips into a moan that with all the Emmys that line her bookshelves in Dallas, there is a monument of discontent on her third finger.

Darian listens patiently like the good friend he's always been.

Then Nikki smoothly sways into a pretestament of how he "pissed off a lot of top brass people by suddenly leaving."

"Oh, Hollywood's going to be just fine without me."

"Wait a minute," she catches him, "did you say, *just fine without me?*"

"I did."

"Well, I hope you don't plan on using the same rehearsed lines to my questions that you threw at the WAA conference."

"Such as?"

"Such as… 'Hollywood's going to be just fine without me!'"

Darian looks away. "Did I say that?"

"You most certainly did, honey."

"Oh well, it just goes to show ya, Nicks—practice makes perfect."

CHAPTER 31

THE INTERVIEW IS TWENTY MINUTES into full swing and Mr.
Fable—much to the shock of his sisterly friend and
Prime Star producers—is blowing his opinions as
carefree as the elm trees that sway in the camera's panning. Nikki's
covered almost all. From his rocketing shot to stardom, to his mysterious orphanage days in Vermont, to the shocking announcement
heard round the world on March 28th, Darian slams the media and
"backstabbers" of Hollywood as he defends in his own words the
unfair characterization of his BMW, (short for "bitch mogul wife").
He notes that his love for Faith is "irreplaceable" and adds that their
only major difference in belief is that he is *pro-choice*, while she is
pro-life.

On Seymore Testa he scorns harshly, but with perfect tone.

"I personally didn't believe he was a bright enough man to call
my shots. In fact, I've been there when he had to remind himself to
breathe."

On his beliefs between good and evil in society, he scorns the
motion picture industry as having "destroyed the family-values system."

On religion he says, "I do believe in a certain God," but adds, "sometimes he picks on the wrong people."

When asked what the word "star" means to him, he pauses.

"Most of the people on your movie screen are in control for that moment. But just for that very slim moment. After that, many are a reckless roller coaster from the word *cut*. Perhaps because of that infamous labeling, *star*."

He adds, "Most people in the biz have *acquaintances*, not friends."

"And why's that?" Nikki asks.

"Because anyone close to you fears success will win over them, and you know what? In most cases it does."

"So who's your best friend?" Nikki asks.

"My wife, and after this airs, maybe you too," he smiles.

He even hits an explosive opinion on politics, declaring he's a Democrat and slamming Congress and the administrations of past and present. He hints at suspecting they've held out on a cure for AIDS, "because they can't come up with a big enough war to control the over-population of society."

"Now that is a damning accusation, isn't it?" Nikki challenges.

"Maybe," he says, but offers a not-so-damning analogy.

"Let's say a nuclear bomb was on its way in. I think, though we currently claim to have no knowledge of detonating it, somehow we would, don't you agree?"

He then vows he'll give every dime of the supposed billions he's earned, if the government 'fesses up the cure for the disease tomorrow.

On what Hollywood's top brass thinks of his cold split, he says, "You know I really couldn't care less, aside from the people who enjoy my work and a few close acquaintances."

"Well, yeah, but come on, Darian! Look at the great wealth Hollywood has bestowed upon you," Nikki advocates to the camera's pan of geese and elm.

Darian pauses in his longest thought yet.

"Well, I can assure you anyone with an abundance of wealth and power has not achieved it without seriously damaging a soul or two along the way."

"So who do we women fantasize about at night while we're on our way to dreamland?" she teases.

"Well, you could always try the man who's lying next to you," he chalks up a chuckle from the crew in the background.

"What's your view on violence and why is it *out* of your movies?"

"I despise the senseless killings and racist mud-slinging that still roam in today's world. It sickens me. And because black people still have something to prove, it's going to take the greatest unthinkable act by a black man to break the racial barriers of this country. And by the way God's been acting lately, don't be surprised if it happens soon."

He despises guns and says: "The sight of even a blank one on a movie set scares me beyond belief."

"What else scares you?"

"*Hunger,* poverty."

"What's your thought on this silent philanthropist who's donated almost a billion to inner-city schools and run down communities and yet has never come forth?"

"I think it's wonderful," he smiles.

"I think it's *you,* Darian Fable," Nikki smiles back.

He holds his smile to hers, trying not to break in laughter.

"And ... I also think you're being *way* too humble, Mr. Fable."

"Have you met my best friend, Spark?" He reaches down to pet.

So goes the mysterious hero, lover, father, and friend to many by the simple means of their movie screens and entertainment magazines. The inner, private, and exclusive thoughts of one angelic, humane spirit, who made your night content and your day a little more pleasant. A man who no doubt desires to remain chosen, but not forgotten, in the cruel cravings of a *hungry* 21st century.

Do you like Darian Fable?

CHAPTER 32

IN STUDIO CITY, CALIFORNIA, the lights still surge; but the desktop PCs and IBM memories are long vacated, as Faith and Sheila whistle through the Queen Bee's possessions that nested in the hive from which she stung, at *Barsolla Management Company.*

Faith directs Sheila to pluck through several weeks of accumulated manila that slipped the forwarded request of the U.S. Postal's short-lived memory. Sheila swipes into a clear mail bin. The bin, overflowing, holds invites to movie premiers, charity functions, and other PR praisings for the *clicky chosen;* the Fables in billion-to-one odds will attend.

Sheila's sifting for significant pieces, which have BMC's personal monthly code of GOLF transcribed just below its home address. This is to ensure the package was solicited prior to its send-off by a heavyweight colleague. All of the half million *cattle* who roam the streets of Hollywood for fame have a standard 8"x10" airbrushed black-and-white. All have their stapled resume of credits attached to the back of the photo that list work from loft-size playhouse to national car commercials. And *all* read like a sequel to *Liar, Liar.* The majority of cattle, at one time or another, almost always boast a featured role in a *Tales from the Crypt* episode or a Roger Corman bikini flick. But all can't fool the heaviest. This secret code of GOLF stops any "unsolicited" part-timers from wasting valuable look time at a doctored resume' by this elite company that boasts the smallest list but largest client in movie history. The owner's husband.

As Sheila flings and tosses the uncoded tip-earnings of dreamers to the wastebasket, she stumbles on a violet-colored envelope that's addressed to a "Mr. Jose."

"Mr. Jose?" she ponders aloud.

Faith strolls over. "Oh, it's nothing." She drags her smoke. "It's just an old friend of Darian's from his childhood. Oh, Jesus, that Jose, he sneaks through now and then. He's harmless. Darian bought him a house some years ago; I don't remember the full details. I think he helped him out when he was younger."

"Helped who?"

"Helped Darian. Just forget about it. I'll let him know the old padre's still breathing. For now just toss it."

Sheila squints a closer look to notice the post-office stamp of "(something) Park, IL." She starts contemplating. Park in Illinois doesn't rhyme with Rutledge in Vermont, birthplace of the star. *Something's* off.

"Bought him a house? Isn't that a bit overboard?" She fakes more sifting.

"Yes it's overboard. I could have killed him!"

"Wow he's generous, how much was the house?" Sheila noses in.

"About $120,000 cash. Can you believe it?"

"Well, yeah, but then again, how 'bout that guy who's giving these billions away and hasn't come forth yet?" says Sheila.

"Oh, what a joke; I've got two words for him, suck-er!"

"Well you know, Faith, he is helping a lot of unfortunate people in the world."

"Yeah, well, listen Sheila, if people can't shit for themselves, screw 'em. No one helped me out when my mother died."

"Hey Faith, you've ever been to Vermont?"

"No, and what for?"

"You know, to see Darian's birthplace."

"Listen, honey, between you and me, Darian had a horrible childhood and never wanted to talk about it, so I never pried. He likes his little secrets, like we all do, right? Besides, what matters is the present and not the past. If he wants it that way, then so be it. Now just toss that *ugly fucking* Mexican envelope."

Toss it to the trash, Sheila does. But her Boston street-smarts flare up a sudden urge to hunt. Faith knows more and Sheila's growling to know. "You know, I thought something was strange when we couldn't find anyone from his childhood who remembered him from Rutledge."

Faith ignores her packing. "It was David back then, remember?"

"Faulkner, right?"

Faith's hands rest to her hips. "Ah ... yeah."

Sheila takes Faith's irritated cue to back down and continue rapid-firing anything non-coded to the trash. With two bundles down and four to go, she scores another GOLF code. It's another greeting-card envelope. But a prettier one. A bright canary yellow. *Wow, this is strange*, she wonders to herself.

Faith, who's all work but more ears, halts her packing of who's-who photos that once sprawled the five-story main lobby.

"What now, Sheila?"

Sheila doesn't say a word. She turns over the evidence to Faith, who eyes it with embarrassment.

Mr. Darian Fucking Fable
c/o his bitch wife

"Ooh," Faith says, smiling, "wonder who this is from?"

She rips into it with instant wrath, while frowning a cold stare to Sheila. Sheila doesn't understand the instant flare-up or Faith's eagerness to rip inside.

"Goddamn it!" Faith snaps. "You know, we've got a staff of I don't know *how many* to accept this shit and keep it far from my office? Now, I'd like to know *who* and *how* these fuckhead freaks are getting a hold of this code I religiously change like ... every Goddamn month?"

"I don't know," Sheila stands clear.

Faith finally yanks the contents out, as a Polaroid photo innocently floats to the floor, landing face-down.

Hey Daddy O,
Hope your happiness is found outside of moviemaking, and thanks for
the many years of nothing, you stubborn, selfish bastard!!!!
Love, your daughter,
The Bitch!

Faith nibbles her lower lip and mumbles the word "again."

"Again what?" Sheila tiptoes over her back for a peak.

"Nothing, it's just another obsessed bitch claiming to be Darian's kid."

"Do you mind?" Sheila reaches out. Faith hands it over.

"How many of these have you gotten?" Sheila asks with a gleam in her eye. Faith fires a nonfilter and stares through the window to the headlights along rush hour Ventura Boulevard.

"I mean...it's *really* no big deal! It's probably the 100th or so daughter and 70th son this year. Do the math, by now he has a total of 250 kids. What a stud, huh?" Faith jokes and Sheila fakes a smile.

Faith then bends down to snatch up the enclosed picture for a closer view. Suddenly, her face slips to an insecure fear and a hidden rage of envy. Together, she and Sheila explore the 3"x5". It flaunts the sexual poses of a seductive female. It appears from the seedy backdrop of this color Polaroid, it was shot exclusively on location in a 2½-star motel room. The enticing "miss" has a black leather jacket unzipped to her waistline, with panties that match her low cut lacy bra. Her dark eyewear serves and protects her identification. Her loose ringlets of auburn hair are held in place by two butterfly barrettes that are more fit for a 12-year-old.

The thigh-high stockings mold nicely to her thighs, minus the support of a garter belt. Posing as a rodeo bucker riding a bull, the girl holds a bright pink squirt gun with one hand and grabs a firm squeeze of her black-satin crotch with the other.

"Well, I'll give her one thing," Faith puffs her deepest drag yet, "she does strike a weird kind of chord with me."

"Yeah, but...I mean how are these freaking weirdoes getting your personal code?" Sheila's stumped.

"You know what, Sheila?" Faith says looking down on her seriously. "That's a good question," she continues, scrutinizing the snapshot. Firing another smoke, Faith now becomes lost in her thought.

She grabs at her neck and begins fiddling the silver locket from left to right, followed with a nibble to her manicured nail.

"Who would break and give my code of the month," she whispers in a tone that's borderline accusing Sheila.

"What?" Sheila blushes.

"Nothing, where's the postmark from?" she checks the envelope. *Pomona, CA.*

"This is the sixth or so card in several weeks of this naughty little nature. I mean why would this stupid bitch send a photo?"

"Well, yeah, but..."

"But what?"

"Well, she's hot in a weird way," Sheila blushes *again*.

"Sheila Deblin, are you a fucking dyke?"

"No!"

"Come on, Sheila, you can tell me," Faith smirks.

Sheila's face beats red from embarrassment. Faith lets her off quickly.

"I'm just teasing, but what's that comment supposed to mean?"

"Well, it means it's kind of creepy, don't you think? Does Darian know about these little secret cards and letters?"

"No, I never told him. Maybe I'm naïve, but what do I do, show him every naked woman and turn every sick-o death threat over to him? Honey, this is no danger!"

Faith stamps her smoke out to the marble floor, then heads back to her packing.

"Not to sweat, Sheila, this isn't the first. I got it under control, sweetheart. Plus, *believe me*, if a kid's out there, we'd know about it by now."

"Sure," Sheila's eyes *still* roam the photo.

"Besides, Darian and I hold no secrets back, dear," Faith says, continuing to pack.

"Well, you know," Sheila slips, "Darian did have his share of women before you, Faith, and he may have..."

Faith confronts her. "Listen to you! Let's get something straight, Miss Deblin, Darian and I have *no* secrets! We know everything there is to know, he and I only! I don't want to get into it, okay? It's for his ears and mine only! Just toss it! Everything! Get all of this shit out of here *please*. Take it to the shredder downstairs! Now!"

"Well, excuse me," Sheila fires back.

The moment of tension is unbearable for both. In their thirteen-plus years of sisterly teamwork, the two have never raised their voice at each other. Sheila has a hunch there's more than meets the hidden eyes of this 3"x5"; but for now, the bulldog will shred away as ordered. If she keeps the photo, Faith may take to a serious notion that she really is gay, a secret Sheila's never made public.

Faith fights to regain her cool. She reaches for her pill to place the first of two calls she needs—one for Chinese food to make amends with Sheila, and the other to her husband—who, according to her wrist, should be wrapped up from his long day in Westport. But first, to pull her nerves together for the long night ahead, she must take her *pill* which she knows is somewhere afloat in the drawers of her desk. The pill that her concerned and worried husband couldn't smell if he *dared,* some three thousand miles away. It should still be in that drawer that held her morning, noon, and nighttime remedy she hasn't sipped in weeks. She pulls at the bottom drawer on the lower right. But where's the key? *That bottle better still be there, Sheila better be shredding downstairs, and that bitch Nikki Hopkins had better left my grounds.* Bingo. Two for three on the above.

CHAPTER 33

BACK IN WESTPORT, THE TAPING IS A SUCCESS. The crew has wrapped, wound down, and rumbled out from the star's gate, by the late sundown of 8:53 P.M. Darian finishes a lengthy goodbye game with Nikki, who is now staggered from the post-interview $300 bottle of Merlot she and she alone has sipped dry. She's 0 for 20 on come-ons to Darian, who respectfully escorts her to the stretch limousine. Finally, after ten goodbye hugs and a couple of "oopsy daisies," she is on her way. *Darian is drained.* As he heads inside to chat goodnights and thank-yous briefly with Mary, the phone rings, and it's his loving wife from L.A.

"Well, how'd it go, lover?" Faith lazies her words across the time zones.

"Okay. I should have at least a million more enemies by air time next month."

"Good, take some from me. Where's Nikki?" she asks.

"She left about ten minutes ago," Darian yawns, "the wine started taking over."

"Ooh really, about ten minutes ago, huh? You two spent some time together now, did you?"

"Yeah, it was great sex," he teases.

"Well, I wouldn't be surprised. It's no secret she gets a little *too* touchy when she sips."

"You just won't let up on her, will you?"

"Hey, I'm just joking!" She fakes a giggle. "So anyway lover," she yawns, "L.A. still sucks, but I have to stay at the office 'til at least midnight, so don't wait up for me. I'll call you first thing in the morning. Got it?"

"Got it."

"Good. Oh, and listen, Dare … one more thing. I got something weird today in the mail."

"Weird? What kind of weird?"

"Ah, it's nothing; I'll tell you later," she threatens a quick hang up.

"No, wait! Tell me, come on."

"No."

"Yes!"

"No, no, no … "

"Oh, come on, for God's sake, Faith."

"I … don't know, I … "

"Come on!"

"*Beg me, lover,*" she teases.

"What?"

"Relax, it's no big deal! It was someone wishing you well after Hollywood and calling you a fucking asshole. There, ya' happy?"

"So, what's weird about that?"

"Well … "

"Well, what? Wasn't it you who said if everyone loves you, you're nobody in this town?"

"It's *you ain't shit* in this town, and it wasn't me."

"Tell me more about this card. I mean, there must be more than your giving up."

"Well, it's signed … *love, your daughter, the bitch.* She said she was your daughter! Can you believe that one? Darian, do you have a daughter?" she asks.

"Where's Sheila?"

"Oooh, you fucker, you didn't answer me!" she laughs.

"I see you're Miss Nasty Mouth again."

"Oh well, sorry. So, do you have a daughter, Mr. Fable?"

"Yeah, fifty." He's not amused.

"I knew it, you fucker."

Darian's now concerned, and it's not over this *daughter issue*.

"Are you tired? Where's Sheila?"

"She's on the first floor, shredding."

"Shredding?"

"Yes, sir! *Sure—redding*," she giggles.

"Shredding what?"

"Obscenities, like the dirty little picture your girlfriend sent you."

"What are you talking about? What picture?"

"You'll never see. Look, it's no secret you have admirers, but, uh ... honey, this card was definitely *strange*."

"Strange how?"

"How nothing. You ask too many questions! I gotta go!"

"Wait!" He tries to hold her ear.

"Wait for what?" she holds.

"Nothing, just huh, what makes people tick the wrong way."

He hears cubes jingling and smoke blowing through the receiver.

"I don't know. But I *do know* that I think I'm already missing you. Am I sick?"

"No, you're not sick, honey—you're just a funny girl."

With that, Darian sends off his love and Faith follows with hers to Mary and Spark. She even throws in a mention of Santos.

As they disconnect, Darian starts to feel funny. Could it be a relapse of guilt he felt on his last ride from fame? The air through the study window brings the reminiscent smell of late-night L.A. from his younger years, assisted by his wife's slurring tone.

His mind congers up his buried curiosity. What happened to the many women he fled from like a burning bed before Faith set in? Has his own self-absorption slammed shut any memories and feelings towards others in his distant past? And what's going on in Pleasant Park? Why hasn't the phone rung? Surely, someone must have a clue about *David*-turned-Darian. They now have computers and are a little more in tune with the outside world. He dashes upstairs to seek out old photo memories that are buried in one of the many *cluttered closets* in an unoccupied bedroom. The purposely cluttered closets that secure the grown man at sundown from any scampering reminder of darkness at 1933 Maple Avenue.

CHAPTER 34

I**T'S** 2:00 A.M. EASTERN AND 11:00 P.M. on the West Coast. Darian, who's deliriously tired from his final performance, begins the exhausting search of his pictured past. He's checked all but one of the twelve bedrooms' closets, packed full with rubbish and has come up empty-handed. He heads for what was once his wife's sleeping quarters, just three weeks ago. The transfer of her creams and hygiene products to his bedroom was only a hop, a half-day, and a room away. But upon entering, he hunches it could take weeks to move Her Highness wardrobe into his master-chamber.

Tugging open her closet door, he gets a sudden urge at what lies in her walk-in *boutique*. It's cluttered, but neatly organized, with racks of designer shoes still in their boxes, evening gowns dangling with price tags, and everyday wear that overindulges the rows of shelves and racks on the side. He can smell Faith's pheromones. He picks a pink cashmere-wool sweater and brings it to his nose. It breathes the scent of pineapple-and-tangerine lotion. *This* is what he smells from his bed while she's bathing.

He spots a mustard-brown photo album atop a steel briefcase. He's been curious about that briefcase now for years. He's told it stores "valuable documents on him," per his wife's words. Such as early contractual agreements before he was a "somebody." It's been locked, stocked, and stored for safekeeping, some ten years. But while the cat's away, the mice shall play. He pulls the cruel safe case down to investigate its cold exterior. He notices the clamped keyhole won't snap open without the key's possessor, who is miles away from his snooping. He slips the case down and opts for the photo album that lies below *that* navy V-neck sweater Faith sported during the Fall nights in Los Angeles. He then strolls back to his room and hops in bed to picture-flip himself to sleep with briefcase at side, and photo album in hand. He finds a photo of himself and Faith, showcasing his fisted grip of the first Oscar he received from the Academy nearly four years ago. As the *humbled* one skims the many photos of "back when," the many faces beam and scream for his attention. There's he and Nick crashing a movie premiere bash thrown by Nick's late legendary father. Both are smashed, to say the least, while proudly baring their product-placement Heineken label for the camera's lens. There's a picture of Nikki and Nick in a dumpy Hollywood apartment, sifting party goods on a kitchen counter with a razor blade.

There's another of Faith, just days before the two hitched, taken at her father, Frank's, Malibu summer home. He reminisces over Frank, who has his daughter plopped on his lap, with a Miss California ribbon over her swimsuit for a laugh. Without Frank, there would be no Summerville, no Faith, and no one to rescue the orphan from Pleasant Park. He can see the miles of hard work on Frank's trenched, liver-spotted forehead. "Thank you, Frank," he says, touching the photo.

He looks to his dresser mirror and begins to question if his full head of silky hair will desert with age and time.

Seymore enters his mind, but he dumps him quickly and returns his eyes to Frank. He thinks of Faith and looks to the glow of his nightstand. It's now almost 3:30 A.M., time to get some sleep. But first, he wants to boyishly bother her to announce his proud finding of this lost treasure—the photo album. Maybe the call is not a good idea. She'll ask, "Who's in there?" an argument will ensue, and she'll demand all evidence be presented upon her return. How about just a goodnight chat of a minute or so? He reaches for the phone and finishes his dial, but is puzzled when the rings lead into Faith's personal voice mail. It's the first time he's never reached his loved one at her office to speak. If she were ever unavailable, an *assistant* would hunt her down and relay his beckoned wish in under a minute.

He listens with pleasure to the articulate and sultry tone of his wife's pipes. They bring him a soothing security, almost to the point of shut-eye, before the outgoing message beeps. But with the beep, Darian balks to speak, and simply clicks off.

It's now down to one final shot. He'll try her cell phone. She loves that *pill*. She'll snatch it up in a quarter ring, he bets. Maybe he'll get lucky and connect with her on the dusky road of Coldwater Canyon. That's the quickest route that leads over the Valley to the Four Seasons Hotel on Doheny Boulevard. Faith's home away from the 22 they landlord. What perfect timing to safeguard her from the roaming packs of coyotes that scurry the canyon cliffs nightly. But the only voice he's greeted with is that of another powerful female known to millions. *"We're sorry but the cell phone customer you're trying to reach is not available at this time. Please try your call later."*

"That's *odd*," he ponders. Where the hell could she be? He guesses at her having a late-night dinner with Sheila at the Seasons, or maybe her *mania* has taken over and she's digging like a gopher through a rubble of papers into the early-morning sunrise.

Regardless, Sheila's most likely long gone, being she trusts no one and would never drive the 5 Freeway at midnight, in fear of gang cruisers and sleepless semis on a rushing rampage to San Bernardino. He dedicates to retry in ten minutes, but first insists on flipping to more of his treasured past and frozen faces of lost "acquaintances."

CHAPTER 35

A̲T 3:54 A.M. DARIAN FABLE IS DEAD ASLEEP in a fetal position atop his canopy king-size bed. The perfect photos of his *imperfect* past lie beside him, under him, and slither off his bedside with every toss and turn. He's still decorated in his 501's and suede blue button-down, as his barefoot hooves fall pleasantly numb from the cool outdoor breeze that blows through the open French doors of his balcony.

Suddenly, his *coma* is interrupted by the harsh telephone ring that frets his 20 minutes into Dreamville. His senses alert after several rings pass. He has an instant hunch it may be Faith who now wants to play a little, knowing her husband can be *boyishly agitated* when awoken from his deep snooze.

"Hey lover? You sleeping? I love you. I miss you," he can hear her say now.

Darian answers in a playful, monarchy tone, "Yes, my dear."

"Darian Fable?" a deep male voice pierces his ear.

Keep dreaming.

To Darian's alarm, he is blasted with a rich and less than sultry greeting, from a thick and brawly accent, perhaps English, Irish, or something with those cold and frigid tones. Darian rejects the baited offer, presuming it's another lucky prankster who aspires to annoy him for a joke throughout the night. Should he give in, it will cause yet another phone-listing change for the Fables, whose number changes like bed sheets do in hotels.

"Mr. Darian Fable, please!" the voice now commands in military fashion over the passing minute of dead air.

Darian reluctantly gives in, but only nips the tip of the baited wire. "Who is this?" he disguises his voice down to a whisper.

"Mr. Fable, sir! Is that you, I ask?" the voice barrels on.

"No, he's not here!" Darian replies in a gravelly hush. "Who is this?"

"Alrighty then sir, this is Detective Jonathan E. Murray from the Los Angeles Police Department here, and I must speak to Mr. Darian Fable!"

Darian's sleepy body remains weary. He isn't yet buying into this late night hoax. But this funny accent is almost convincing for a B-phone prankster. It sounds like old tricky Nick's had too much of the bottle and has festered up a drunken nerve to phone after countless years of rejection.

"Is this Mr. Fable, I ask?" the voice demands once again.

For Nick, Darian needs more clues, so he tosses the impostor a lazy "Yes."

The voice now proceeds forth like an immoralistic, premeditated gag.

"Alrighty now, listen carefully Mr. Fable! Your wife … ah …" the voice trips a second, "Faith Barsolla, has been involved in a serious car accident, sir, and I'm sorry to inform you that your presence is required immediately in Los Angeles."

Darian now fully awakes. "Wait a minute! Now just wait a fucking minute! Who is this? Nick? Come on, Nick? This isn't funny … who is this!"

"Who's this?" the voice challenges back.

This game player is out of line. This is no longer amusing, and old Nick wouldn't be *that* tasteless. Darian wants to slam the receiver, but curiosity causes the mouse to listen on, while his paw begins to quiver.

"Answer me God damn it! Who is this!" Darian yells.

"Once again, sir, this is Detective Jonathan E. Murray from the Los

Angeles Police Department, sir! You must listen to me! This is no joking matter, gosh damn it!"

Darian now braces for the possible worst. He flashes back to how he didn't buy the call from his drunken whore aunt some 22 years ago on New Year's Eve. Then Christmas had passed and it was *too good* to be true.

The caller's frustrated tone validates his credibility.

"Okay, hold on … just hold on a minute," Darian quickly gathers himself. "Is, is she all right?"

"Well, Mr. Fable, she's been rushed to Cedar Sinai Medical in Los Angeles. But as for now, sir, I must demand that your presence is needed at once *in* Los Angeles!"

Darian's mind is made up, but his fear won't allow him to accept. He needs just a bit more.

"Who did you say you were?"

"You listen to me sir—loud and clear! I am Detective Jonathan E. Murray, sir, and you may call me back to authenticate! Hold on a second, aye?"

There's a pause, as Darian's ear hones into background jabbering. Whispering and phone rings are heard over the partially muffled receiver. The Detective loses credibility as he snaps at someone in anger. "What do I have to do for a gosh damn number here, aye!"

He returns in carefree fashion. "Alrighty then, sir, here's the number. You ready for a jot?"

"Go ahead," Darian speaks penless.

"310-824-6765—did you copy that, sir?"

Silence.

"Hello? Mr. Fable?"

"All right. Okay, okay, I'll be there!"

Darian drops the receiver and scurries from his bed. His heart races, while his mind freezes. The pane on the French doors reflect silhouette shadows from the tree branches that sway from the yard. He hears the sounds of a hooting owl that excites and triggers scampering raccoons. He reacts quickly in fear and slams the French doors shut. He stares at himself in the mirror, and reaches for the receiver to phone back the scribbled digits his frazzled brain remarkably jotted. But once he connects, he hears the scariest voice of American authenticity.

Good morning, the Beverly Hills Police Department.

PART THREE

CHAPTER 36

THE *CHARTERED* 737 LANDS ON RUNWAY 35 and taxis for a half mile before halting far from Terminal 6 Gate, 21B. Mary and Santos assist the dazed and confused legend as he unboards to the toxic runway fumes that swarm the air of his unkingly arrival. Darian can't deny the familiar dew of polluted mist he ran from several weeks ago. Then, his tolerance was a few moments away from final freedom. But now, his red-eye return has triggered frightened flashbacks of when the orphan from Pleasant Park landed with little more than his bag of crinkled laundry and his lost mother's smoking jacket.

He studies the overcast glow of skyline beyond the miles of serenely lit runways before he steps down from the jet. Checking his watch in the still of 4:12 A.M., he's safely reassured that the millions of roaming lions are now peacefully asleep in their dens in the city they *still* have the nerve to call "angels."

Awaiting below the jet's wings are the flashing red of three unmarked sedans with six officers, who meet him without smiles but with sober nods. They then whisk the trio in stately speeds of 95 through the sloped freeway and misty mountain blackness of the 405

South, which is clear the entire way to Cedar Sinai Medical Center in Beverly Hills.

Huddled between Mary and Santos in the back seat, Darian begins to bargain with his Lord. He asks to awaken him from this hellish dream and he will never abandon his wife's side again. But the dream deal is off when inhaling the back breeze of nicotine, compliments of the impervious mustache of the law, who passengers *shotgun.*

Mary, as expected, is holding it together, consoling the distraught one who rests his tense grip in her calming hands. Darian looks to Santos, who's all *ears* with *stares,* infatuated with the radio dispatchings and a double-barrelled-shotgun that's locked to the front of the dashboard. The *loaded* shotgun that's ready to blast, smoke, and no doubt shred, should it ever be called upon.

• • •

PAPARAZZI AND NEWS PHOTOGRAPHERS gather in dozens outside Cedars, to hear what police have so far only released as "a serious car wreck" involving the icon's wife. As the three sedans slip past all at the east entrance, the frenzy of flashbulb poppings illuminate off any glass from the media vultures who swarm upon the speeding convoy for a frame or two of the "chosen one" in "panic mode."

Once safely isolated underground, the trio is quickly hustled to the intensive care unit on the fourth floor of the wing. As they exit the freight elevator and swing the corner of doom, Darian sights three men in a distance. They look to be holding secret court in a huddled circle. The convoy's heels clicking on the shiny tile sends notice to the mammoth one of the bunch, who breaks their huddle and begins to observe the approaching trio but fixates his sight on Darian. The mammoth one and Darian make eye-to-eye contact and it sticks, even from 60-something steps apart. The mammoth one transmits his blue eyes, beefy face, and tweed undercoverings in a funny-*challenging* way to the distraught husband.

Darian recognizes the short and frail figure of the bunch, in his angel-white scrubs, who lowers his surgical mask as they near. It's none other than the notable surgeon of Cedar's, Dr. Marcus W. Freidman. The two have exchanged hellos and smiles at a fund-raising event that the star and his wife would sneak in and out of quickly.

Though the tweed suit and the tiny surgeon appear semi-collected, Darian spots a troubling look from the third and sleek *blue suit.* His honest, dark eyes are transmitting hopeless signals of empathy.

The trio and their six escorting badges reach their destination. Doctor Freidman extends his hands to embrace Darian. But the sadness in the doctor's watery eyes tells all before his voice *proclaims the mystery of Faith.*

"I'm sorry, Darian, but we've lost her. She's gone."

The verdict is in.

CHAPTER 37

DARIAN SWARMS ABOUT, HEADING NOWHERE, while burying his face in his hands. He flees into the farthest corner and falls to his knees.

"No, no, my God! No! Why? God! Why?" he cries like a boy.

Mary follows and joins in with an uncontrollable cry of her own. Santos cradles his boss, who's crouched to the chilled tile and down for a count of tearful hysteria.

Mary attempts to console. "Darian, I'm here. I'm with you." Darian tries to rise on his own, but stumbles into Santos's arms that guide him to a nearby sofa.

Darian looks at the strangers who pity his loss and study his reaction. The mammoth tweed-suit must be in his late fifties. He has a handlebar mustache, slicked well with tonic oil. Strangely, he projects a comforting, grandfatherly vibe to Darian. He reminds him of that shark hunter in the movie *Jaws*. Darian's forgotten his name. The blue-suit is 30-something, who vibes more like a Hollywood agent, from perhaps ICM. His sneaky movements and that toothpick in his mouth don't comfort the star, who sees him slither off to a nearby corner to spy. Darian's peek at the holster under his suit jacket validates any doubt he's not present to solicit the paranoid and suddenly *free agent.*

"I want to see her now," Darian orders to the doctor.

Freidman and the blue-suit look at the tweed-suit who takes a step to center stage. He kneels to the sitting star.

"I'm sorry, but you can't see her now," the voice replies in a peaceful, sympathetic tone. *It's him,* the *Gaelic one.* The prankster who's now face to face. Darian looks up slowly, only to be greeted by a bulbous, potholed beak.

He turns to Santos who looks the stranger over from his peppered curly hair, to size-fourteen patent-leather shoes.

"You're Murray, aren't you?" Darian speaks.

"Yes, I am, Mr. Fable. Detective Jonathan E. Murray and this is my partner Mike Campbell, Los Angeles Homicide," he modestly replies.

The blue-suit nods. Murray proceeds.

"Sir, we're deeply sorry about your wife. And I apologize for the alarm I might of caused you hours ago. It's all just a terrible shame."

Darian wipes tears on his windbreaker's sleeve. He looks up at Murray, who seems as though he's preparing to scold the man.

"Did you just say Homicide?" Darian fears.

Murray clears his throat. "I reckon I did, sir."

He then gently motions with his hand for Darian to follow him.

"Can I have a word with you please, Mr. Fable ... over there, sir?" he points with his eyes. Darian rises and obliges. Santos proceeds to follow close behind, but Campbell's gentle forearm signals the puppy to stay put. The two make their way from all ears but well within everyone's view. They stroll to a partition that overlooks the pre-dawn traffic lights of quiet San Vicente Boulevard.

Murray checks the gold-chain watch that hangs from his caramel colored vest. He then reaches into his suit's inner pocket and pulls a pack of nonfiltered Camels.

"Smoke?" he offers.

Darian, startled, looks to Freidman, who's peacefully chatting with Mary.

"No thanks."

Murray puts the smoke to his mouth, but doesn't fire up. He then reaches into his jacket and pulls out a silver flask.

"Swig?"

Darian again looks to the bright lights of the corridor. *What's up with this drink and smoke stuff at Cedar?* Maybe he really is dreaming. "No thank you … Detective."

"This," Murray takes a swig, "is between *you and me.*"

"Whatever, Detective."

"Call me Jonathan, and don't worry about this," he jiggles the flask. "It's nothing. It's just our little secret." *Five more haunting words.*

Murray sucks away in view of the party in the next room, as *that* Hard Rock Cafe's Thunderbird taillights in the rooftop across the street blink off Darian's face. Darian suddenly becomes a lookout for Murray, to Freidman and the party, who aren't paying any attention. Things seemed to be settling in there, he notices. Settling almost *too much.* He and Murray are probably silhouettes from the view of the x-rayed lobby. Darian now feels more of a loss than he did minutes ago. *Who is this man they call Detective? Nothing more than an Irish drunk for the loss of my precious wife.* Is this all the city has on hand? But then again, van Gogh, and, God knows, Jack have had their share of the bottle. Not to mention his dead wife. Suddenly, Murray's the best L.A. has to offer.

"Ah, look at this city. Bunch of animals out there, lad," Murray says. "Where are you from Mr.—can I call you Darian?"

"Vermont," he says, staring to his taillight blinking view.

"Vermont, aye! Now there's a peaceful, but *boring* state. Me, I came here from Northern Ireland some twelve years ago to escape the animals of territorial boundaries, and ended up right back in a jungle. A jungle of greed. It doesn't make sense, you know, all these killings every minute on the half-hour. Welcome back to Hollywood, my boy."

Darian hears violin strings.

Murray swigs again. Darian senses this guy's a heavy chucker, judging by his scarred, potholed beak and *that* accent.

"Detective, do you mind please telling me what the hell happened?"

"Oh, I will, son, that you can bet on. But first, I want you to know between you and me, that I'm with you all the way," Murray winks.

"What do you mean by 'you and me?'"

"Oh, I … I know who you are. You're a good kid. Look lad, I'm terribly sorry about the loss of your wife. I myself lost a wife many years ago, who was caught in a crossfire of rebels while grocery shopping one day. But that's then and many years past."

Violins.

"Look, ah, what's this about, Detective?"

"Well, I hate to break it to you, son, but this is far beyond a routine car fatality."

Darian turns to the lobby again. Santos is now chatting casually with Campbell.

"Just what the hell are you trying to say, Detective?"

"Well, Darian, you see, *yes* your wife was involved in a terrible car accident, now that we know for sure. But upon arrival to the scene, *sir*, we found she did not die from the impact of a car wreck alone. In fact, the car wreck itself wasn't even a factor. It was the wreckage *in* the car. You see, Darian," he rest his hands on his shoulders, "it's been discovered that your wife was stabbed to death. Savagely murdered, just cut up real badly, sir, you really don't want to see her, we have dental records and ... "

Darian loses his breath. Suddenly Murray's a prized boxer who's just punched a blow to his heart. He stumbles from the roped corner back to his entourage in the lobby.

Just before reaching Mary and Santos, his 6'2" frame collapses, and his cheekbone slaps to the cold and squeaky-clean tile of the floor. The doctor and a nearby nurse rush to his aid. Freidman pushes away Campbell who tries to assist the *star*.

"Just back off a minute!" he warns Campbell. "Darian," Freidman gently holds him by the head, "are you okay?"

Darian struggles to crawl for a chair. He leans his head back and stares to the fluorescent ceiling tiles that burn his irritated eyes. Murray, who was watching all the way, now casually strolls over like a lion tamer in a circus. Campbell, on a cue from the veteran Murray, now takes over. "Darian," he confronts on a first-name basis, "are you okay?"

Darian doesn't respond.

"Look, we'll know more in the next few hours about this tragedy, but for now we desperately need your help. *Help* on any information you may have for us. You understand, don't you?"

Darian still doesn't respond, and Mary's now heard enough.

"Excuse me, Detective, you want to tell me what the hell is going on here?"

"Ma'am."

"Don't 'ma'am' me! Darian, should I call Sid?"

"No," he shakes his head. "There's no need to, Mary, I'll pull it together. Don't worry," he assures her.

Murray reaches for another nonfilter, as Campbell gets the evil eye from Santos, whose patience to sit like a good puppy is growing thin.

Darian rises and composes himself to semi-normal.

"Where do we start?" he says, *suddenly* pulling it together.

Campbell and Murray look at each other. Murray nods. Campbell continues.

"Darian, this is not what it seems. We just want to question you a little down at headquarters. It's only twenty minutes away."

"That's it. I'm calling Sid!" Mary snaps.

Santos rises.

"Now hold on a moment, miss," Murray speaks to calm her and the others.

"Darian, as of now you are *not* a suspect! I want you all to know that right now and right here! We just want some answers to kick our investigation into a higher gear," he adds.

Darian donates a suspecting look to Campbell. He can't believe where this so-called investigation is leading. This fatherly-looking figure, Murray, is insinuating Darian may be hiding something. And this punk rookie's too cute for a cop. *Something's up his designer sleeve.*

"Let me get this straight. Are you guys saying I'm not a suspect in this? Or are you saying you need information?"

Campbell injects again.

"Look, Darian, we need information, but we also need your cooperation. Come on, man, we just want to *get* to the bottom of this, you understand, don't you?"

Suddenly Campbell hits a bad nerve.

"No, you understand, Detective," Darian rises. "You understand that I'm going to go down to your headquarters. You, Mr. Murray, and I. Then, I'm going to give you everything you want and anything you need. And then you're going to find the animal that butchered my wife. And I'm not going to take some episode of *Unsolved Mysteries* for an answer. Do you understand?"

The neutral Murray was waiting for the fire to begin, and the screen idol has finally lit it. His plan has worked. Darian hates Campbell but, so far, likes him. Murray's won his trust and can now pry into anything he likes. It's a perfect partnership. The mild and the cocky.

But now this *somebody* named Darian has insulted the frail ego of Campbell, who broadens his shoulders and speaks.

"Ah, Mr. Fable, with all due respect, we don't tell you how to do your job, so please don't advise us on ours. We'll find your wife's killer, but for now, can we all just get along?"

Murray reads the tension between his slick-dick partner and the legend's studded ego. He bids with a trusting wink to his *lad* Darian to carry on before the star sways into a stubborn need to call on *that guy* named "Sid."

"Alrighty then! Shall we hit it, Darian?" Murray motions towards the exit.

Darian looks at Mary, who shows no reaction, then on to Santos, who strokes his mustache with a *frown.*

"Detective?" Darian looks to Murray.

"Go ahead."

"They're coming with me."

"Well, I have no problem with that, my good friend; how 'bout you, Mike?"

"Not at all. No problem here, *Darian.*"

CHAPTER 38

Iᴛ's ʙᴇᴇɴ ᴏᴠᴇʀ ᴛᴡᴏ ʜᴏᴜʀs at Parker Center Police Headquarters in downtown Los Angeles. The same downtown that weeks ago showered the star and his *living* half with heaps of warmth and red-carpet royalty, now has the "messiah of film" in a 12'x9' room, with bulbs beaming hotter than a cafeteria buffet. The star *perk* on this center stage is coffee by the Styrofoam cup, as two civil servants who earn in a year what his dead wife earned in an hour bluntly pry for gossip on their terms.

Without that *guy* Sid present, Murray dances Irish jigs, in and out of routine questions the law asks when a spouse is murdered. Were there any infidelity problems? The answer is yes throughout rumorville, but, according to Darian, not in his fifteen years. Murray then asks, *just for the record*, if any financial problems are brewing in the couple's estimated $30 billion kingdom. Before Darian's response, Murray checks it off before killing himself from laughter.

"I've got to go through this for the record, Darian, you understand, don't you?"

"I understand. I have nothing to hide."

Murray concludes that it's a slim to zero chance the wonder boy of film was involved in such a satanic butchering on the pitch-dark road of Coldwater Canyon. Sure, big money will buy you a murder or clean hit, but in the end, the dead always speak from their grave. Just ask a guy named O.J. On the other hand, a hundred bucks will get you blood by the buckets from a homeless street junkie on any corner in America. Then you're safe. No identity, no residence, and no more than a year or two before the desperado who did the sloppy hit is found pulseless in a restaurant Dumpster. The witty Irishman's ploy to plant his seed of trust to Darian the first hour has won. But now the second hour has his boy becoming feisty and drained from tear-shedding and jet lag. Murray knows his limits, and, like a smart cop, will reach for the jugular in the final minutes. The old-timer from County Cork wants to ensure himself that he hasn't a football Hall of Famer on his turf. The same Hall of Famer that sang and danced in '96, only to get off and return years later, with his newly found God in one pocket, his mug on *People* magazine in the other, and the pay-per-view profits of $150 million for his confessional detail in the slicing and dicing of his beloved wife. O.J. tried, but couldn't allow his broken and guilty conscience to rest any longer in the poverty of his peace. *In time.*

But unlike the Simpson case that could have filled the Grand Canyon with physical evidence, this one has fled the gate; without a print to pull, a passing headlight to reflect, or a coyote's plaintive wail for time of death, some five hours from the gruesome discovery.

• • •

THE 39-YEAR-OLD IS SQUEAKY CLEAN—no surprise from "the poster man of decency." There's not even a trace of a jay-walking ticket from when angry David stumbled across a flashing "don't walk," with his drunken theater nobodies back "when."

A holding room away sits the most valuable witness of the night. The person who not only spoke to, but was last present with Faith Barsolla. The one and only Sheila Deblin. She describes to the note-taking Campbell her boss's demeanor of being normal and upbeat early on, but then bewildered and sluggish later.

"Sluggish? When?" Campbell questions.

"After some bizarre fan mail was discovered, addressed with satin and lace," Sheila colors.

Campbell asks why a provocative photo with a sexual connotation would upset the wife and manager of the biggest sex symbol in the world?

"I don't know," Sheila plays dumb, "but for the first time in almost thirteen years she seemed to lose control. Complete control. I remember I left the office around ten, because I never drive the freeways after eleven. Anyway, it was clear we would meet early the next morning to send off some final few boxes of personals to a summer residence in Naples."

"What do you mean by 'personals'?"

"Things people acquire in their offices, mostly pictures of the famous or their family. Faith treasured pictures of friends in the business. I mean, she was born into it."

"And did *she* have a lot of friends in Hollywood?"

Sheila pauses. "I don't know, when you're famous you can't tell. I mean, I have a lot of friends ... I think."

"And what about that sexy photo and dirty card from this woman? Could it still be at the office?"

The solid and sturdy Sheila breaks and weeps, but quickly recovers to attempt to save her guilty conscience.

"She told me to shred it with the other junk mail from weeks gone by, and I did exactly what she ordered. I had to. You see, when Faith Barsolla orders, it's 'do what you're told, or forever be scold.'" Besides, it really wasn't that strange, you know, the card and note. I mean it posed a threat to her only because any woman did; that was Faith. She had to be in the center, like she was *still* Miss California. She *was* Miss California, you know."

"I know, please go on," he nods and smiles, "but first, what do you mean by 'do what you're told, or forever be scold?'"

"Well, there's the story of Amanda Richardson."

"Who's that?"

"Someone who worked for Faith early on. She was a longtime friend and former Miss San Diego."

"And?"

"She's dead."

"Dead? So what's that to do with Faith?"

"Her husband killed her."

"Whose husband?"

"Amanda's."

"Why?"

"Because Faith told him she was carrying a black actor's baby."

"Was she?"

"The autopsy revealed her unborn had Cherokee blood."

"I don't understand."

"It matched Amanda's drunken husband's."

"So, why would Faith lie?"

"Because Amanda was getting *too friendly* with Darian, so rumor had it."

"What do you mean by '*too friendly*'?"

"Figure it out, Detective, I've been with the Fables ever since then."

The bright light figures it out for Campbell. *Her face is a mess. Not with a ten-foot pole or Murray's dick.*

"Back to last night, did you get an address or postmark on the envelope?"

"Yeah, I did. It was mailed from Pomona, California."

"What about a name?"

"Only initials. W.F."

"And it *was* a white female in the picture, right?"

"Oh, yeah! She was white, and she was no slouchy-looking one, either."

"What do you mean?"

"Well, I'm sure *you* wouldn't kick her out of bed," she laughs.

Campbell excuses her after forty minutes, but warns he may have another session in store if needed. Sheila wobbles out to sit with Santos and Mary, who have already volunteered small-chat with Campbell.

He finishes jotting his notes on Sheila. Maybe another interview, not enough mourning. Too nonchalant. Motive? Unlikely. Pay another to her home in Glendale, he scratches. *This week.* Secret crush on D.F.? Maybe. Him? Interest? *Never.* Hollywood? *Maybe.*

CHAPTER 39

MURRAY AND CAMPBELL GATHER THEIR NOTES and huddle for their next move. They're summoned to the phone by a crime-scene tech, who has recovered what's believed to be the personal belongings of Faith Barsolla. Recovered is a measly $19 in cash and small silver, along with some jewelry valued in the five-digit range that was undisturbed and lay innocently among her blood-drenched clothing and carved flesh.

It's confirmed already by a speedy autopsy that she *was* indeed semi-conscious just before blades shut her down. Her head plummeted into the Mercedes airbag upon collision with a boulder that sat at the lonely cliffside. The bag did little in saving her life, but a lot in protecting the ID of the sneak attacker, who plowed in with over eighty jabs, stings, and twists that stung Her Highness's blindfolded vision. Over fifty quickies to her cheeks, two dozen to her eyes, neck, and countless more to her arms, chest, deflated air bag, and grayish custom-leather interior.

Disconnecting, Murray relays the info to his rookie who salivates for the veteran's theory.

"Pit-stop timing, one-two-three," Murray unfires another Camel to his mouth.

"Pit-stop timing? That's a new one, whatta ya mean?"

"Pit-stop timing!" Murray snarls. "In and out, that's what I say, lad! A minute or so at the most! Now what did you get out of the old lady. Mary's her name, right?"

"She's a little stunned. Says they had a clean marital record. According to her, normal sex life. Hotter than usual the last few weeks."

Murray looks in confusion. "Normal sex life? Now how without the Lord's eyes would she know that?" he grins before a gulp. "What about the Mexican ox in the lobby?"

Campbell shrugs. "Bodyguard. Nothing. He said Faith Barsolla was kind to him and that Darian's a big-brother figure, who he looks up to and loves."

"Yeah, I'll bet he loves him. What about the bag lady?"

"Publicist."

"No kidding?"

"She had nothing. Just another note from another fan. She destroyed it upon orders from Miss Barsolla."

"Well, what did it say?"

"Nothing a star wouldn't expect."

"That publicist is an ugly woman," Murray strokes his oily mustache. "*Mmm...* interesting."

"Interesting what?" Campbell asks.

Murray unfolds a thick magazine, which was rolled tighter than a diploma, from inside his suit jacket. The weighted glossy settles when tossed to Campbell. It's a three-month-old issue of *Glamour* magazine, sporting the dead victim's face: The headline innocently pokes, "The Faith Hollywood Loves to Hate."

"Nice. Older, but God, what a face," Campbell fascinates for a moment.

"Never mind her beauty, Campy! Who amongst us is not telling the damned truth?"

"Wait a minute, where did you dig this up from so quickly?"

"Never mind your business," Murray scolds like father to son. "Everyone hated this woman. It's no secret, look at her, Campy, there's miles of bitch patrol under that bratty smirk. Homework, my boy! You've got to do your homework!" he says, snagging and tucking it away, then retrieving another refill to his Styrofoam cup.

He then boasts a lesson to the "green one," while he pours from the flask his secret cream.

"Slow drinking and long thinking will mend unanswered questions in life, my son, but age," he pauses his pour, "age and Jonathan E. Murray will outwit even the wittiest. Now let's get back to work. But first! Two words, Campy, and what are they?" he quizzes along their stride.

"Rage killing."

"And how do we know that?"

"Jabs to the face."

"And who did it?"

"Someone who had a personal vendetta."

"Or has! And that *someone* is?"

"Someone close to her."

"Bingo, my boy!"

CHAPTER 40

MURRAY AND CAMPBELL RETURN TO DARIAN, who, with the help of the sun's rays at 6:50 A.M., sports the haggard look of a "beaten favorite" at *Hollywood Park*. Murray does the talking and ups his volume per his sixth jolt of caffeinated mud.

"Darian, my friend, we're going to wind this up quickly, but first I want you to dig hard! I want you to pull from your sleeve anyone you think *had* or *has* a hatred. And I remind you, it doesn't have to be a burning one to your wife or even to *you*."

The star's bloodshot eyes swing to a map of L.A. that masks the good portion of a wall. Sure it's a start, but holds too few millions of suspects.

He then rubs his burning eyelids and mutters into the stale air, "Seymore." "Seymore," he repeats in a stare to the oak desk, scarred with nicks and scuffmarks of past decades.

"Seymore? Seymore who?" Murray calls out.

"Seymore," Darian repeats. "Yeah, Seymore." Adrenaline gushes through his sluggish mind and feeds alertness. Campbell finally catches his clue.

"You mean the chairman of Summerville Studios? Seymore Testa?"

"That's right!" Darian quickly paces the room. "He disliked me, but couldn't stand my wife."

"Such as?" Campbell asks.

"Such as he wanted one of us to pay for my walking out. Now he's made us both pay."

Darian reaches for one of Murray's smokes on the desk and fiddles it between his fingers.

Campbell gets testy and becomes defensive.

"Now wait a minute, Darian. With all due respect, you can't go throwing in the wind that a billion-dollar corporation had a part in your wife's murder."

"Damn right I can!" he slams his fist down. "What do you think, Mr. Campbell, those people over there are a bunch of animated angels? In fact, you just hit it on the head without even realizing it. Billions! Money! Greed and *power*. More and more billions and *billions more!* Think about it, Detective. They killed to make me who I am, and I burned them. So why shouldn't they continue to kill?"

Campbell looks to Murray, who nods his fatherly approval to proceed.

"Darian, are you sure about what you're saying? Because I have to tell you, it's a rough call to investigate someone as powerful and influential as Testa, with what is up until now, little physical evidence from a cold-blooded murder."

Darian reaches to his windbreaker to put a flame to the fiddling nicotine he's bummed. He takes a long hard drag and releases a vapor of smoke that dissipates to a rusty air vent above.

He then chooses his words calmly and slowly.

"Mr. Campbell *and* Mr. Murray. I'm as sure about what I'm saying as I am of this first cigarette I've dragged in over fifteen years. I mean, don't you get it? They're no studio; they're the fucking lowest. Let me tell you now, gentlemen, with all due respect—you either get some suspects quick, or I'll hire my own goddamn force of power. Because this bastard that butchered my wife is not only going to be found, but is going to pay. And he's going to pay on my terms. Now," he coolly drags on, "is this *interview* over with?"

Murray's impressed with the star's finesse and boldness.

"Mike! Out here!"

They leave to gather their thoughts. "What do you think, Campy?"

"I think a lot of things right now, what about you?"

Murray pulls his flask out for some thinking juice.

"Do you want to know what I think, lad? I think there's a ghost in the Fables' closet. Perhaps an ex-lover of hers, maybe much before they were an item. Or maybe even as we speak. What do we do, Campy, let the kid go for now?" he quizzes.

"I don't know. I've got my own theory, would you like to hear it?"

"Shoot me down," Murray accepts.

"I've seen all of Fable's movies, every one of them. And, yeah, he's without a doubt the greatest actor ever, but he scares me. I get a feeling this guy could act his way out of death if he had to."

"Oh now, I wouldn't overexaggerate, Campy!" Murray says and snaps his suspenders in a smile. "Alrighty then, let's release him. But first, let's get him to check off the personals the lab's sent over."

• • •

DARIAN GATHERS UP FOR HIS EXIT, but Murray stops him with a morning smile. "Ah, Darian, one more thing I have to ask of you. I know this has been a very painful night for you, lad—but, I'd like you to just skim over a list of personal belongings of your wife's we now hold. Keep in mind that this will be a quick but painful few minutes. We must hold and preserve the actual items recovered for forensic testing. You understand, don't you?"

Darian nods.

"Is that a yes?"

He nods again.

Campbell retrieves the faxed evidence list titled "2112" and lays the one page atop the desk for viewing. Topping the list in bold type is a pair of ruby earrings Darian gave his wife on their 14th wedding anniversary last December. *Check.*

An 18-carat gold diamond-face Ebel sports watch that was on her *trapped* wrists. *Check.*

Her 4-carat wedding band, which was on her severed finger at the time of the swiping. *Check.*

The Gucci purse and billfold that sounds like his wife's taste. *Check.*

The platinum credit cards he hasn't a clue about, nor did he care to, for all those years. *Check.*

The keys, a charm bracelet, that briefcase, and that *fucking pill* that failed his calling from Westport. *Check, check, check, check.* He has a tearful last check from the last sound of her voice on voice ail. Then he has a feeling something of great importance is missing amongst the estimated $60,000 in personal items.

He fights with his tired brain to remember what's missing. His eyes wander astray from left to right and up and down. Finally, it all *checks.*

"The necklace!" he screams, "the necklace! Where's the necklace?"

"What necklace?" Campbell shouts back.

"The necklace is gone! The necklace!"

"Now *simmer down,* Darian," Murray directs.

"She wore it day and night! Never took it off, it was a silver heart, and … and inside there was my photo!"

He loses his breath and wrestles with his words.

"I gave it to her when we first met many years ago."

"What was the value of it?" Campbell gets in his face.

"Slow down!" Murray shouts.

"That has nothing to do with it! I mean it was worth maybe $150. I gave it to her when we first met. I was broke. It was a sentimental thing. She slept in it! Showered in it! Worked in it! Never took it off! It's gone, isn't it?"

The room comes to an eerie pause of silence. Murray and Campbell review Darian's fatigued performance.

"Take it outta here, Mike," Murray orders the list away.

Campbell flees the room to call into the crime scene.

Murray becomes agitated. He's had enough. "Alrighty, Darian, you're free to go."

Now Darian's suspicious. "Free to go? What about the necklace, wasn't that a clue?"

"Of course it's a clue, but let's get this straight. You say inside the necklace, your picture lay?"

"That's right."

"And what's the face value again?"

"No more than a couple hundred."

"Okay, I'll figure it out, now go home. Maybe go to that woman Sheila's house. But keep it a secret, the necklace that is. I have a 'copter on the roof. You aren't going to make it on ground. It's a madhouse out there. And do yourself a favor, don't read the papers.

You're here, they know it, *and* you're guilty. Now get out and get some rest, and don't worry about anything, Darian. I'm the best, and will find your wife's killer."

Darian's escorted to his waiting family members—Mary, Sheila, and Santos. They will be shuttled by air to Sheila's where he'll no doubt get little sleep and much grief as he makes his way back to the public's eye today, with the help of headlines that launch every newsstand around the globe.

"It's going to be a long one, Campy. Freshen up," Murray warns.

"You hit it on the head again, didn't you?" the rookie praises his superior.

"What, the fact that she was brutally murdered for a lousy necklace valued at a buck and a half? Of course I hit it on the head! The old saying, 'a picture is worth a thousand words,' is suddenly true to form, is it not, Detective Campbell?"

But hidden under Murray's stubborn and witty confidence are silent doubts which way to run or *who* and *where* to head for. Is the missing necklace a link to his lad's "faithful" wife's secret lover with whom she broke it off? A lover infuriated and berserk at her loyalty to spend an eternity with her loving husband?

Or was it a possessive disciple, who hit and ran with the biggest souvenir that sat snuggled in the crevice of her beating cleavage? Or is this a "Godfather" send off from Summerville, relaying farewell blessings from their cold-hearted barrack? A blessing to not only this "fabled one," but other pieces of robotic *meat* who must now be reminded to, *love your family second but your obligations first.*

CHAPTER 41

A BRUTAL PIT-STOP SLICING" is the five-word statement from the "bushed" Murray outside Parker Center to a flock of bewildered media, who tug for insight on his three-hour-plus exclusive with the man he proclaims "is *not* a suspect at this time." A nation is in disbelief over the hit-and-run gashing. Many shed tears throughout the world—no tears for the victim herself but a downpour of pity for the widowed star, Darian.

In Hollywood, veterans and *flavors of the month* are on a paranoid lookout over their shoulders for a sneak hit, for what the media has dubbed "the Mysterious Blade Runner of Coldwater Canyon." Productions are lazy for the day, patience is short, and concentration is shorter. Most shoot only half the "keeper" footage over their 12-hour grinding day in wardrobe trailers. Wall Street to blue-collar servants in the thousands are suddenly blessed with their own 24-hour bug. Many have bluffed off work, while setting up television snackings for round-the-clock coverage and a possible peek of the widower, who, rumor has it, hides behind closed doors of the Deblin home in Glendale, California.

• • •

YELLOW TAPE, YELLOW WOODEN BARRICADES, vans from outer space, and more wardrobe trailers (*just in case*), agitate the peaceful habitation of Midvale Avenue, residential side street of Sheila Deblin. Cameras stalk, launch, and invade up close, to many *unfamiliar* faces that revolve by the minute in and out of her stuccoed two-story colonial home. Reporters are foaming at the mouth for a "somebody" besides the dry Sid Greenspan, who's in dire need of the Florida sun, and floral-delivery boys who arrive by the minute, to emerge and step up to the microphone's podium on the front lawn to update the star's current state of grief. They're sure the "humbled one" is hiding out somewhere inside the valley villa, because they were scooped by the delirious rookie Campbell, who slipped in his morning fatigue to spit, "Mr. Fable is in seclusion with his publicist."

But the cameras on the sprawling lawn aren't the only nightly gravy of blood for America's steak-dinner chatting tonight. The hits to www.falsefable.com are multiplying by $59.50 a jab to the fortune of The Fly, who holds no vigil on his Web site for the star widower. His three pages boldly conclude, "The actor was outraged with his mogul wife's dictatorship and non-interest for family life the *lonely orphan* never had." He theorizes, "Then, as a perfect *act* to release the pented evil inside of his honorable and moral soul, he (Darian) ordered the butchery hit on his *faithful* wife. The same perfect timing he mastered on the silver screen is a dead ringer for the bloody and gruesome hit on his dead bitch wife!"

Clyve's assumptions weary many of his left wing with cold-hearted accusations, but warm a possibility to many heartlanders in the blue-collar Midwest, when he reminds all, "The rich always buy their way from at least *one* murder."

He closes his Agatha Christie mystery with one final word for thought. The initials "O.J."

CHAPTER 42

ANDY WARHOL RIGHTFULLY PREDICTED: "everyone will get their fifteen minutes." This afternoon, at 2:10 Mountain Time, on Midvale Avenue in Glendale, California, intern Gigi is again about to prove the prophet true. Timing and climbing beats masters and bachelors in Hollywood. And with that, in the words of the dead Queen Bee, "the fucking bimbos" couldn't be more perfect.

With her sheet of words in one hand and her bosom buddy Missy along for her *fifteen* in the other, Gigi beams her way to the podium, like a *Seventeen* magazine angel of *cool*. The two girlies are escorted by the old shark, Sid, who limps like a wounded dinosaur with his walking cane in hand. Sid's along to assure Gigi correctly carries on her leading role of fumbling vital info to the vulture media, who few would have the nerve to outwit. But the vultures should know better. Little people are the perfect cover for dirty chores in the field of power. And who better to throw to the wolves, a Beverly Hills brunette named Monica or a bleached-blond intern named Gigi?

Gigi hits her mark to the podium and poses with *grinning remorse* to the countless flickers and flashes. She then recites her prepared statement of half-hearted honesty with Oscar-winning persuasion.

"Good afternoon," she begins. "Since learning of this horrible tragedy, Darian Fable is in deep mourning over the loss of his wife of thirteen years, Faith. This is a grievous shock to not only him, but to the entire entertainment community. He is devastated and does not wish to comment on what he calls 'the most horrific tragedy and greatest loss of his lifetime.' A private memorial service for close friends and family members will be held at Forest Lawn tomorrow for Miss Barsolla. Mr. Fable wishes you to respect his need for privacy, then and *now*. Thank you."

"Won't he come out for just a word or two," shouts a reporter.

"He will *not*," she boldly snaps. *Gigi's getting warmed up.*

"Is he in there?" shouts another.

Gigi looks to Sid whose cane softly pokes her to cut. She takes his cue and is quickly hustled up the cluttered pathway, where she enters the gates of the home's front courtyard.

Chaperoning the live coverage from a television set many miles away, Sheila applauds her scapegoat.

"Very well done, Gigi," she blows into her soaked Kleenex.

The armored bulldog is down to a frail wobble, as Sheila wanders in and out of this *stranger's* eccentric, four-bedroom canyon home that hides the entourage. Darian, who also watched, scores Gigi an A for reassuring him continued privacy to mourn in the master bedroom of his reunited friend. There, he lies, studying his smoke rings that drift upward to the spinning ceiling fan. It's the same cigarettes, and the same smell of morbidity in the air he's accustomed to, from his neglected childhood. Faith's body will be released for the planned memorial tomorrow, but now he's toying with the possibility of cremation. He fights with his pride at burying his wife's cut up and butchered corpse in a box that will never be opened.

But who really gives a damn around this town? His thoughts run wild. You're either slaughtered, OD on pills, or an over-the-hill, dried-up piece of meat. *Hero today, gone tomorrow*, then reminisced during a pimpy three-minute Oscar tribute, before a seven-minute break away to sponsors.

I'll dispose of her ashes peacefully, his mind makes the call, *in the calm breezes of the Catalina Island. And who will cover the moment of dust in the wind? No one. They'll all be too busy shoving for camera position over the turf of the dead. Then I'll say goodbye, but not for long. Then it's goodbye to my lonely friend, Nick. The one "true friend," who was so kind and so silent in allowing friends and myself peace from the madness that's packed and headed for Forest Lawn. Now Mary, Santos, and I can sneak from this closet of smog and return to the green clippings of decent Westport. But then my dimly lit future must start, minus the light I depended on for an eternity. It's a sad day, but an enticing possibility.* He shoots a smoky circle.

This dirty little game of hide-and-seek with the press is a dirty little trick. But then again, it's a dirty little world with dirty little secrets. But now, it's my fucking world.

Darian Fable is angry.

CHAPTER 43

THERE WAS A SEA OF CAMERAS that famished for 36 hours. Helicopters circled for miles, as scores of "somebodys" arrived by black shiny motorcades to the smile of network commercial breakaway dollars, on a sunny spring morning, on the lawns of Forest Lawn Cemetery in Burbank, California.

At 10:00 A.M. Mountain Time, the cameras were snapping, while the heavies were aspiring. But soon came word that a wise man had fooled all, balking to bare his gold urn of ashes that rested the "dead bitch's" soul.

It was an upset at the highest. Bigger than any in Oscar history, and more offensive than the wise man's no show almost a year ago at Morton's. The ceremonial "hoax" was a humiliation from the mysterious one, who chose to hold his own peaceful service many miles away in the pre-dawn darkness of Catalina Island.

It's now noon Pacific Time, and Darian Fable is safely back in Westport. Meanwhile, the press is printing blood of their own on the *ungrateful one*, as Murray and Campbell anxiously await their own eulogy from one of the many who also gathered but in the end was shunned. *Seymore Testa.*

Murray and Campbell sit tolerantly in the lavish lobby that over-looks a tip of the Santa Monica beach.

"Business as usual," Campbell shrugs, as the two can't help but glance at every fine detail of a black-and-white poster that floats high above the lobby. The giant shot portrays a man walking a dusty dirt road, barefoot in cream-colored baggies, a loose white shirt, tan sus-penders, and a mint-green tie that was hand-colored into the photo. His face is stubbly, unshaven, and scraggly hair blows wildly in his face. He sports a tweed fedora hat. A willow hinges from his lips. He makes his way with a folk guitar swung over his back. He tugs with frustrated protection his golden-locks flower-child costar in his first Oscar-winning performance titled *The Balance*. The film that kicked off the fabled streak of three take-homes for the man on display, Darian Fable. It's the story of a vagabond jazz guitarist in the farm trappings of Kansas City way back in the 1940s. Darian's character, Trevor Clewly, struggles to raise his 7-year-old daughter, Chloe, by day, pick his *A minors* by night, and battle his nightly addiction to the bottle, while hopping one bluesy café to another after the vanishing of his restless wife. So right was the star's perfect timing at delivering this natural performance to the silver screen.

"I like that tie, Campy," Murray comments to the framed *god*.

"I like those." Campbell gazes low to the pins of Candace that seductively twist below her desktop.

Suddenly, from the double doors of Seymore's office, bolts an anx-ious and stunning brunette. She stops by Candace, who hands off an envelope for her lunchtime *services*. Meanwhile, the servicer tries to disguise the ever-obvious by smirking the dicks a sensuous freebie.

But Murray's and Campbell's eyes shoot away from her toned calves, back to the hanging photo. She then flings her designer backpack and flips her silky mane for her exit. Her strapped sandals tap loudly, but tease silently, *"the best lunch you'll never eat,"* as her shapely stride echoes on the lobby's marble floors. Murray's forehead drops some sweat over her *locomotive steam*. He quickly reaches to his jacket for some cooling juice.

"$2,500 an hour," he swigs.

Campbell giggles as he eyes the girl's ass that Jell-Os her way to-ward the elevators.

Candace rises and the two are escorted into the sleaze-king's play-pen. Upon their entrance, Seymore looks too relieved and too mellow, with his feet resting on his desk, slouching low in his high-back leather throne. He looks lost in joy and doesn't appear to be making any effort to rise and greet his *little people*. Instead, he basks in the wall of tanked salt water, while he swirls his afternoon cigar to his lips.

Finally, he swings around and makes his way down from his mini-platform. With a smile, he extends his clammy hands and offers politely, "Gentlemen of the law, how are you?"

Murray shakes and nods, unimpressed. Campbell shakes, while his eyes look away at every corner. He eyes the mammoth fish tanks, the art deco furniture, the fine art on the wall, and the mini-bar Seymore makes his way to.

"How 'bout a drink, gentlemen? Perhaps a soda, an iced tea, or a fine shot of this Irish whiskey I only share with *special* people," he grins to Murray.

Purposely missing his warmth, Murray begins an informal formality. "Mr. Testa, I'm Jonathan E. Murray of the Los Angeles Police Department, and this is my partner, Mr. Michael Campbell."

"Campbell and Murray!" Seymore jolts. "That's a thick Irish accent, Mr. Murray! Now just what brings you boys down here to Summerville? You wanna be in the movies?" he giggles.

Murray looks to Campbell, who pecks to his pant leg, trying to hold back the laughter *he prays to God doesn't follow*.

"You're a good-looking kid," Seymore aims a wink to him.

Murray looks at Campbell, who's flattered and taken in by Seymore's keen eye for talent. But the veteran isn't amused.

"He's already taken, and please don't call me 'boy,' *son*. We're here to talk about serious business."

"Oh well, excuse me, serious business," Seymore shakes his cube,s moseying to his throne. Then says, "*Serious* business," dosing his fish their lunch. "Serious business, such as?"

"Such as Faith Barsolla," Murray speaks.

"Oh, Faith Barsolla!" Seymore frowns. "What a shame, they had it all. Love, fame, and now she's gone!" he settles to his throne. "You know, I even sent over a nice floral piece. Ole Darian Fable isn't in any position to be playing tricks on this thing we call the media. I mean, his ratings are sinking fast in public opinion and will float to the bottom of the ocean after today's *performance*," he nods to the fish tanks.

Campbell toys in.

"Seymore, let's hold off on the ratings and the flowers for a moment please. We want to know what your relationship was to Ms. Barsolla?"

"Relationship? What do you mean relationship?" he asks.

"You know what we mean." Murray stares cold and hard.

"All right, look, both of you and *all* the business, know I could give a David Geffen fuck about Faith Barsolla. I mean, I'm sorry she died the way she did, but gentlemen, I hope you don't think I, or anyone around here, had a part in this … do you?"

"Well," Campbell straightens up in his seat, "just for fun: Darian Fable has cost you millions, and perhaps billions, in lost revenues since he walked out. So, Seymore, why are we not to believe you would want revenge?"

Seymore barrels out a gagging spit and yanks the Cuban from his mouth.

"Gentlemen!" He catches his breath. "You've got it all wrong! Has Darian Fable made us billions? *Yes!* Will he continue to make us billions? *Yes!* But let me assure you both here today, Hollywood and Summerville Studios will be just *fine* without the *great* Darian Fable! I mean look. I liked the kid; he was a great piece of meat. But her," his expression turns sour, "she just kept this bitterness towards me ever since that fucking wrap party at Swifty Lacrosse's house some umpteen years ago."

"Whose house?" Campbell leans forward.

"Swifty's!"

"And? What happened there?" he follows up.

"What happened there?" Seymore snarls, "What do you think happens at all Hollywood parties? It's what *doesn't* happen once the hors d'oeuvres are laid out."

"Can you be more specific about Ms. Barsolla and you?" Murray digs in.

"Alright, I fucked around with her a little bit when Darian was schmoozing the place, eating relishes and drinking fucking cranberry juice."

Murray and Campbell stare to each other in disbelief.

Seymore holds straight face. He dares them to make a move. Campbell can't believe it. *Say it ain't so, Seymore.* The rookie rises and begins to pace the office like a defense lawyer.

"Wait a minute now, hold on, let me get this straight. You fucked around with Faith Barsolla?" he fights back laughter.

Seymore ignores him and puffs a dragon-sized drag.

Campbell repeats for the record, "In what way did you *fuck around* with Faith Barsolla?"

"In what way? I'll tell you *what way*," he offers. "I was president of Platinum Records, and she was way out of pageant queen competition. You know, she was a beauty queen. Now you put two and two together. What do beauty queens aspire to be? Entertainment correspondents? Yes! Actresses? Yes! Singers? Yes and foremost *yes*! They all want to fucking sing their way onto the charts and into the movies as leading ladies. They all want *power*. Just like you and me. Power rules and power tools suck! And you know what? The beauty queens all *suck*! Every one of them, except that black piece...what was her name? Many years, the one from *Penthouse*...Vanessa Williams, that's it! One out of a fucking million with a real voice!"

Seymore slays on without a thought or a pause, spewing like a locker-room chat with old buddies.

"Let's just say ole Faith Barsolla wasn't a good holder of her wine that night, and once the heat's on, guys, I'm cooking the meat, you know what I mean? Oh god, what a fun fucking night that was! Oh, Swifty says I did quite a performance on tape that night."

"What do you mean, 'a *performance* on tape,' Mr. Testa?" Murray holds onto his every word.

"Are you guys naive? Everyone has cameras rolling in their homes. Wanna see a clip of old Jack taking a dump at my house?" he giggles. "Shit, I'd like to bet Faith never had a drink since then, but I'd be wrong now, wouldn't I? God knows her husband hasn't."

Campbell isn't yet falling for Seymore's *fable*, but Murray doesn't rule out the storyteller's story. Something stinks, and his gut feeling says it's nothing to do with the cloud from Seymore's Cuban cigar.

"Look," Seymore playfully offers, "I know what you guys are thinking, a big fat Dago-Jew like me and all, but hey, it happened real quick and we were both smashed. The kid, I'm assuming, never knew about it, so do me a favor guys? Old Dare's in serious pain right now, so leave this little *secret* of ours out. Don't jab the kid anymore," he winks.

"Did you continue to see her after that night?" Campbell wishes.

"Hell no! She couldn't stand me after that 'performance.' But I did make good for her guilty conscience. I told her the kid had something. I was top brass in the music world and it was *my* soundtracks that saved her old man's safe floppings! I told her to bag her dream-singing career, stick with the kid, and they'd both be bigger than life itself. And guess what? The proof is in the pudding. You know she never forgot my advice, but I know she resented my vision. It frustrated her to do the dirty work all those years for her husband, *the real star*. But as we all know, gentlemen, frustration is where anger and drive come from. Sure, she had help from her father, who put the kid on the map, but wait 'til I got my hands on him."

He rises from his throne, with a funny look of regret to his face. Seymore closes his performance with food for thought.

"Detectives, if you're insinuating I had an obsession for Faith Barsolla, you're dead wrong. Because if you really knew the one and only *Seymore Testa*, you'd know I always pay for my pleasures, and rarely touch anything over 21. So! If you gentlemen are finished, I must get back to ruling the empire I have been blessed by Frank Barsolla to rule."

Campbell looks to Murray, who eyes back.

"We'll be in touch again, Mr. Testa," Murray adjourns court.

"My door is always open, gentlemen," he smiles and waves from behind his desk.

"I'm sure we will be in touch," Murray threatens so kindly.

"Thank you for your time, Seymore," Campbell *strokes* in.

Upon their exit to the towering double doors, Seymore once again whales across the final word.

"Hey!"

They both turn.

"Thanks, guys," he salutes his drink up, "and by the way, I wasn't kidding when I said about getting you in the movies, kid!"

"Thanks, but no thanks, *Seymore*," Campbell kindly waves.

• • •

BACK TO HEADQUARTERS, the rookie becomes impatient by the afternoon traffic of Wilshire Boulevard, while the cool veteran swigs in thought from his flask.

"Fucking Hollywood murder," Campbell grunts and moans, 'I'm fucking her, he's fucking me, and she's fucking her!' Where does it all end?"

"Campy, be patient, my boy—we just may have a luncher on our hands," Murray sighs.

Campbell knows the term "luncher." It's a common term of uncertainty in the field of police investigations. It's short for no clues, no leads, and no arrests.

"How 'bout we tell Fable about the mistake his *perfect* and *faithful* wife made back then?" Campbell hints.

"Absolutely not!" Murray says, "it's just another play by Seymore to get another jab to him."

"Fine, if you say so, E, I mean after all, I really can't see *her* sleeping with that fat bastard, now can you?" he tests Murray.

"How do we know it was consensual?" Murray tests back.

"Well I … "

"Well, my son, how's this for a motive?"

"I'm all ears."

"The fat man throws himself on her, and she hides it for years. Then one night, like every woman eventually does, she spits it out to her husband, probably after a session of hot sex and a cigarette. They retaliate years after it sinks in, by dumping Summerville on its ass."

Campbell falls silent at the red light. "Hmm … interesting."

"Interesting? Son, let me bring you back down to this earth. In the world today, anything *interesting* is either a reality or on its way to becoming a Hollywood script."

"Now *that's* interesting," Campbell nods.

"*No,* that's reality. It's a sick world out there, and I wish you would wake up, gosh damn it, Campy. Now pull over for a bite to eat. But first, let's hunt for a quick refill of the witty one's favorite drink."

CHAPTER 44

WESTPORT, CONNECTICUT STILL BOASTS one of the lowest crime rates in the Western hemisphere, but you'd never guess it by the alarms that decorate this castle, like ornaments in December during this sticky month of May. Or you'd never guess it by the dozen foot soldiers that bake in military greens while blatantly striking poses for overhead flying copters, who hover high above the chosen one's acres daily. To top it off, at the helm of this high-tech militant operation is the fully appointed commander in chief himself, Mr. Santos Lupe, who prepares his mini-army by day and maps their ground stalkings by night, as they roam the private acres with semi-automatic rifles, *fully loaded*.

It's been a mysterious 31 days since the gruesome last night of Faith Barsolla. The public is losing patience with the Los Angeles Police Department, while the media pairs the *ungrateful* and *mysterious* one with a crazed halfback Hall of Famer some 23-odd years ago. But the hungry wolves that roam the streets of modern-day civilization will not wait for this killer to turn to his saving Lord a decade or two from now. They want their bloody rib-eye gossip served nightly to their supper plates off the juicy fix called "nightly news at six," and

167

they want it now. Meanwhile, every television station, every radio talk show, and every publication from *Time* to its chief competitor the *National Enquirer,* is offering millions in rewards to know *why* and *who* killed Faith Barsolla. Everyone, except the widowed billionaire himself, who mysteriously hides behind the steel gates of his castle on the hill.

• • •

HIS ONCE GLOWING COMPLEXION and well-honed alertness has now altered to one of a full-blown manic. He now emulates a mountain man, with his flourishing beard sprouting faster than the wasted day of eleven hours he sleeps. Darian fancies bathing once a week, as his once 185 pounds of chiseled structure is now chiseled too deep into his former handsomely shaped jawline. The screen idol to millions, who once sported a glow of health, success, and *looks that could kill,* now resembles a death-row inmate in his final hour before leaking his trousers. Darian Fable is protesting to the hypocritical world and, in his tired and stubborn mind, *rightfully so.*

This is the payback for his charity that will never be matched by any single humanitarian again. No salad-dressing profits, no AIDS awareness in the millions, and no MS celebrity-carnival event. His *billions* will never be matched.

And who will ever know?

No one.

And who will ever believe?

No one.

And who cares?

No one.

And why not?

Because a full belly nurtures the selfish world we all starve for.

Now, what reason is there to live? he asks himself daily. Life is over with. He's made his statement and done his time. Now he's ready to suffer the piercing stings his wife endured. Like it or not. His daily regime of running and healthy eating has now turned 180 degrees, *backwards.*

He awakes no earlier than 4:00 P.M., then drags his daily two packs of filterless smokes to the television news. After an hour of verbal depression, the stereo surround-sound takes over, as the operatic cryings of his favorite tenor of the month scream away. His nibblings of crackers and soup (sometimes bean, mostly chicken) are delivered to him by the distressed Mary, who enters like clockwork at 6:00 and returns early morning at 5:00, to draw the curtains shut from any sunrise of hope that may threaten his ordered day of doom.

Mary only receives from her loving employer a small nod, barely a smile, and no acclaim of her hot, homemade squashing.

Darian's denied all daily correspondence from Sheila, the weekly ones Nikki "promised" several weeks ago, and the dozen hourly ones his concerned buddy Nick won't let up on.

The only calls open to his bed are from the *witty one* himself, who's now eating a *brunch* of media criticism. But without a break in the case from that fatal night, the only small talk from Murray to the star is his well-being, which Darian always closes, then poses a threat, after their 60 short seconds, to assemble his own team of personal investigators. But Murray doesn't panic at the star's hostility, nor does he let his Irish pride or stubborn, witty ego lose faith. After all, they're the same threats and warnings the rich king vowed on the morning he bummed his first smoke down at Parker Center.

CHAPTER 45

THIS AFTERNOON THE FABLE HOME IS *TOO* QUIET. At 1-some-thing P.M., and it being Saturday, Darian senses Mary may be in the nearby town of Norwalk or Fairfield, doing her annual search for a bargain antique at a front yard or cottage estate sale, and surely Santos and his foreign-armed cronies are tucked well into dreamland in their cottage bunkers. Curiosity might have killed his queen that fatal night, but today the cigarettes, the crackers, or his frail well-being are not enough to keep this king from checking the downstairs quarters of his castle he hasn't dared to roam for weeks.

The air is a slimy humidity outdoors, but from the ajar windows, Darian hits on the lower level breezy dampness that swarms to his cobweb brain. The overcast sunlight penetrates and stings his sleepy pupils. He walks far from the window's breeze and spies the clattering of a dozen groundskeepers who snip and trim at tree branches that hover too far over the cobblestone drive. He sniffs the smell of freshly cut grass that flows through the main living-room shutters. Sweaty Hispanic landscapers, mostly in their mid-fifties, buzz the walkways with their gas blowers, as hurried younger men scratch at the plush green sod with their rakes just outside the study's windows. The smell of freshly cut greens does little to brighten Darian's afternoon journey. Instead, it reminisces to his childhood days as a slaving houseboy in that ugly brownstone bungalow he *paralyzed* in.

Darian moves closer and quietly into the study where, once inside, he ceases his steps. He views the huge oil portrait of his deceased wife that hangs high above a brick fireplace. As he reaches for his white cotton robe, he fires up a smoke and pays a silent moment of homage to his lost half. His heart and swirling stomach *twist* from the anxiety of surviving his future days and nights without her. He never really wanted much more than to own an upper-class home in the suburbs, hailing from a family of a lower-class bond. All he asked for was just a small light of hope and that trusting wife to guide him through life's speeding tunnel. But he got more. Maybe *too* much more. Maybe the rich really *can* buy a murder or two, but maybe the Lord's fate has him now face-to-face with a portrait of reality. The reality that money may buy luxury, but luxury does have its price.

His eyes burn with every blink, as he moves his afternoon respects a doorway down to the adjoining game room. Upon his careful descent, he enters the dark dome, to a sense of deadpan stillness. High above him, the Sistine Chapel painting of angels and saints seems to glide in motion from his pupils' reaction from light to darkness. There's an eerie mist throughout the room. The ticking of an eight-foot grandfather clock taps for his attention onto the back wall. His eyes see nothing but dark and fuzzy dots. Everything is blurry along that back wall. *Everything*, but the sealed labels of destructive alcohol that appear in double vision from the mirror's reflection behind the lavish wet bar. This vision pulls his steps closer like a magnet, and now has him face to face with his "bottled enemies." The same enemies that, until now, haven't befriended David Faulkner in over fifteen years. But now temptation may be breaking up his unhappy home. The future of his once contempt domain now lays a mere twelve steps away. Darian moves slowly but closely to the *altar* of his friends he betrayed, named Jack and Crown, who, judging by their color, have preserved and behaved so well after so many forgotten years. Surely, they deserve a second chance.

He looks about the room to make certain he's alone. He moves ever so slowly to the ray of light that shines from a connecting doorway off the kitchen. He must clear the way of his snooping, like a little boy stealing change from his mother's purse while she fiddles in the yard on a sunny day. The coast is clear, so, he steps up to the altar of the devil's potion. He reaches for a dusty crystal rock glass, still being ever so quiet. Suddenly he hears a small tussle of laughter. His movements freeze at the haunting laugh. Is it a ghost frowning upon his mischievous action? He looks to the ceiling. The angels have stopped gliding, but now all eyes are frowning upon him. He hears the laughter once more. He retraces his steps quickly, back to the study. From his view in the picture window, his ears hone a hard listen to his hallucination. It was nothing more than echoes from breaking workers who are clowning over a "chilled one" in the driveway. He almost jogs back to the room with the glass in hand and barrels it into the altar's cooler. Ice cubes fill his crystal chalice to the brim.

He then reaches for his forgotten friend named Crown, and snaps his sealed head open. He and Crown were always the best of friends. His tongue salivates as the cubes shrink from the royal potion of his pour. Then, without even a half-second hesitation, he chucks a healthy mouthful. The cold cubes ram his dried, stinging lips. His head tips back to the ceiling above. *Everyone's still watching.* He sets the glass down and turns face to face with himself in the mirror. The grim look in his glazed eye speaks guilty on the broken sobriety he washed away, per the help of his only real friend in life—*himself.* It's a different time and different place, but it's the same mirror and same friend his father spoke to nightly for so many years. Suddenly the mirror turns no longer friendly and he must now transform it to a camera for rehearsal. His rehearsal for "the killer" he knows he will ultimately confront. He stares hard at his beaten face.

"Fuck the world, the time has come," he recites.

His courage turns bold, his posture broadens proud, but his voice slumps in bitterness.

"I'll give you Mr. Fucking Nice Guy, Mr. Perfect," he bullies the camera with a smudge from his finger. "You took my *life* when you took my wife."

He then softens his tone and looks above to the stares of his audience, whose eyes have frozen in suspense. He returns to his invented camera.

"I gave you my soul, but for what? For what, you sick fucking vultures!" he screams.

Then, in a *beat*, he slams his forehead to the padding of the bar and sobs uncontrollably. His body sweats anger and frustration. He reaches for his diced glass then steps out from behind the altar. He cocks back and whips. It bull's-eyes into the custom framed Time magazine cover, that penned the phrase from *Mr. Imperfect* to "Mr. Perfect," causing a splattering boom. Upon the thunderous splatter, he awes with pride his perfect aim of destruction. The cubes cling for dear life, as they quickly melt their suction and trickle rapidly down the bare shiny gloss of the matted frame. A siren of noise similar to a car alarm fires off. Darian hears manly hollers that echo with *panic* from some two rooms away.

CHAPTER 46

POURING A SECOND ROUND, Darian is rudely intruded on by Mary, who never was yard shopping, and Santos, who has awoken from his afternoon napping. Santos has his pistol aimed, cocked, and ready at the startled homeowner, who freezes any movement from his fuzzy corner.

"Boss?" the voice doubts.

"It's me, Santos, put that gun away!" Darian orders.

Mary steps in closely and cautiously behind Santos, who drops his aim. Santos turns away in a look of embarrassment, hoping for his boss's forgiveness.

"Sorry boss," he calls like a frightened boy, then looks to Mary.

Mary shoos the puppy from the room to be alone with Darian, who proceeds with his pouring as if nothing has happened.

"I see I can't throw a drink in my own house without having the *A-Team* show up," he carries on.

Mary holds her ground in the doorway, as she observes the proof of destruction pouring into his rock glass.

"Darian," she politely calls out, "the house is severely alarmed now and any suspicious noises, little or loud, will be responded to quickly, you understand, don't you?"

"Any suspicious noises will be responded to quickly," he mimics her.

He slams his buddy Crown down. "And just who are you?" he proclaims from his corner, "my fucking mother?" he smiles.

Mary's blood freezes. She has to remind herself to breathe. It's clear her rescue attempt is a drink or maybe *three* too late. She doesn't know how to react to this newfound *stranger* in such an intimate setting. The clock's ticking counts their uncomfortable seconds of silence. The look in his eyes, from her blurred view, is not the look of an innocent, nor the trusted one she's known for all these years. She must think how to win control of this unfortunate showdown. Should she be delicate and pacify? Or should she take a bold and motherly stance? Faith crosses her mind. She splits it down the middle.

"Look at you, what are you trying to do? What's happening here?" she speaks.

"And loving every minute of it!" He clutches the bottle tightly and stares down her every step that approaches slowly. As Mary moves in, Darian's eyes are piercing with the intensity of a junkyard dog set for a surprised lunge. He *dares* her to stop now in her pushy tracks, but Mary continues to close in.

"I'm feeling your anger, Darian. I understand your pain. Every day, I feel the loss of Faith, but we have to get by now. We have to get to the bottom of this and find out who's responsible." She steps softly, *moving closer.*

"Mary," he whispers.

"What is it?" she pulls up.

"Do you know who the fuck I am?"

She stops in her pushy tracks to think things over. *Who is this beast that has trampled the grounds of my fairy-tale garden?* She looks above and prays for Santos's return.

"Mary," he whispers.

She doesn't answer.

"Mary?" he speaks louder.

"What?" she says and swallows the dry lump in her throat.

"Do you know how hard I've been robbed of life?"

"We've all..." she tries to spit it out.

He makes his way forward and walks six of the twelve steps that once separated them.

"No, no you don't, now do you Mary?" he smiles.

Darian is now twelve inches from Mary. He touches her hair softly with his fingers. She doesn't dare move in her shiver.

"You don't Mary, and I knew it. The public doesn't and you know what? No one does," his fingers now partially grab. "Do you fucking hear me!" he grabs firmly and spits his words to her frightened eyes.

She crumbles weakly to the floor weeping into her trembling palms. He slips his grip and trance and attends to her grief. He rushes to set aside his drink, then rushes back to aid his *victim*. He gives her a cradling hug and emphatically apologizes, "Oh my God, Mary, I'm so sorry. I don't know what's come over me, you know I love you, Mary; it's not you, it's me, it's my fault," he cries.

Darian wipes Mary's tears along with his and paces the room, circling from embarrassment, as he musters up a resolution. A resolution he must pitch to her at her weakest moment. It sounds like the perfect apology from him, according to his new buddy, Crown.

"Mary, I'm sorry. You know I love you, don't you?"

She nods her head.

"And you know, I need you to remain with me here forever, don't you?"

She nods again.

But ... I may just need some time and space right now. I mean, I don't know ... I want to send you into Greenwich for a while. What do you think?"

He's referring to his unoccupied loft in Greenwich Village. It's a luxurious crib with all the nightly hipster hopping of fashion models and social elite that spill from all sides of Manhattan. But Mary has never slept a night outside the calm suburb of Westport since she first landed.

But this is *his* place. Then again, she's held *his* fort down.

She's confused.

"No, I'm not leaving you alone," she refuses, to his surprise.

"*Shhhh*," he places his finger to her lips, "listen to me Mary, I'm a big boy now, I just need some time to myself, for just a few days. Just a *few* days, Mary," he begs.

"And what do you plan on doing for just your ... *few* days?" she sniffles.

"Mary, Mary," he smiles, "look at me, I'm Darian Fable! I can take care of myself! I'm a big boy now, with a fucking army outside to protect me! I'll be all right. You go to the city and stay at the loft for a couple of weeks." His "few days" slip.

Mary affords him slack. He's delirious and she damn well knows it. After all, Sheila will be arriving in New Jersey for a short visit with her mother, and she can always turn to her to post bail.

"Just a few days? That's all, right?" she contemplates.

"Just a *few* days," he reassures.

Darian knows, he's now won a "yes" without Mary's final word. It's time to celebrate with another pour, but first it's time to push his limit for one more request.

"Mary, before you leave, can you do me just one small favor?" he measures with his shaky fingers.

"What?" she answers, suspicious.

"Get rid of Santos and his patrol boys."

"Absolutely not! They're not leaving. I'll give you your space, but *they* stay. Listen to me, someone is after you and it's not to be taken lightly."

"Okay, okay, you're right," he calms her. "They can stay. But I better not have them running in with guns every time I drop a glass."

She eyes the devastated frame of Mr. Perfect, who did more than just "drop his glass."

"How long do you plan on letting yourself go and carrying on with this kind of behavior?" she mothers him.

"Mary," he sips on, "I give you my word, when you return I will be a new man and things will be back to normal. Please, trust me, my word is, and always has been, *good.*"

And so they have agreed on a short-term pact between them. Darian has won his space for a *few days* and Mary will monitor him by phone from the Village loft.

Then, when all fails, as Mary suspects, she will designate the only one to sew back the unraveled pieces of his once purest soul. The one and only Sheila Deblin.

CHAPTER 47

THEY DIE IN THREES. Just two days after Mary's departure from Westport, a four-sentence item appears in the Arts & Entertainment section of the *New York Times*, which announces number two in the personal circle of Darian Fable. At 74 years old, Sid Greenspan's heart finally gave in. Maybe to the gruesome loss of his best friend's daughter, or maybe to the burning heat of Florida. But it was a peaceful death for the "old shark," as he lay ocean-side, napping off into the afternoon rays of sunlight. Sid followed his Faith right into the heavenly lighted tunnel.

Darian does little mourning and zero sobbing over old Sid's death. Instead, he salutes him with a tip and hourly mumble of "*Here's to ya, old Sid*" throughout his drinking day. After all, the old man did have a good life and a better death than his best friend's daughter. He had colleagues who respected him and friends who nurtured him, long after the death of his wife, Mae, those many years ago. The shark wasn't forced to gasp for air while he *suffered* his last seconds. Instead, he was invited peacefully to rest high and will be respectively lowered after a small service in his residing town of Beverly Hills. Darian will send the lavish sympathy of flowers and typical profound statement to the press, which was rendered in three minutes and two sentences by Sheila. Presumably and understandably, the *distraught one* will not be present amongst the fifty or so expected for prayer service, held at a synagogue on LaBrea Avenue in West Hollywood.

• • •

MEANWHILE, DARIAN CONTINUES to duck Sheila, in fear of the big-sister-like scolding he'll receive for his return to the juice. But Sheila's one step ahead of him, having already nipped Mary's ear, assuring she'll pay him a respectful visit of her own after she attends Sid's service. Mary warns Sheila to beware of Darian's sudden mood swings. But Sheila vows to the motherly one that his days of sobbing and sipping will foreclose promptly when she visits with a flight plan to the Betty Ford Center in Palm Springs.

Meanwhile, it would take a shuttle to launch Darian from his new crashing space in the downstairs den. There, he lies plopped day and night on the sofa, sipping away by the half pint to round-the-clock news coverage that still obsesses on the never-ending mystery of his dead wife. After more than a few *jugs on the rocks,* he taunts back to the tube in slurred rebuttals, which panics barking from Spark, who quickly calms with a smile and pet from his boisterous master.

Surprisingly, Darian's had an increase in his appetite. He's now managing to scarf away more than just a couple of crackers soaked in leftover chicken noodle soup. He's even befriended the many foreign foot soldiers, who now have a green light to roam freely throughout his main house, any time, day and night. This traffic and the smell of Italian and Mexican spices have lured the star's appetite for more than a daily nibble that's prepared by the *chef* of the newly founded boys' camp, Mr. Santos Lupe.

Darian takes a liking to the guards and their clownish sense of humor. They speak rapidly, but their hand and facial gestures guide a good translation of the English language for him. He respects that they're not star-struck, or intimidated by his presence, and repays their friendship by allowing them to sprawl freely on the floor or nearby corner for some small chat and nightly news. There's only one rule Darian requests of his newfound buddies: to check their guns and ammo into the study. The guards chug their beer out of cans as one of the bunch known as "Gabby," a witty Italian, plays

MC, ridiculing several news reporters' *rugs*. Darian also amuses in observing the guards' flirting comments to the cleaning ladies', who hurry out after their few minutes of feather-dusting the star's *dorm room*. He occasionally treats the guards to the World Cup soccer channel, while observing the playful bickering and competition tally counts of world titles. *It's one big manly pajama party*. Darian's won their trust and they've won his. So much so, he's recommended that Santos, now turned *yes man*, tone down the outside patrols, suggesting they sport a more "camouflaged" presence throughout his acres of land. This is, in his words, "to begin a slow return to normal living," not to mention it will ease tensions from the jittery and curious passers-by on the bottom of the road. "Oh, yes boss, great idea," the yes-man Santos excites. But there's one smaller chore the boss must turn over to his *chief*. He hands Santos the steel briefcase that lay beneath those photo memories in the shelves of his wife's cluttered closet. He requests of Santos, under his supervision, to have one of the maintenance workers "saw open its combination clamp."

"Don't snoop or pry into its contents," Darian warns. "It's personal and professional paperwork; you understand, don't you?" he clears his throat.

Santos smiles and strokes his mustache.

"Yes boss, I understand."

The chief is beaming at his big brother's trust in him. He's finally worth something of value and importance, more than fetching a latte or directing the traffic of workers and maids on the grounds. He's achieved more than his planned goal of cheering up his brother to a quick recovery and perhaps *normal living*. Santos attributes this to the vacationing and unwatchful eye of Mother Mary, who is far away from her residence next door. He applauds his mini-army and their addictive foreign humor. Laughter is working. It has brightened his boss's mood. The best medicine prescribed to man is now living proof through his grieving brother, whose other half was always *too bitchy and way too serious in the morning*.

God rest her soul.

CHAPTER 48

SANTOS'S SECRET MISSION IS ACCOMPLISHED one hour from his boss's request, as he delivers proudly the busted-up briefcase that's now fastened shut with a bungee cord. The puppy dog couldn't wait until morning and took matters into his own bear-strength hands. He and Darian confer in the study, away from the guards. Darian instructed him not to snoop, but now invites Santos to the unveiling of the mysterious vault. The chief stands aside with his arms folded on the lookout, as "boss" studies the inner contents. Darian is flustered upon the vault's opening. It doesn't hold the "contractual papers" on the star's early days. Instead, he discovers it packed with bundles of rubber-banded envelopes. All are open, and appear to be personal letters. Letters that are surprisingly addressed to him, Darian, but, unsurprisingly, in care of his wife. There must be at least a hundred in neat bundles of ten. Darian's confused. They seem grouped by time. On the top lay whites brighter than the bottom ones of faded manila. As he begins to unravel them, he and Santos are both interrupted by the head groundskeeper, Roberto, who appears frantic in his nightly sleepwear of just a white tank top and matching boxer shorts.

Santos is startled over the rude intruder. *Is Roberto sleepwalking? He's not welcome into our private slumber party, nor does he have the green light to roam the grounds freely after dark.* But Roberto saves his face of embarrassment. He relays an emergency message in Spanish to Santos, who passes it to Darian.

"Detective Murray is trying to get in touch with you, boss. Roberto says it's an emergency."

Darian instantly closes his chopped case and retrieves it back to the den.

Santos shoos the drinking guards out from the living room to patrol.

"Foot, foot," he yells, signaling their start to pace the entire grounds.

• • •

SOME 3,000 MILES FROM WESTPORT, the rain shows no mercy, the traffic won't budge, and the blood of Faith Barsolla from Coldwater Canyon has now splashed the walls of suite 1526 at the Four Seasons Hotel in Beverly Hills, California.

"It's a slaughterhouse suite," Detective Jonathan E. Murray frowns with a hint of savor to reporters who weave and scurry throughout the stalled traffic on Doheny Drive. Murray flees the many microphones, then ducks to his car and dials directly to Darian, who unblocks his private line and accepts the call.

Darian opens with his routine delivery to Murray, "I hope you have good news, Detective."

"Alrighty now, Darian," Murray shouts over the evident chaos in the street. "I'm calling you from a crime scene and wanted to let you know before it hit the airwaves. Seymore Testa's body was found about two hours ago here at the Seasons Hotel. He's dead, stabbed to death, in the same brutality as your wife."

Darian's eyes squint to Santos who studies his boss's look of suspense.

"Oh, *Jesus*," is Darian's only response.

Murray cuts it short. "I can't speak to you now, I'll get back to you tomorrow, but before I hang up, there's one more thing. Is your security team still beefed up there?"

Darian again looks to Santos.

"Yes," he replies.

"Okay then, lad, I just want you to stay put and we'll talk more tomorrow," Murray closes.

Darian disconnects. He's relieved and stunned. The hate he had for Seymore and the gut suspicion he held all along has dissolved in less than two minutes.

It's not that he feels remorse over Murray's inside scoop. It's the confusion, and the more questions. Silently, he now begins to panic. Darian Fable knows the "domino theory" all too well. Set quietly in perfect line, and topple in unsuspecting time. This late-breaking evening news has induced him with fright beyond any he's ever endured as a child, man, screen idol, or widower.

And frightened he should be.

PART
FOUR

CHAPTER 49

THE SYLMAR CRIME LAB AND THE LAPD conclude a connection between the Barsolla and Testa slicings. Their biggest clue is Seymore's assets of gold chains in the six digits, which marinated in the pool of his blood. The 230-pound chairman was defenseless, handcuffed to a bedpost, while his murderer sliced away his bloated kingly flab. Face wounds, ear wounds, eye wounds and a plunge to his balls, up and out of his intestines. Then, for a final curtain call, a razor-sharp whack that severed his *cock,* which lay tighter than a pipe's fitting down his whining esophagus.

By all accounts, the penguins slaying appeared to play out the makings of consensual sex with a satanic climax. But this time, the FBI is on the forensic gathering of evidence, plucking their clues from the bloody, drenched bedsheets, which dabble in traces of smeared semen. Just an hour after discovery, two 16-inch strands of synthetic-looking hairs were found, glued to the butchered meat of Seymore's belly. But now the next question the FBI must deal with is if Seymore's sexual preference on this night was that for a female, or was it his casual appetite of a flavor-of-the-month cover *boy.*

The hotel staff on duty "has nothing" as to who came in and out on this rain-pouring night, because of the secret side entrance the chairman's regulars would enter when slipping to his suite away from home. It was a secret entrance that was formed after Seymore was busted two years ago by his third wife, Mia, who overheard an *afternoon delight* inquire his room number while she was to have been sunbathing poolside. *Only the good die young*. So they say.

• • •

IT WAS A STAR-STUDDED PREMIERE in Hollywood. Cameras, 'copters, and horses. Police escorts, *escorts*, and a mile of star-studded opportunists whose "live performances" on camera failed to shed a tear of remorse over the dead pig's slab from under their Chanel shades, at this closed-casket premiere held at *Forest Lawn*. There it was, in hypocritical black-and-white, for the world to enjoy in living color. By invitation only, it was a final *respect* from the many, who in reality "disrespected" the sleaze-king chairman of Summerville. Over 600 of the industry's heaviest on display for television tubes around the globe. Murray and Campbell even found time to drop in for their *fifteen*. It was a star's opportunity and a publicist's dream. You couldn't wish for a better plug on your newest project, or a greater royalty in a farewell song's single, since the death of a British princess some two decades ago.

Instantly, after the two-hour tribute, the fake sniffling stopped and everyone was back to high spirits again. Reaching out in smiles to old faces and flavors of the month, while they inched their way purposely to the sea of reporters' annoying microphones, who flocked on some thirteen scattered broadcast scaffolds. Once the stars were entrapped in PR *heaven,* they reflected their favorite memory of "funnyman Seymore" with a surrealism of high spirits. Sure, they sobered a few words on the *penguin*—like "God rest his soul"—but used the airtime to plug the grand finale that debuts this weekend everywhere. The long and "awaited" first live interview of *Prime Star's* "Mr. Perfect," who still remains "Mr. Mysterious" since the first drop of this soap opera slaughtering was introduced by his wife some 91 days ago.

Meanwhile, L.A. is losing business as stars make sudden leaps and evacuate La-La Land. Sets and locations are relocating from the West to the East and at little concern for the hassle of an actor or studio's location cost. But the stars and the craft-service trucks aren't about to "park and fly" anywhere close to Westport, Connecticut. Not after the FBI forecasts Seymore's *rainy-night killer* is most likely enroute, heading eastbound towards his *last supper.*

CHAPTER 50

THE PAJAMA PARTIES OVER, the guards are back on trail, and Santos is pestered by more than just the August humidity, as he prepares for real-life combat. Darian, in a bold move, has decided (with the advice of his buddy Crown) to open his phone line of communication to whoever dares to place a call of threat or harm. And with that invitation of stubborn boldness, Clyve Barlow's landing this afternoon couldn't be more perfect to annoy the dismantled brain of Darian Fable. It's going to be a no-holds-barred interview, The Fly promises his subscribers. Unannounced, uninvited, and fed live right into the Web site of www.falsefable.com.

Darian *sways* over to the phone this afternoon, thinking it's Mary, Sheila, or Murray, whose latest clue is the elimination of Faith's strongest suspect by death. But upon answering after four rings, he's greeted with the pipes of a Southerner whose research paid off, being the Fables' number hasn't been changed since the night of that fatal phone call. The Fly buzzes Darian's ear in a cool and relaxed demeanor, almost as if the two are old-time buddies who have some catching up to do.

"Thought for sure you'd hop a plane and be at Testa's funeral today," Clyve opens in a lazy swang. "How 'bout that crowd on television? Shit, I guessed it was bigger than the one ya hoaxed over to your wife's gig, don't you?"

Darian is neither startled nor annoyed. His emotional courage is relaxed by his current blood-alcohol level of .11 percent.

He's going to sip on, and play along with this old buddy he can't stand. He remembers an old dig from an old dead comedian over the death of a former movie chairman who was also despised in showbiz by most.

"Well, it just goes to show you, Barlow—give the people what they want and they'll show up," Darian kids.

But Clyve doesn't loosen up to stolen humor from the dead. He needs to dig harder and push the humble one's anger button. His on-liners don't want small chat or a head count of the Countess's burial. They want mud. *Start slinging, Clyve.*

"You missed a good one today, Fable. Or should I call you *Faulkner?*"

Darian isn't surprised. He knew Clyve knew all along by showing his hand the day after the Oscars. He throws him a B+ for tying *David* to *Faulkner*. But now Clyve's going to get some of his own medicine. Darian's no dummy. He knows audiotape is rolling. He reaches for some ammo and whips up a convincing Southern accent. This will confuse the credibility issue, of who Clyve's really taunting.

"Oh, I see you've been doing your research, Clyve! You're too smart a boy for a stupid redneck like me."

The onliners are confused and stumped. This *big* scoop the editor promised online sounds more like a hoaxed morning radio show, than an articulate legend millions *used* to adore. This just can't be, the "one and only."

Listeners are dropping like flies. Clyve needs to take control.

"So you think farmers are stupid, Faulkner?" he says, trying to regain momentum.

"Yeah, I *tink* farmers are stupid, not all dem, just the ones from Oklahoma! How's dat? Got enough dirt yet, *Cleeve?*"

The skeptics who hang around aren't amused. They've been had at $22.50 after that free minute that's now passed. Clyve's in deeper manure than he can barrel out of, and the desperation in his voice validates.

"You know, I'm a little smarter than you think, Fable," he plows forth.

"Oh, yeah, now how's that, Clyve The *Fly*!" Darian reverses his tone to a bullish New Yorker.

"I know all about Pleasant Park, your whore aunt you used to fuck, and your slut wife who claims to have never given it up," Clyve rips.

There's silence. Clyve's grade point average just jumped to an A, and Darian knows it. Clyve laughs hard as Darian plays dead, but hangs on for more assault.

"Old Jane Robel from the *Pleasant Post* in Pleasant Park has a bigger mouth than I do! You 'member Jane, dontcha, David?"

Darian switches over to a British accent, "Hmm, Jane, no I can't say I do now, my boy. Can you please tell me about her?" he politely requests.

"Shit, don't you fuckin' lie to me, *David*," Clyve snickers. "You know Goddamn well who she is! She's the only one running 'round town with her big mouth, claiming you grew up there! And guess what? No one's listening! But I fucking am! The people in that shithole are too ignorant to buy the fact *you* fell from their ugly sky!"

Darian's had enough fun. It's time to sign off. He was willing to play, but now Clyve's crossed the line.

"So what's your point?" Darian returns to his drunken tone.

"My point?" Clyve stumbles.

"Yeah, get to your point, dumb ass!" he slaps him in plain English.

"My point is, Fable, when this is all over with, you're gonna wish you stayed home and fucked your aunt!"

Darian knew Clyve's longing dream, to dig the deepest gossip that smears dirtier than the sweaty crack of his fat Southern ass. But he's not going there. Instead he punches out with a closing blow of his own.

"Hey, Clyve, speaking of whores, did that ex of yours ever get that chicken suit before she dumped your stupid ass?"

You can slice the air of hate from Clyve's end of the wire. If he had his wish, *they'd die in fours*.

Once again, Darian's instinct is right. Now for the hanger.

"You didn't think she really loved your fat-cow ass, now did ya?"

"Fuck you, Fable!"

Darian disconnects in the middle of his laughter. Spark howls several barks. The Fly has brought painful memories to Darian, but also has brightened up his gloomy day. He couldn't care less if he "dug any dirt." Who's going to believe Clyve Barlow? He's a nobody, a fake, "the roaring mouth from the South," who never got his guest to identify. It was just an afternoon circus. He's got about as much credibility to Hollywood as the Englishman he appeared with on McBride's show. Which suddenly reminds him to place a call to his old friend before Darian's incredible and *credible* interview from *Prime Star* debuts tonight.

CHAPTER 51

FORGET THE SMALL CHAT OF CRIMES FOR THE WEEK, such as the death of the notorious Manson Family leader "Sir Charles," who, after a luxurious 45-year prison term, died peacefully in his cell. Forget a spraying of bullets by a working-class black elementary student in a wealthy white schoolyard in the Midwest, which pecked 42 innocent "honkies" to their death. Tonight, being Saturday and the closing of network sweeps week, this is the biggest news of the decade and the biggest barrel of blood and power one can ever whip up for a weekend feast. It all starts at 6:00 Central and 9:00 Eastern Daylight time, beginning with the investigation of Faith Barsolla's murder, moving on to Seymore Testa's fortune of fate, and ending up in a grand finale of sorrow for a man who finally *dared to speak,* after many unspoken years.

But the star of the evening is far from a stabilized box-office king of the 21st century, as he urinates and shakes his penis over his bathroom's washbowl.

Darian faces off in the vanity mirror with the dark circles that trace his bloodshot, beaten eyes. The eyes that now sparkle more like a burnt-out rock star from the eighties, who nourishes with nightly runs of Jack Daniels by the fifth and cold pizza from a week gone by.

Darian tries to imagine a workout plan with the hope of putting himself together. Maybe then he'll look *halfway decent*. He needs a quick solution to free the pent-up tension in his pupils. He notices lines are invading his forehead, like they did Frank's. The thought of running again slowly enters, but quickly exits as he dissects himself in the mirror. He guesses it would take weeks to detox *this* polluted soul. And he should know. He's done that; but never alone. Maybe he needs another soul mate. But not so quickly. Maybe he needs a good dose of sex to distract his tension from the round-the-clock murder coverage. It would most likely have to be a high-class call girl whom he wouldn't have to carry on small chat of any kind with. This idea he likes. He could have his way with her in any perverted sense he desires, while he sexually punished her for 60-something minutes. He scurries to the downstairs and contemplates more on this *desire* and Nick, whom he owes a return call.

"Old Nick would find me a good piece of ass," he smiles down to his best friend, Spark. *Someone I could pay off for the night, maybe five thousand or so, then be done with.* He mixes another round to think it over.

In the back of his paranoid mind, he fears he may be setting up for a scandalous tale of indecent proposal. This whole "call-girl sex thing," he ponders, would detour and backfire from the murder investigation. It would leave the few who still defend his honor to sway over. "We knew it all along" would be the new calling from the streets. Like that popular "king of all media," who bragged his successful career on being a loyal and loving husband to his wife only to finally 'fess up to the devil's temptation of lust with his favorite *Penthouse* pet who now claims to have secretly borne his sixteen-year-old child—before he was divorced. Maybe pleasure's not a good idea, *but wishful fantasy sure is.*

Darian walks to the outdoor terrace to view the sun's final moments, before the giant orange in the sky waves goodbye. As he squints to silhouettes of soldiers that lazily pace out of boredom, he notices a passing couple on the bottom of the road in their matching designer jogging suits. Remarkably, his 20/15 vision picks up their expression of *disgust* from his view a football field away. Ignorant to American snobbery, Gabby and another guard at opposite ends of the gate salute a smile, then wave to the lovely passer-by.

But there's no return smile coming to Gabby and the other guard from the conservative housewife, who salutes them with the oldest wave known to mankind. The American middle finger—stiff and proud. Darian now begins to sense there's fear in the air, insecurity in him, and hate applied by his neighbors. He should have made friends when he jogged those back roads, back when. After all, it was this snobby but bookish small village that ignored and respected the star's sudden exit from "Ka-Ka Land." And it was *this* village that pitied the loss of his loving wife they never knew. But now, it's evident he's in a place that's hostile and fearful over the darkness that he and he alone has instigated to their fine, decent community.

What does the real world now think of Darian Fable? he wonders. But what does it matter? he realizes. It may be too late. *Maybe in another life*, he contends, *I will find lasting happiness. Hopefully, I'll reincarnate as a small and innocent bug. Hopefully, a bug without wings, or maybe an animal of some sort. An animal who means no harm or danger to anyone.* An animal, hopefully, like his best friend, who sniffs his damp nose to the pant leg of his martyred master. The master, deep in thought, ignores his friend's calling and swats a fly that grazes his frizzy beard. For now, Darian must find the strength to rebel against society's hold on him. He now contemplates ways to sneak off the grounds of his barricaded castle. He has a sudden craving to flee into town. Flee to that *pub*, rumored from the guards, that's located beside the Spic and Span meat market some few winding curves down the graveled road. And who will notice the Grim Reaper in disguise with his flourishing decoy of facial hair? *No one.*

He likes this new adventure. It's a challenge to him, and right now, his isolated living needs one. But first he must gather up some costume wardrobe. He runs to his chambers, where he throws a white cotton button-down over his black V-neck T-shirt. He heads to his cluttered closet and parks his bare feet into some black Italian loafers. Then onto the bathroom washbowl, where he splashes his scraggly hair down for easy flexing to a ponytail. He tries to camouflage the threaded lines of his forehead by dropping his bangs forward. This will also help blur the one dead giveaway of his true identification—*his eyes.* But the bangs don't blur the bloodshot sparkle enough, so he opts for some sandy-tan specs to conceal them for good. He tops his "incognito" look with a baseball cap. A black cap that reads in white stitching, Chicago White Sox. In the full-length mirror, his eyes are barely visible; his jawline is concealed by his mountain-man beard, and his frail weight of 159 pounds resembles to the bone a wanted fugitive from *Unsolved Mysteries*.

The long days of drinking and imprisonment have canceled any fear in Darian Fable's bullish mind. He now begs for the killer to prey on this wandering bait that lurks the seaport village, for he doesn't seem to fret the fear of death right now. In his hungry mind, living safe was over with after the murder of his wife, and there can't be anything else in life *worth acting for*. Now's the time to confront that cloud which rained heavily on his sunny days. But not so immediately. He must wait to escape *after* his sermon airs for the estimated 500-million-plus disciples who sit and chow munchies while awaiting their pre-game episode.

CHAPTER 52

TONIGHT, TELEVISION WAS KING. Everyone watched. From the former first lady, to her former first husband. Princes and princesses, Tony Rubenstein (the new head of Summerville Studios), and even the guards, who deserted their post in rotation for the never-before private thoughts of the charismatic leader they honorably protect. But while the whole world barely blinked during Darian Fable's views on violence and moralistic beliefs, the robot laid himself to rest a little longer than he bargained for.

The visor on his baseball cap shaded any light from a lamp, as he snored and clutched his diluted rocks glass that snuggled in the flesh cup holder of his bloated potbelly.

It's now a little after midnight in Westport, as he slowly awakes, feeling refreshingly charged from his three-hour "nap."

Squinting at the view from his balcony, Darian tallies with the help of the floodlights glare eight figures that gather at the front gate. The smoke rises from their cigarette drags and dissipates to clouds in the syrupy air on this humid night. He does the math and declares four guards MIA.

Hopefully, they're with Santos in his bunker, or maybe they've split up and stalked the trails extra hard. If the latter, this could be a dangerous mission to freedom. If any silhouette is spotted or any sound of footsteps heard on his bike trail at this hour, they'll most likely empty their chambers of bullets. Suspect or no suspect—raccoon or no raccoon—legend or no legend. They haven't seen action and are getting itchier by the day since being assigned to an agreeable two weeks of duty, which has now spewed into months. They have families they miss, and wives they have to fuck in their respective countries. Sure they're being paid a year's salary during duty thus far, but in their honest minds, making a living is still the old-fashioned American way, by earning it, and earning it with pride. Even if it entails snipering Mary's Persian cat who sluggishly walks across their path of short-wick patience.

Checking his watch at 12:14 A.M, Darian decides to make his move. He'll exit the back way, out through the kitchen and into the eclipse of his backyard. Spark, who thought he was invited for the journey, is barred by the screen door that whacks his whimpering nose.

"*Shhh…*be good Sparky, I'll be back boy!" Darian whispers to his buddy's panting weep. He then dodges toward the mammoth elm trees that bend slowly, like dark towering feathers amidst the backdrop of the moon. He camouflages his shadow and cautiously continues past the mini-lake, where two geese glide side by side. The same lake and same geese that painted his perfect and peaceful living less than thirty minutes ago on TV, now has the king sneaking from his own-trapped self-misery.

• • •

HE DASHES INTO TOTAL DARKNESS, as sand from the bike trail sneaks into his loafers. He's escaped and has now safely landed in the back woods that map his route through the half-mile trail. His heart jumps, as a sprinting rabbit dashes across his path. He starts to jog up and down the mini-humps of the trail, as he pushes on in determination. It's pitch dark on these trails, but he knows the path like the back of a book. He's also aware that at the end of his half-mile journey, the one thing that will separate him from freedom will be a tall, flimsy cyclone fence that weaves with tumble weeds and partitions the boundaries of neighboring territories, which he's passed but has never stepped foot on. Nearing his destination, he spots Willow Road.

High above the hushed side road shines the brightest street lamp ever known to man, that swarms with the flock of at least a thousand spastic insects. Leave it to his streak of never-ending bad luck. Out of the countless village roads darker than a cave after dawn, he happens to hit a jackpot of light he doesn't need for guidance. Now, he must streak down grassy knoll just inside of this *stranger's* property. From his distant view, the neighboring house lights are dim, but clues hint they're not home. There are no cars in the drive from his 50-yard point, and no movement through the kitchen's sheers. He takes off and descends down the slope as his momentum carries him faster than he anticipated. But there's no stopping now, for he must ride the ride with whatever endurance his bony legs can muster. The wind to his face is cool as the *Marathon Man* breaks sweat. Toxins pour from his flesh and induce his eyes to burn. His legs remarkably straddle the downhill ride, while he snatches his baseball cap before it has a chance to airlift to the wind. *Run, legend, run.*

Finally, he hits the lamppost mark and throttles up a sprint to the finish line. He must continue this for at least a half block more to escape Willow Road's light. He races for any darkness, fearing the headlight from an approaching motorist, who creeps closer up the dark tunneled road. He finally settles and begins desperately gasping for air. His ears hear the whistling winds from a canyon of wilderness to his left. To his right is an entrance road to a neighboring villa, whose iron gates are chained ever since *you know who* arrived. Suddenly chills run over his limbs. He fights to hold on for dear breath as he belts a cough and spills phlegm.

His lungs can feel this three-quarter-mile journey. Short of breath, he reaches to his pants pocket and fires up a smoke. *Suddenly he has oxygen.*

He continues to beware his surroundings. Ahead, up the road, seeing nothing but blackness. Behind him, left to right, *blackness.* He moves in his lengthy stride, holding on to any air, while clutching a fist to his sweaty button-down. A few leaves in dust sweep over his feet. He listens to the creaking of tree limbs along his route. He wishes he had some thick, *white* cotton socks or some jogging shoes, for his bare feet in these stiff leather loafers are stinging and ripping the skin of his heel and big toe on his left foot.

His mind now becomes illusioned. His ears hone in on an orchestra of low cello strings and high operatic chantings that mix beautifully in unison.

Chumchum! Chumchumchum! Chumchum! replays in his head over and over. It fuels him with the endurance he needs for the struggle of his destination. But suddenly the hallucinated symphony is interrupted.

"Get tough you little bastard!" a voice screams out of nowhere.

After those words, nothing but eerie silence follows. Tree branches limp to a calm, similar to the moment before a tornado. His symphony has vanished. He can now only hear the restless ocean waves from far up ahead off the *Island Sound.* He thinks of Faith and the night she was murdered. The faraway ocean reflects her peaceful rest, but the near silence reminisces her neglected screams. How frightened she must have been, with nowhere to run and no one to safeguard her. The stinging she took that awful night his blistered hooves will never match. He wants escape from this morbid thought.

He forces his brain to his rebellious years of early Hollywood. To the countless nights when he and Nick would sip to their last silver in change, then hobble by foot several miles down Sunset after a few hundred rounds at the Coach and Horses. Then, be faced with the gruesome task of an uphill climb of a quarter mile to Nick's ranch on Laurel Canyon, the sister canyon to Coldwater. Little to zero passing traffic after 3:00 A.M. and stuffier than a can of sardines minutes after sunrise. Now, he's alone, on this pitch-dark road, with no bully father for falsified protection, no bitchy wife with a verbal sword, and no drunken friend from England to assist in battle. A sitting duck, just waiting to be plucked. The man who pleasured millions tonight with their popcorn, pizza, and jaws in awe, is now on a mission with a thirst to burn twenty at the corner pub.

Ah, the lights of freedom. The bright-red neon CLOSED on the Spic and Span meat market signals he's almost home. To its left, a door down, the yellow OPEN of P. J. Patrick's bolts energy to his thirsty blood as he nears the finish line. Almost to the gate, he must now search for an alias, should a stranger try small-talking him.

He'd like to carry on a friendly conversation with a working-class one, but it would be too dangerous for this robot, who's unrehearsed to public socializing for more than a decade. He searches for creativity, as he slacks in closer to his neon target. Suddenly he lands a character, with the help of his sore arches and tobacco tongue. Tonight, he'll play a business owner who's in search of a cold one after a twelve-hour day at a print shop. He has his front. *But wait a minute;* he reneges, realizing it's too weak. It's way too unbelievable, this whole *printer thing*. After all, the only ones who work late nights in Westport are the best-sellers he passed, who are still tapping their typewriters. He needs another, and it comes to him with the help of the ocean's roll. "Tonight!" he declares into the lazy lighthouse, blinking miles away in salt water, "tonight my character will be one of a nature photographer."

"I visit from South America," he recites. "Perfect!" he gloats.

The shy photographer, the eccentric down-and-out struggling photographer. His confidence rises. He preps more on his character, *one who barely gets by and is staying in a rented cottage up a side road.*

"I do not speak good English," he fakes an accent. "I am here to shoot seagulls on the *Hoodson* Bay for *Reader's Digest.*"

That'll work, I'm good. So what if I may look like Darian Fable with a beard and thirty pounds lighter in the flesh—I'm not.

"So fucky off!" he laughs and drops the lit butt he extinguishes with his stepping loafer. He simmers his hot foreigner blood down. He must low-key his entrance to the crowded American bar; playing opposite the shy, but commanding entrance many welcomed for so many years. He tugs at the double-glass pane doors and slyly slips his way in.

CHAPTER 53

DARIAN'S CURIOSITY IS PLEASED and his paranoia is resting, as he journeys into a thin Saturday-night crowd. The patrons, two fraternity preppies in collar button-downs, and a bored female barmaid, scrutinize his every *lost* stride to the end stool that sits opposite the trio's triangle of small town small talk.

But the thin turnout at this late hour doesn't allow the fabled one in disguise to marvel so quickly. Across the nation, almost all have passed on their noisy weekend meat-markets, for an unruffled listen of the man who's never spoken. *Pain* sells, and if tonight's turnout is any proof, the nation has *bought*. From his corner view, under his tinted specs, Darian is wary of two husky preppies, who, judging by their empty half-pints, are headed for half-in-the-bag. They flaunt no empathy in their chuckling that's loaded, aimed, and fired in the direction of the rambled *sea monster*.

Planted close to the jukebox, Darian's ears separate the sports arena cheers that echo from the big-screen tube in the pub. Instead, his ears hook to the pop music, from an old top-ten single in an older motion picture, *City of Angels*. The track spinning behind him is titled "Uninvited," and by the looks of daggers that shoot his way, the song's opening lyrics couldn't be more coincidental, directed at the *freaky foreigner*. His facade seems to mock the rich preppies, who now could care less about the boring NBA opener that was taped delayed, thanks to Mr. Hollywood's interview, who, rumor has it—litters "somewhere" up a private road. The game's a first-half blowout, between the still "regrouping" Chicago Bulls and the defending world champion New York Knicks. It's a given victory to the Knicks thanks to Michael Jordan, who, after two decades, *still* left Chicagoan's court too soon. As for the Knicks, they praise their veteran head coach, Ewing, and thank the good Lord for finally trading his jersey for a ring in his *three piece*.

Darian reaches to his back pocket for his wallet, as the woman of 40-something, with a waistline stuffing of 50 or more, lethargically strolls his way. He immediately senses dejavu. She reminds him of someone, but he can't place it. Suddenly he finds it. *Pammy at Swiggs*. A blast from the past, but not all that bad. He liked Pammy. She was okay. She had a pleasant smile and pitied his slap from the German. *Both of them.*

"Heenakin and shoot of clown loyal on d'rocks please," he perfectly inflects with a polite smile.

Waiting acclaim on his warm and friendly delivery, he searches for the tinniest break in the barmaid's tightly sealed lips, but she denies him any ovation for that delivery. Instead, she flips him a coaster and coldly retrieves the *sewer rat's* beer. Darian's uncomfortable with the cold ambiance of his newfound habitat and now fears he may be in trouble. There's a gross addiction to Polo and DKNY roaming this yuppie village. It has to be his vagabond wardrobe that's keeping the Pammy-clone distant and causing one husky to jitter his leg, which vibrates the entire foot-post along the bar. Surely it can't be his mountain-man facial hair he hasn't trimmed in months or his greasy biker ponytail he hasn't shampooed in eight days? Surely it couldn't be his tinted shades at midnight?

Or maybe her rudeness is just a substitute for her nervousness. Maybe she's looked beyond his fake facade and has figured him out. Maybe she's laughing at his disguise and laughing at his shades and dopey White Sox cap, who's MLB tag dangles and lies unnoticed by him on his ponytail. Darian shifts his authenticity by swapping his crinkled twenty for a smooth hundred. The Pammy-clone raises the

Franklin in the backlight to verify. She then returns with the sea monster's change. Through his burning cigarette that sticks his dry lips, Darian flips her a twenty for her fine service, and, like he planned all along, it buys him more than a peek of her chipped chops.

"Why, thank you!" she lights up and blushes.

He takes a deep breath after his long swallow from his medicine.

"So this is life in the real world," he whispers through his smoke rings. His eyes drift from the peanuts and chips that hang the back wall down to the friendly server who's now grinning on the phone, while smiling his way.

Her expression now causes concern to the legend in disguise. He's not one to be fooled so easily. He knows her body language all too well and now senses he *may* be busted.

"Who are you trying to fool?" he scolds down to his fellow conspirator, Crown.

Darian knows the game, and she's played it perfect. It's the same game he reluctantly participated in a thousand times over when spotted never in public. She's on the phone, trying to persuade her best friend, of the sudden landing of Mr. Perfect at his imperfect lowest. Seeing the LEGEND in such an unlikely environment is out of the norm. He should be tucked safely in his castle with his army of guards fearing his life and grieving the loss of his dead bitch wife.

"It's him, I'm telling you!" he reads her lipped plea to the phone's receiver. It's now only a matter of seconds, he panics, before some natural-born "others" like her happen to blow in with the wind. What a drag, he thinks—his freedom for the night is closing to an end. He now wishes he'd thrown her a measly buck tip, like a real sea photographer *wouldn't* have. Though his ankle's scalding and this journey may be short-lived, it was all worthwhile to escape the armored trap of his infested castle, the rat reminisces.

CHAPTER 54

THE SIDE DOOR AT P.J.'S SWINGS OPEN, and in blows a cover-girl essence. With her billfold in grip and quick determination to the bar, it appears this *steamy* brunette has dropped in for nothing more *than change to go.* The gossiping barmaid doesn't budge her phone jabberings to acknowledge the long legged impatient one. Darian inhales the back breeze of her aroma that sweetens up his cigarette's smoke and spellbinds the two gawking preppies. The husky preppie's neck jerks from the big-screen blow out.

"Blow me," he slurs loudly enough to the tall brunette whose fidgeting finally wins a notice from the barmaid.

The girl has a healthy, seductive steam that vaporizes from her cocoa-tanned complexion.

Darian, the quiet foreigner, acts as judge amongst the three other favored American panelists in house. He scores her a 9.3 in her snug, summer skirt that showcases her towered pins, shapes tightly to her womanly hips, and throws all eyes to her silver-hooped navel piercing. The steamy beauty is becoming restless. She flings back her black mane, stomps her sandal for notice, and cocks her head around to catch the foreigner playing favorite to her, the *contestant.*

"Hey!" she slaps five whacks to the bar's oak top. The barmaid squints an eye to the rude patron and puts her gossiping on hold.

"Change," the girl flings a buck while she snaps her gum in bitch fashion.

She finally gets her change and a look from the Pammy-clone. She then moves on to the pay phone, which is located by the entrance. The husky preppie is now searching for a male counterpart to assist him in his lustful thoughts. Earlier, he jittered his leg, but now he tosses the *sea monster* a friendly toast of "cheers." His preppy partner joins in the toast.

The sea monster raises his beer bottle and plays along with the huskies' wishful fantasies. Darian guesses the poor girl is lost, heading to or from someone's home in the area. Or maybe she's had boyfriend or car trouble. Whatever the case may be, something of her Saturday-night landing is not right. Carnal steam like hers does not routinely blow through this safe suburban village. Not that there's a shortage of good-looking women throughout town, it's just that history shows those born into *this* section have the three B's of breeding, baking, and babies; in a Volvo village with green picket fences and husband's receding in their late twenties. Westport is miles away from the nightly stomping grounds of a continental woman more determined than a shark in bloody waters. That kind of predator you can easily net at a corner pub in *Mother Mary's* temporary living quarters.

The girl finishes her call, on what looks to be an uneasy note, then roams up to the bar for a spot to sit. She halts a stool away from the "scraggly one" and a dozen *still* not far enough away from the two hopeless romantics. Darian just stares straight ahead, as he relies on his peripheral vision to do the snooping. He purposely disregards her key jingling and fumbling through her bag, while sucking on his cigarette and the stinging sweetness from his good buddy in a shot glass. It's a smart male trick to win attention over the obviousness of *starers,* who may have a dib on this girl, *never* in another lifetime. But Darian's no dummy. The girl fumbles in and out of her bag for more "nothings." The foreigner can tell her nervous and fidgety movements are per his refusal to acknowledge. The barmaid strolls over and tries to make amends, forcing a phony smile. But her sluggish service for change is not so easily forgiven.

"Jack and Coke," the bitch demands straight up.

Hmm... Now she's really moved the foreign judge by her drink of choice. She's a pro pounder. Could be a lush. Déjà vu occurs. *Auntie Judy.* Her stool swings his way and Darian opens his door of "therapy to a stranger."

"Whew! What a night," she says, brushing back her long bangs with her fingers.

"Is that so?" he mumbles in *plain English.* She lights one up and her juice arrives.

"Here," he offers, to which the confused barmaid gives him a look. *Suddenly he's an American citizen,* and the barmaid now has confirmation on what she was 50-50 on. "Take it out of here," he pushes a twenty forward.

"Thank you," the brunette stranger accepts the round on him, almost as though he was obligated.

"Where the hell am I, anyway?" she looks about, speaking to no one.

"You're in Westport, Connecticut," he clears his throat.

"Westport, Connecticut? Shit, I've got to get back to the city."

She means New York, which means the *judge* is losing time.

"New York?" he tries for conversation. "How'd you end up here?"

She blows a thick cloud of smoke and swirls her cubes with her straw.

"It's kind of a long story. I don't know if I want to go there, if you know what I mean. Anyway," she volunteers, "I came down to write with sort of a stranger who lives in... Fairfield? Is that it?"

"Fairfield," he nods.

"Well, anyway, it turns out he wanted to do more than just write, and I said *see ya!* I mean sorry, but uh, he's like, not my type," she turns a look to the preppies.

Darian nods again, "So, what are you writing?"

"Well, it was supposed to have been a one-woman play, and *he* was supposed to help with the editing," she blushes.

"Oh, it's finished?"

"Just about."

She then stretches backwards, as Darian sneaks a glance to what's under her "perky" cotton pullover.

"Do you mind if I?" she points to a stool that separates them.

"No, of course not."

"Hi," she smiles, "I'm Gwen."

"Hello, Gwen," he barely touches the tips of her fingers.

"And you are?" she grins.

"I'm ..." he pauses.

"*You're* is nobody's business in *here*. Right?" she winks.

He's been caught off guard. Where's the fucking sea character when he needed him most. His timing is off and his accent has long left. No time to ad-lib. He's been caught in a netted trap through the bad directing of his good buddy Crown.

Gwen continues with her playful tease in a girlie smile that's sneakier than his escape route tonight.

"You know, I *am* kind of in the business," she stirs her cubes.

"Oh well," he now couldn't care less. "But, hey, my cover-up got me this far, and I do appreciate you respecting my privacy, *Gwen*." He tips his drink.

She glances to the preppies and the barmaid, who are no doubt gossiping about "them," the "outsiders."

"It's perfectly okay. We'll just keep it right here, between you and me, our little secret."

Little secret. First his whore aunt, then Murray at his wife's death-bed. And now this, a complete stranger.

"That it is," he winks, "our little secret."

Gwen's cool demeanor is slowly but surely winning him over. Most would fold from the screen god's presence. They'd go over the top and lose him in five seconds from some ridiculous jubilation.

"So how are you doin'?" she asks.

"How am I what?" he's stumped by her nerve.

"I know you've been through a lot lately, and I just want you to know from one human being to another, I'm feeling for you," she tips her drink, swallows, then taps her empty glass for a refill. The barmaid comes over in lightning speed.

"Another," she orders.

Darian looks hard into her dark chestnut eyes that look him back in a serious, warm intensity. He senses a feel of honesty in their "comfortable" ten seconds of thought.

"Thanks for your concern," he looks to his rock glass.

"You're welcome," she says, blowing smoke his way as she rises and hits the ladies room.

Left alone, Darian's now confused. He does a suspicious mind search for the unanswered thoughts. Like where is this one getting the nerve to treat me like a human being? He's quickly becoming too comfortable with her poised demeanor. This has to be a cloud of friendship that has fallen from the sky, like a rare occasion when you meet someone and exchange maybe five or six words and suddenly it becomes months, even decades of loyal friendship.

Gwen has oozed into Darian Fable's soul, and he now has a feeling of strange attachment. There's something about her. Maybe in another lifetime, he searches, or like the dreams we all experience of a familiar face and voice of a trusting friend. A friend you've never met, nor seen, in your entire awakened life. Or like that attraction at a stoplight that ends with the color green.

Is this a sign, or is this his loving wife tossing a magical soul for him to unload his loneliness on? Or is this a mystery person who will be long gone after one more round? This is strange, he concludes, and *stupid*. I should have a wall up; I'm a legend! How dare some struggling up-and-comer not be intimidated by me, the great Darian Fable! his ego speaks.

Gwen returns with a fresh seal of lip gloss as the scent of watermelon mingles with his cigarette smoke.

"Have you had any of your work published?" he tries more small talk.

"No. I've only been seriously writing for about, *mmm*...I'd say...the last two years."

"So where you from, New York?"

"I grew up in California," she boasts.

"Really," he raises a concealed eyebrow, "whereabouts?"

"Hmm..." she hums and thinks, "I don't know, I mean, promise you won't laugh? I mean it's kind of embarrassing."

"Try me."

"Inglewood."

"Inglewood? Well that's not so bad—home of the Lakers. It's kind of a rough area though." he adds.

Gwen's cheery mood now turns somber.

"Look," she cocks her head, "I don't like to talk about my childhood. I mean it wasn't so nice. I didn't have much to do growing up." She swirls her straw fast. "It was just drink and do drugs, drink and do drugs! But I did manage to make my way into Hollywood a lot, so, it wasn't too bad," she smiles.

For real family morals, he wants to say, but doesn't.

"Well, I didn't have a great childhood either, if it's any consolation," he tries to take the burden.

Yeah right, she wants to say, but doesn't.

"Are you married or do you have a boyfriend?"

"What's with the fifty questions!" she giggles.

Darian's winning *control.* Gwen's gone in twenty minutes from a tall cool woman to the girl she really is, of probably nineteen. The *juice* is kicking in, and so has his need for a background check. "I'm not prying, just small talking," he smiles.

"Okay, no biggie! But to answer your question, no boyfriend, and *no* husband! Besides most guys are assholes these days anyway."

"Just these days?"

"Yeah, they either want to fuck and forget you or they're psycho and won't leave you alone. You know what I mean?"

"Well, I wouldn't know too much about relationships and dating," he looks to his blistered heel.

"Oh shit!" her hand smothers her lips, "What am I saying? I'm sorry, I mean, I forgot! I don't know you and all, but what I've read and heard, I know you were both *really* in love."

"Yeah, well, welcome to the price of fame."

"Hey, can I ask you something?" she nudges her stool closer.

"Maybe," he takes a drag.

"What the hell are you doin' *here*, all by yourself in *this* place?"

"Well, I live up the road, and just had to get out and get some, let's say, human touch."

"Human touch? Okay, I could see that. I mean, it must be hard dealing with all the bullshit of fame and then losing someone you've loved an entire life." She looks at him concerned.

Darian is silent.

"Well, anyway," she says beginning to gather up, "I'd better make my way back to the city, I'm driving to the West Coast in the morning."

"Wait, hold on a minute, you're *driving* back to L.A.?"

"Sure, why not? Hey you, I've got two things in life. A pretty face and a reliable car."

Darian has a thought.

"Well, wait a minute," he nudges her shoulder bag strap. "How would you like to come back to my place and maybe just, you know ... chat a while?"

Gwen smiles, blushes, then nibbles her fingernail.

"Can't you come up with a better line than that? Chat? I mean this is insane, you're Darian-freakin'-Fable and I'm just, you know, some crazy chick who ran from some dude's obsession."

"No, really, I'm dead serious. I mean I could even make arrangements for you and your car to get to L.A. without driving."

Gwen taps her nail to her tooth.

"Wait, let me ask you something? Are you really that lonely that you could use *my* company tonight?"

Darian looks the other way, almost giving up, but Gwen spares him.

"You know, fuck it, why not! Come on, let's blow this pop stand," she says and tugs his sleeve.

Through the doors they go, as Gwen leads *the sea monster* to her vehicle, which happens to be a Range Rover.

A sea-green Range Rover. *A pretty face and a reliable car.*

CHAPTER 55

HEADLIGHTS BEAM THE EYES OF FOUR GUARDS, who through the iron gate have their shotgun barrels pointed at the brightly lit *strangers*. Santos sprints towards the gate barefoot with his leather suspenders slapping below his flabby waist. He's bare-chested and is screaming in a bloody fury, "Hold! Hold!" to his soldiers, who'd love to empty an entire round in a tire or four. He pulls up on his reigns and enters through the watchman's booth, approaching the foreign vehicle. Carefully moving to the driver's side with his .45 drawn, the brightness of a giant spotlight illuminates every dead insect that's glued to the plastic bug shield of the Rover. The bright light blinds Gwen's vision of the pointed barrels.

The passenger *landlord* is more than amused by the frenzy of attention his little brother and his army display. Peering into the passenger's window, Santos is shocked to see his star prisoner has slipped his sleepy army's grasp. Smartly, though, he downplays his frustration by not embarrassing his boss or humiliating his dummy guards in the presence of this visiting *señorita*.

"Oh, Mr. Fable, so nice to see you, sir," he greets the couple.

He then snaps his fingers for a watch guard to switch open the heavy iron gate.

"Why, thank you, Santos." Darian politely smiles, as Gwen proceeds onto the cobblestone driveway. Through her rearview mirror she can see Santos slapping upside the soldiers' helmets, who take their brief lickings, then flee to resume their posts. His boisterous screams of "Foot! Foot!" echoes the still night, like a coyote in heat.

Inside, Gwen is overwhelmed at the movie legend's house. The two first invade the game room, where Darian remotes the stereo on and hustles to his fully stocked *altar*. He dims the lights, darkening the room's corners, leaving just enough over the pool table. Gwen eyes in awe the towering cathedral ceiling above, with the impeccable detail of the Sistine Chapel artwork. Her eyes wander over the paintings on the walls, which have to cost in the millions. But the originals of Picasso, van Gogh, da Vinci, Southard, and Mauriello do nothing to impress her, more than the *freshly* framed *Time* magazine cover of "Mr. Perfect." She makes no attempt to hide her girlish excitement.

"Wow, this place is fucking incredible!"

"Thanks, I painted it myself," Darian looks to the ceiling.

"How many rooms are in this place?" She misses his humor, and glances to the "Mr. Perfect" cover.

"All together, about a hundred and something. That includes the main house, which we're in, and the four guest homes buried somewhere out there" he points to a picture window of darkness. "Not including the closets," he notes.

Gwen has a delusion of grandeur. *The guest homes. The home for me.*

"Who lives in the guest houses?"

"Groundskeepers, maintenance men, and, of course, my 'A-1' security team," he says in slight disgust returning with drinks. "But all that's going to change real soon, 'cause after this week I'm gonna start winning my space back. You know what I mean? Here's to you," he toasts, "to my new friend, Gwen—and it's funny 'cause it rhymes," he smiles. They tap, tip, and sip.

He makes his way to the plush sofa and Gwen unarms her leather shoulder bag to the floor. His eyes pleasure her every fine curve as she bends over to her bag and searches for a smoke. Gwen strolls to the sofa, but before settling in close comfort, surprises him and lays a friendly wet one to Darian's lips.

"Be careful, you might get yourself in trouble," he says and shyly smiles. She ignores his warning and invites in with three more quick ones, before finally taming herself.

"So what's it like to be Darian Fable?" her eyes wander.

And with those eight childish words, her age now drops from nineteen to nine.

"Hey, hold on a minute, I didn't bring you here to talk about me. I want to know about you. Are you really from L.A?"

"Yep," she reaches over to untie his ponytail, her chest pressing his face.

"You need a shave." She runs her fingers through his beard.

"How old are you Gwen?" he tries to ditch what's coming.

"How old are you Darian?" she takes him on.

"Come on, don't put me on the spot."

"Put you on the spot?" she works up to his hair. "Let's just say I'm *old enough*. Besides, older men turn me on." She begins a nibbling to his ear. Goosebumps shower his entire body and her lips once more reach their destination of his. Her once brief and innocent pecks have now propelled to heated passion. The pheromones of this "new friend" named Gwen have now piqued a sexual curiosity for Darian Fable. The scent of the neck he begins to lick and the firmness of the ribcage he wraps his fingers around influence his sinful wishes.

Suddenly his grip guides her to her feet.

"Go over there," he points several feet away to the pool table. Gwen obeys his command. Darian's in control and he *likes* it.

"Do you trust me?" he speaks.

"I trust you," she whispers.

"Take down your skirt," he orders.

She obeys and proceeds to unzip, never losing her stare to him, nor he to her, as she awaits his next command in her white cotton panties and lacy bra.

"You're absolutely stunning," he compliments from his safe distance.

"Thanks," she blushes, then returns to the sofa where she begins performing to his sudden desire. He proceeds to devour her with every ounce of sexual frustration he has in his aching moralistic soul.

During a minute that feels like twenty, Gwen suddenly halts all passion and nervously rushes to retrieve her clothes.

"I'm sorry," he apologizes almost in fear.

"So am I. I don't want to move too fast," she speaks quickly and clothes herself quicker. "So you think because you're Darian Fable you can just have your *way* with me, now don't you?" she snaps through the cigarette that dangles from her lips, while zippering up the back of her skirt.

Darian also zippers up, as the once few desires he held are suddenly replaced by the hundred guilty ones he now holds. He starts to question himself. Maybe he moved too fast? *"Hello? What the fuck Darian! How dare you!"* he can hear Faith scolding from the den.

After all, shouldn't he be mourning her longer? And what would Mother Mary think? Guilt's up to a *thousand* and counting.

"I'm sorry," he begs for Gwen's forgiveness. "I'm confused, I mean, it's just that you're the first woman I've made a move on in a long time." He sighs heavily.

"Oh, come on, you really expect me to believe you? I mean aren't you Mr. Perfect, with all the *right* lines?"

He ignores her and heads over to the bar to freshen his drink while Gwen sings on to his deaf ears. "You know what? Who really gives a shit! I mean why should it matter, I'm the stupid one! I should of known you'd try and fuck me like everyone else does, then kick me out in the morning."

Make it a million and counting. "Well, I hate to break the bad news to you, Gwen, but that's where you're wrong."

"Yeah, right!"

"Hey, wait a minute, just hold it. For some reason you're gravitating to me like no one else has in a long time. But on the other hand, I'm also finding this to be a guilty experience. Do you want another?" he offers from the bar.

Finally the four magic words Gwen's ego has longed to hear—"No-one-else-has." She's won his respect. Maybe she won't have to hit the road tomorrow. Maybe a guest "house" is now her guest "home." *Hell, even a closet in this castle will do.*

"Well, can you really blame yourself?" she poses to his flattering words.

"Hey, can I ask you something?" he misses her playful conceit.

"Yeah, go ahead."

"Who are you?"

"Who am I?"

She pauses and fires up a cigarette that buys her three lengthy seconds to think.

"Like you care who *I* really am?" her words blow through smoke.

"Yeah, I do care. I want to know more about you," he says, now face to face with her.

"Look, I'm sorry," she tries to duck out. "I just don't want to talk about *me*. Can't you understand?" She bows her head.

"No, I can't. What are you hiding?"

"Nothing. Hey, I've got an idea! Wanna do a bump?" her eyes light up.

"What?" he looks confused.

"Let's do some coke! Come on, it's a perfect conversation piece! I mean you might even get me to open up a little bit."

"Oh, Jesus, I don't know."

"Oh, come on! I'll bet you haven't done drugs in the longest time, have you?"

"Well, I haven't drank in almost twenty years either." He jiggles his cubes.

She pulls from her bag two tiny plastic vials packed with white substance. She quickly uncaps one and scrapes along its dusty rim with the tip of her fingernail.

She sniffs it up a nostril and sets *that* vial aside. "This one's for you," her eyes smile.

"What's in the other?" he dares to ask.

"Nothing, it's too harsh for you," she just about ignores.

"Why, what is it, crank?" he half kids.

"Almost," she smiles and chops meticulously with a razor to the glass table.

"Gwen, why do you do that shit?"

"Trust me, if you had my life, *you* would too," she chops on.

She separates the powdered portions. She pulls a bill out from her purse and rolls it tightly, while admiring her meticulous chalky lines.

The once-glamour-king and role model to millions, who lived on a daily jog and nibbled four vegetable servings a day, has suddenly resorted to a liquid diet of whiskey on the rocks, countless smokes, and now this—the devil's doom—*cocaine*. To top it off, he has a complete stranger in his home. The *home* that suddenly resembles the darkest flashback of his father's *house* on Maple Avenue. But fuck it, experiment a little. Just pull this night off, then start with a clean slate, he tells himself.

How dare you.

CHAPTER 56

I'S BEEN A LONG EVENING OF SMALL-TALKING, from political views to pop culture, as the laser disc player burns the greatest hits of *that band,* Cheap Trick, on elevator volume. The smoky glass-top table is severely beaten with cake-powdered smudges.

"Your eyelid," Darian stares.

"What about my eyelid?" Gwen sniffles.

"It arches up and curves just like my wife's did."

She hands him the rolled up fifty. "You're up."

He snorts into the chalk line. His nostrils sting, but it's a *pleasurable* sting.

"Years of substance control down the drain," he moans with regret over this guilt he *loves.*

"Oh well. Life's short, ya' gotta play hard," Gwen reaches for the straw currency.

"Where's your family?" he follows up.

"I don't have a family," she stares numbly at the overcast gloom of 5:07 A.M.

"But where's your mother and father?" he tries again.

Gwen's reaction matches her view while she slips her jacket on from the dampness that roams the room and heads to the bar for another refill.

"My mother died when I was 3," she offers.

"I'm sorry."

"You're sorry? Why should you be sorry? You know, why do people say they're sorry, like it's their fault or something?"

"What did your mother die of?"

"She ODed."

"What kind of drug?"

"Heroin. It started out with coke, moved onto ludes, then onto desperation."

"Where was your father when all this was happening?"

"I never met him, who knows. Then again, who cares? He split shortly after I was born. My aunt raised me till I was 16. Since then, I've been on my own."

"Really? You know my aunt raised me after my parents died when I was young."

"Oh, yeah? And how old were you?"

"Twelve."

"Both of 'em died together?"

"Well, my mother when I was 2, and my father when I was 16."

"You're kidding? How'd they die?" her eyebrow arches.

"Mom had cancer."

"Wow, bummer. What about your old man?"

Suddenly a slight grin overcomes Darian's somber face.

"Bud? I'm back, come home please?" he imitates.

"What? Do that again!"

"Bud, I'm back, it's me, *please come home!*"

"What in the fuck? You're freaking me fucking out! I mean, you sound like a fucking woman! And who's Bud?" She gets in his face.

Darian slips from his performance.

"Hah?"

"Answer me! Who's Bud?"

"Oh, that was my dad. He died in a car accident."

"Your dad? You're speaking of your dead father? I think you're a little weird," she squints up close into his eyes.

"I ain't so weird. Maybe good," he grins, "but not weird."

"Well!" she springs to her feet from the sofa, "that's a drag and all, but you know what? You *can* remember your parents. I have to blank my mom out and the deadbeat who knocked her up."

"Oh, come on, things aren't so bad. I mean look at you, you're beautiful, and from what I can tell, a very intelligent person who's done all right for herself in life. Personally, I commend your strength," he toasts.

"Oh, yeah, all right for myself!"

She grabs for her laminated driver's license to scrape up any caked residue to form another line.

"I don't know," she goes on, "a pretty face and reliable car, I mean big fucking deal. All right for myself. But what about love? Does that matter? Tell me, what do you really know about *love*, Mr. Fable?" she laughs. "Come on, I dare you, tell me about love?"

"Love is like an apple, it's oh so bitter sweet," he mumbles flatly.

"Please, don't try to get heavy on me. Is that supposed to be Shakespeare or something?"

"Nope. Fable."

"Oh well, *maybe* it's different," she's half impressed.

Gwen then pries to the question the whole world was wondering, but Nikki never asked. The question of, if he loved his wife so much, why didn't they bear a child?

"We were afraid to have a child." He looks at the baby angels above.

"You don't like children, do you?" she says brattily.

"Of course I do, but look at this world we live in. It's a surprise we're all still here. I mean, shit, at any moment we could all be disintegrated by some *sicko* leader of a nation because he's had a bad day or maybe even a bad lay. Besides, Faith and I weren't ever in a position to have children. It just wasn't feasible to reach my goal as an actor and her dream at, well, I don't know ... I guess power. It sounds selfish doesn't it?"

Gwen shrugs and listens on.

"I mean don't get me wrong, the wonders of a child are *rewarding*, but I've seen the responsibility shut a lot of people's creative dreams down. Besides, who wanted to raise a kid in that filthy town called Hollywood."

"Well, look at me. I'm normal, aren't I?"

There is a brief moment of silence that breaks with laughter from both.

"That's what I mean!" he points to her playfully. "I think deep down inside, Gwen, you're a fucking nut!"

"Oh no, I'm not! I think deep down inside you may have a few Darian Fables roaming this world!" she laughs.

Suddenly, the laughter and smiles shut off for Darian. Gwen's innocent poke has hit a sour note.

"Sorry, did I say something?" she fears.

"No, it's just that that's such a *stereotype* of the famous."

"Oh, man, I'm sorry. Hey, can I ask you something just a little bit more personal?"

Darian says yes with his shrug.

"How many women did you sleep with before or during your marriage to your wife?"

"Do you know Nikki Hopkins?" he smiles.

"Who?"

"Forget it. I slept with no one during my marriage to Faith. Now let me ask you something, Gwen. Have you ever seen my wife? Have you ever seen such beauty?"

Gwen thinks and smiles, "Well to be perfectly honest with you, yeah! I mean I've seen her many times."

"Many times? How many times?"

"I do watch a little TV, you know. So answer me another one. How many women did you sleep with, let's say *before* your wife?"

"Many. And it didn't pay off. It was so empty, so bullshit. The whole thing they call *a fuck*. Besides, it takes the right kind of woman to put up with someone like me."

"Really? Why? I mean aren't you 'Mr. Perfect,'" she says looking to his photo.

"Well, I guess I was, until now," he looks to his diluted drink. His eyes begin to water and wander the room. Maybe he should spill some more personal beans. And what the hell, why not? Gwen, from all appearances, is not a kiss-and-teller. She's held her cool well. She's confident, plus she's got steam. The *steamy* are the ones whose closets overflow with ghosts.

"My wife and I were ready to give it a shot," he offers. "We were actually trying for a child." He stops himself. "Hey, can we talk about something else?"

"No, I want to know!" she grabs hold of his hand.

"Can I tell you a little secret?"

Her attentive eyes answer *yes.*

"We never consummated our marriage. It was a problem I had growing up, and one Faith had sometime before we met."

"What problem?"

"Well you see, my wife, had been raped. She couldn't handle intimacy, and God knows I had enough sex before fame kicked in, so her problem didn't faze me a bit. I turned her on to this thing called Tantra. Have you ever heard of it?"

"No."

"It's spiritual. Tantra's all about touching and feeling the soul's energy. If you really concentrate, you can reach orgasms without physical contact. It's such a real love. You see, Gwen, I never had love as a child, so any love from my wife was a safe and rewarding one. We were perfect for each other."

Gwen wipes his forehead, and uses her thumb to force the tears that refuse to leak from Darian's eyes.

CHAPTER 57

DARIAN TAKES HER LEAD, AS THEY EXIT the venomous den to the bedroom's staircase. To the upstairs, hand in hand, he grabs to the banister for strength. Proceeding slowly up the flight of steps, Gwen asks during their climb which room is his. He hooks a right for his answer. They reach his giant bed and fall exhausted on it. The daylight sneaks through the crack of a curtain and alters the darkened room into a mood of perfect romance. Darian flips on his sore back. With his eyes shut, he peacefully embraces Gwen's hand.

"I don't think this is a good idea," he whispers.

"What do you mean," she caresses, "don't you want to finish the night off? Or do you have a heart and feel like you may owe me something more in the morning?"

Darian now wishes he hadn't ventured out from his *prison castle*. His energy is whipped, and Gwen's childish second-wind is draining what little he has left in his throbbing brain and sore bones.

"It's Faith," he mumbles. "I'm still mourning. Besides, we've been talking for quite some time now, and my attraction to you has fallen to strictly mental. I have too much respect for you, Gwen, even though you are stunningly beautiful. I just don't want to lose you as a friend."

A friend. The guest cottage. The luxury of the almighty is now and forever hers, amongst the billions of wishful bidders. But only if she plays her final cards right. *Gwen's* no dummy. It's time to shut down shop while she's still ahead.

She takes her finger and grazes his lips. "I completely understand. I don't want to jeopardize our friendship either."

"Good!" he exalts from his sleepy trance, escorting her with sudden energy up another winding staircase to the fourth floor wing. "This is where you'll stay tonight," he swings open a door.

Curtains dim the morning light, but the French doors are wide open to the bedroom's terrace. Two hummingbirds loiter about a flower basket on the terrace's ledge. They chirp in a fairy-tale portrait to the background bubbling of cascading fountains directly below in the front yard. The queen-size, four-poster canopy bed is draped with pastel prints and linen sheers. Vases of yellow and white tulips purify sweetness throughout the room. The pink bedroom set serves more for a 12-year-old princess than a guestroom for an adult. The walls are wallpapered in violet pastels, with baby angels barely visible.

"This is a guestroom? It looks more like a little girl's room," Gwen comments uneasily.

"Well, if you'd like, rough it up a little," he jokes. "It's yours for as long as you'd like."

"But should I not return tomorrow?" She recites like a princess. Darian's impressed. "That's not bad," he smiles, "do you have work in L.A., Gwen?"

"No."

"Do you have any commitments soon in L.A?"

"No … not really."

"Well, then," he smiles again. "I mean, I dig you and would like you around. We'll talk in the morning." He winks and exits.

Gwen studies her new surroundings, as she now finds herself left alone to wonder, *and* wander. She examines every porcelain cow, pig, and other pinkish knickknack that invade any shelf of the room. She poses in front of a long closet mirror to admire her new curvaceous royalty.

These lavish surroundings are what she's yearned for her entire life. To grow up in a room of such safe comfort and plush innocence lends her stability for the moment, as her feet sink into the thick plush-plum carpet. A normal upbringing is all she ever wished for. Just some parents who cared and a boy on the block "who dared." *Just like the boy one story below.* As she surveys to the mirror, a strong feeling of guilt stares back into her eyes. She starts doubting her morals of the evening. The sexual escapading may not have played out properly for her dream of becoming more than a friend to Darian. "Or was it?" she asks herself. After all, "what is proper?" she questions her tired mind.

The hummingbirds' chirp and water fountains' flow is interrupting the investigation of her dark and deepest thought. She rushes to slam shut the French doors and rips the curtains closed to exclude any pleasant chirp or trace of sunlight. She's now burning with guilt over her actions of the night. She turns hostile and rebellious to this *fairy-tale setting.* She approaches closer to the mirror and ponders at what lies behind its doors. She opens the mirrored doors, while the closet succumbs to internal light. Her eyes are met with surprise from the neatly lined shelves and a garment rod that doesn't seem to end. Inside, lies a squash of clothing whose designer labels and price tags still dangle, *unworn* garments. She notices these garments aren't fit for a princess of 12, but more for a *rich bitch* in modern time. She yanks a black silk evening gown from Dolce and Gabbana. She tosses it to the bed and quickly yanks for another. This time she lands on a pant suit. She runs her hands along the *walk-in boutique*'s rack, becoming hostile in confusion as her heart begins to pump.

She rips the shoebox tops open that stack three high. Reading the boxes' labels only adds to her fire, when she notices they're custom-fit perfectly to her size of 9. She pulls more shoes, digging like a woman on a last-minute change while her blind date waits. She lands on a platform mule-style wedge and fiercely wings it into the air where it topples over the vase of tulips and nicks the window's shutter. The hummingbirds flutter off. This may be fashion paradise to some women, but a fashion disaster of confusion to Gwen. She turns and approaches the nine dresser drawers, whose top holds Zaharoff, Jil Sander, Calvin Klein, and other heavenly bottles. She pulls the top drawer, and her eyes are met with sporty everyday cotton wear. In the bottom drawer, she eyes undies, bras, and lingerie, all tagged, all new, and ever more confusing to her snoopy urge. She finally gives up and falls on the designer *rags* in piles on the bed. Her mind searches desperately to sum up why she has stumbled into a fashion wonderland. Even more strange, fit perfectly for a woman of her proportions. Perhaps this was his and his wife's way of dealing with not having the presence of the child they longed for? But why not fit the size of a young child and not one of a woman?

Maybe it's just a sick compulsion, but an understandable one for a couple who could afford any fantasy in life. Maybe he was preparing for the perfect woman to perfectly slip into his wife's shoes? Or maybe this whole setup is a selfish mindfuck? A prop to lure someone into his miserable dark world to substitute for his miserable dead half? Or maybe this is just unworn hand-me-downs from the queen herself, who could afford anything money could buy; *anything* except life itself. Gwen fires a smoke with a bratty intent to toxic up the fresh linens of the bed and those fresh-cut tulips. She lifts a few of the garments with her bare toes and drops them to the floor below. She then walks over to the perfume bottles to inhale essence in her cakey and clogged nostrils.

She roams her way over to an oak nightstand beside the bed. What lies in one of these two drawers? she wonders. Maybe it's stashed with sapphire diamonds. Sliding the top drawer, her heart pounds, from what sparkles brighter than any cut from Tiffany and holds more power than any lace from Victoria's Secret. For in this top drawer, all by its lonesome self, lies the weapon of power, destruction, and, to her, protection. It's the chromed and shiny magnum force of a .45 caliber. Gwen reaches to the drawer for the weapon.

The wallpaper angels *blend* with the porcelain knickknacks, the hummingbirds match the summertime tulips, and the shoes fit with most of the designer apparel. But now a gun. Why would this lounge in a room of decency? she searches. Its weight indicates the evil toy is *fully* stocked with *killing* lead. She adores the cool steel about her face and even slides it along her thighs. She'd love to stick the barrel in her steamy oven for a kick, but balks at the danger of blowing her precious floral garden to pieces. She smiles and cuddles it to her face, whiffing the toy's shiny steel barrel. Its scent flashes back to the aroma of a lead pencil that reminisces to her last year in the seventh grade. She then places the gun carefully back to its bed. Dipping a finger to her mouth, she kisses her killing pet goodnight "like a good little girl." It's now time for one final activity of the evening. She sprinkles more dust for a bedtime tooting—*before thy little girl lay her precious self to sleep.*

CHAPTER 58

A T 2:00 P.M., IT'S SUNNY OUTDOORS as Gwen makes her way to the kitchen dressed in a black silk robe she snagged from her walk-in boutique. But where to begin searching for her morning coffee is another mystery. She spots a filter and gets lucky on the first of eight canisters that hold some fresh grounds.

After a minute or so, the machine begins perking. She eyes inside the fridge for something to nibble on, but the nicotine tang in her dehydrated mouth tells her to wait till her *java* has finished brewing. She searches for a simple mug that holds *hot* along the wall of cabinets, but strikes out, running into juice glass after tall cool glass. Frantically puffing and slamming cabinets that echo into the front courtyard, she flinches in surprise and embarrassment when Santos barges through the swinging kitchen door. He's dressed impeccably in black pleated trousers, a pressed white shirt, and his trademark brown-leather suspenders snapped tightly over his broad shoulders, as his holster snugs unconcealed to his hips.

Both are startled.

"Oh, excuse me, ma'am," he says, looking away from a thigh that slips her robe.

"Oh, hey," she smiles. "I'm Gwen."

"Oh, hello, Miss Gwen—I'm Santos," he blushes.

"Oh, yeah, Santos! You're one of those guards."

"Oh, no," he frowns, "not me, I'm the *chief* security officer."

"*Ooh*, the chief, hah?" She raises an eyebrow, impressed.

His need, like a little boy to proclaim his manly title reassures Gwen of who's really "chief." *Her*. The spotlight was bright last night, and Gwen's vision spotted his droopy eyes lit in fear, while he barely hung on to his falling trousers.

Who's this softy in my kitchen?

"Do you want some coffee Santos?" she turns away, as his eyes disrobe her.

"Oh, no thank you, maybe not now, Miss Gwen." He motions to be on his way.

"Wait a minute! Where ya' going?" She tugs his holster.

Santos's face turns flush. His eyes roam the ceiling.

"Is that a real gun Santos?"

He looks down, into her eyes, but the moment is smeared by the rude roar of a leaf blower from a passing worker. *He was sure she was going for his zipper next.*

Mary's Persian mopes on by their path.

"What's the matter, Santos? Cat got your tongue?" Gwen smiles. "You know where I can get a mug and some cream?"

Santos moves to the fridge and pulls a half-pint carton that was buried deep and high on the top shelf. He sets it beside her pot of coffee, then reaches to a tall cabinet and pulls a mug down. He still refuses to speak. He just behaves with his hands folded in front of him awaiting the *princess's* next request. He's gone from chief officer trying to have a pleasant Saturday, to serving this sexy stranger, who choke-holds him in 3.2 minutes.

"So, Santos, tell me?" Gwen pours to her cup, "how's the investigation going?"

Santos isn't sure, but believes her to mean the murder investigation. He thinks it over carefully, to buy more spy time to her nipples that perk under her silk robe.

"Oh, I don't know," he makes up anything, "I just watch the grounds and protect Mr. Fable, you know."

Like a smart officer, Santos avoids publicly commenting on the case, which so far has produced less DNA than the semen that leaks inside his bulging trousers.

"Detective Murray," he offers more than he should, "he's in charge of the investigation."

"Oh...I see. Detective Murray. Interesting."

There's an uncomfortable moment of silence. Santos can't keep his eyes off the *wrong* thing. He needs to split fast, before the good Lord slaps his dirty thoughts down. He excuses himself and bolts out through the swinging screen door. Gwen smiles at him. Santos waves and looks for a return wave that causes him to collide with Spark, who almost manages to trip up the 260-something-pound cubby bear.

CHAPTER 59

AT A LITTLE PAST THREE, Darian has finally risen. Downstairs, Gwen now makes her way from the kitchen to start a journey throughout the bottom floor. She snoops a peek at the various rooms just off the long main hallway, carefully not veering *too far off*, in fear she may need a compass to guide her back to the kitchen. She uses the ticking of a grandfather clock in the den as her reference point. She revisits that familiar room with the Sistine Chapel ceiling. She's impressed at the cleanliness and the shiny clean slate on the smoked-glass table she and her *future husband* smudged up last night. *The maids are good, can't wait to meet 'em.* Making her way closer to the tick-tocks, she wins an eerie sense. Her steps are told to pause and "enter" into the cozy den. As she looks into the room, her eyes are met with the force of a freight train.

It's the giant painting staring at her.

Gwen's bullied in closer by this *strange* force.

Suddenly she hears a women's grave voice echoing, "Darian? Ohh, Darian?"

She becomes frightened and takes two steps back, imagining that the voice is calling from its frame.

As she steps back slowly, it continues, "Yoo-hoo! Oh, Darian?"

She listens closely, then compasses her way back quickly, with the help of café vanilla that vaporizes from the kitchen. She reaches her destination and confronts the mysterious voice that was calling.

It's none other than the innocent bullhorn of *Miss Sheila Deblin*. Their eyes meet, the piercing greens of a "bloodshot beast" and the almond eyes of a "junkie princess."

Sheila stares at Gwen, who doesn't flinch. Sheila's face beads with anger to this scantily dressed *stranger,* who must be some cheap one-night stand-in for her deceased girlfriend.

"Excuse me, who're you?" Sheila snaps.

Gwen throws down a sip of vanilla Roca. Her eyes roam top to bottom in blatant disgust at Sheila's pudgy calves, brown eyeliner, and caked-on-powder, that couldn't smooth out the million potholes of her ugly mug if it was steamrolled on by *Mary Kay* herself. *How dare someone who's here to clean out a stable get sassy with me?*

"Ah, excuse me, but who're you?" she raises a hand to her hip.

"None of *your* fucking business that's who!" Sheila holds her stand. "Now where's Darian, little *whoever the fuck you are!*"

Gwen throws in the towel to the cleaning lady with the filthy tongue. She's obviously a somebody, who has now clued Gwen to attempt a decent introduction some other time. Perhaps, *some other lifetime.*

"He's upstairs," Gwen tugs over a lapel of her robe.

Sheila storms from the kitchen with thunderous claps from her cleated flats, proceeding to rumble quickly up the marble stairway. Gwen, barefoot, sneaks and trails behind her, until she hears Darian's bedroom being barged in on. She then sprints to her bedroom on the fourth floor and loiters on the balcony, directly above his. His French doors are open, making it easy for Gwen to eavesdrop.

"What the fuck is going on here!" echoes in the wind, across the courtyard, and halts the garden clippings of Rosa.

"You don't know who the fuck she is!" Sheila's voice carries as clear as the day's sky. "Look at you! You're a wreck!"

Gwen now wonders, *just who is this woman?* The laughter from Santos, who huddles with breaking workers below, indicates this person has carte blanche around here.

It's gotta be a relative, maybe his sister? Can't be. Not cute enough. *She's* uglier than sin. Maybe Faith's relative? *Ditto.* She's gotta be a close friend of his for years, who's showed up to rescue the wrecked superstar. *Warmer.* Whoever it is, Gwen's title a half hour ago as ruling princess has now vanished. Suddenly, she's the underdog in this house of *aliens,* and feels grossly insecure. There's now someone on the grounds with influential power. A power greater than the fire between her thighs that could have melted frail king's sword last night. Suddenly Gwen hears the bedroom door open. Now the tone of the ugly bitch's anger is more overt and to the bottom line.

"I'll be back tomorrow morning, so get yourself together!"

Gwen holds still and spies Sheila's departure from the main doorway to the driveway. Overtones of Santos's voice carry well, but pronounciate weak. Any hope of eavesdropping is quickly ended by the yard's sprinkling system that has triggered on. Sheila hops in her black Lexus and makes a racecar exit to the gates. She's waved off by two guards, who envy her shiny sports car.

Gwen hears her friend gagging from a balcony below. *Who was that little ugly bitch,* loops over and over in her thought. She scampers down to the kitchen. There, she refreshes her coffee mug and, without thinking, sips it *creamless.*

She fires another nicotine stick to help calm her shaky nerves. Looking out from the kitchen's bay window to the plush greens of neighboring hills, Gwen notices the gardeners detailing with pride their clipping, trimming, and wheelbarrowings black-dirt deliveries to the rose garden. Santos, who's suddenly in Gwen's mind, *the traitor*, plays with Spark, who fetches a flying Frisbee in a yard bigger than a public park. Santos had what looked to be friendly gestures with *that angry bitch.* The party may soon be over, Gwen fears.

As Gwen observes this Sunday afternoon, she can't help but envy the lifestyle of a man who has it all—power, fame, and the beckoned call of service and loyalty from anyone he pleases. But although her conscience is shaken, and her destiny now uncertain, her ego is restored when she reminds herself of the one earthly possession fame and power cannot buy.

The poorest clue to his wife's mysterious murder.

CHAPTER 60

WELL, HELLO THERE," DARIAN SAYS, smiling out of no-where making his way into the kitchen. His eyes roam to Gwen's bare feet, as he hustles to a nearby cupboard to retrieve his "cocktail" breakfast mug. Snatching a tall one on his first strike, he stuffs it to the rim with ice cubes from the freezer. He then reaches further beyond the cubes, and like the magician he is, pulls from nowhere a bottle of chilled vodka. It's then onto a swing of the neighboring door below, which houses the Bloody Mary mix. His hair is slicked and shiny from the shower. He reaches for his horn-rimmed reading wear that's held by a nylon chain around his neck, and substitutes it for a barrette to his falling bangs. Gwen notices a physical difference in Darian. His beard is trimmed as closely as a clipping shear could snip. The cross breeze knocks about his scent of tangerine—most likely compliments of his shampoo—and more than a subtle smell of musky talcum powder that overpowers the scent of vanilla. On his black terry cloth bathrobe is an inscription of the tiniest gold letters that sews the initials DF.

His body movements are much too alert and much too calm. He should be dying a slow death in hangover city from the eight or nine rails he

231

shot up his nose last night. Something's not right with his bubbly demeanor. Gwen becomes envious of him.

He's much perkier and more vibrant than those tulips upstairs.

"So how did you sleep last night, my new friend?" he smiles.

"Oh, just fine," she answers to his swirling spoon, which mixes his tomato-and-potato-juice potion on the rocks.

"Ah, nothing like a Bloody Mary to cure the morning blues," he salutes while grinning at the playful yard antics of Santos and Spark.

Gwen's now suspicious. This small talk is just a setup for what she now suspects, after the ugly bitch's visit, to be his "ship-off" sermon to her, but she plays along and fakes a grin or two. She makes her way over to a swivel chair at the table. There's a minute of silence, as Darian stares into the yard in deep thought. He finally breaks it with the barking of Spark, who demands the exhausted Santos keep the Frisbee-tossing. The three foot soldiers look on and belt with laughter over their fatigued boss, who throws in the towel to Darian's 8-year-old *best friend.*

"God I love that dog," Darian turns to Gwen. "So! What do you say we go for a swim and then grab a little something to eat and then, you know, just hang out."

Her eyes squint, but it's not from the rays of sunlight. "Just hang out?"

"Sure! What do you want to do?"

She fiddles with the cellophane from her empty cigarette box. *Fuck the food and fuck the swim,* Gwen wants to find out who that intruder was and get to the bottom of her uncertain fate. Then, maybe she'll play nicely in her friend's castle—like a good little girl.

She hangs her head down. Her crossed leg rocks faster. Darian's waiting on her answer.

"Who was that raging bitch that was here this morning?"

"Wow, *raging bitch,*" his forearm shields his face, "aren't you one with words. That my dear, was my close friend and personal publicist, Sheila, and I do apologize. Let's just say Sheila's not too happy with *Dare* these days," he swallows a gulp. "But, hey, you have to respect someone who made me who I am. I mean without a good publicist, honey, you're nothing in a field of dreamers."

Gwen straightens up from her sluggish sitting.

"Well, I wouldn't know about dreams and fame. I mean, I'm just an average nobody to your *big-wig* Hollywood friends."

"Oh, come on, don't take it personally. Look at the bright side, you didn't have a press badge on. Besides, fame isn't cracked up to be what people think it is. I mean look at me, drinking it up with you, snorting coke, and having a wild night at P. J. Patrick's. *Whoopee*," he rattles the cubes in his glass.

She doesn't smile, causing Darian's to quickly vanish. He looks to the window and surveys more of the afternoon activity.

"I have a confession to make, Gwen," he turns to her in a frown.

Her leg stops fidgeting. Her cellophane-twisting silents. *This* is the *bomb*.

"I'm so unhappy right now, in fact, I'm a fucking wreck. But last night, Gwen, you really, and I mean really, *brought* something to me."

"Really? How's that?" She listens carefully.

"Just by treating me like a normal person. Can you understand that?"

"Yeah, I guess I can," she lies to him.

"Good, 'cause after today, I'm gonna get focused and clean up my act."

"What do you mean clean up your *act*?" She fears the worst.

"Well, under strict orders from Sheila, I've got 24 hours before she kidnaps me away to dry out."

Bingo. He dries out and she ships out. Gwen knew it all along. It's classic manipulation.

"Wait a minute, I mean, what are you trying to say?"

"What I'm trying to say is, your publicist is always right. I mean maybe I should clear my head a little and focus on the investigation of my murdered wife. Don't you agree?"

She stares beyond him into a spacey thought. He reads fear on her face. Her blank expression invites him to share in her regret. The regret of that *fake* love last night. The regret of his promised jetting her back to L.A.

Darian attempts to comfort her boggled brain.

"Hey, don't worry, you're my responsibility, too," he brushes a strand of hair from her forehead.

"Yeah, right," she swats his hand of comfort. "Well at least I didn't screw you, so I'm not completely burned!" She rises.

"Hey, listen to me, Gwen," he follows her stubborn pace in the room. "I do care for you, and as soon as I have some closure, we're going to be *long* together, I'm telling you! Listen to me, I have intuition, I know a feeling when I get one, and right now, I'm getting a feeling about *us*."

"*Us?* Did you forget? I have a pretty face and I've heard that line of bullshit too many times like everyone else from fucking L.A.! But you know what? I'm used to it!"

"Now wait just a minute..."

"No, *you* wait a minute!" She tries to freeze her tongue. "Just," she says, throwing her arms up, "just let me get myself together and leave, okay? Nice meeting you, Mr. Whatever."

Her tone was stubborn and his message was bold, but now Gwen's weakness is silently begging for sympathy from him. Her tongue snapped fast in anger, but now her stride exits the slowest pace. She stops to drop her empty mug to the sink, hoping to pull an ounce of guilt-ridden concern from Darian's heart. Even if they're more false promises, her slow pacing around is all ears. But hope's running thin from the air of silence as she makes a sluggish exit towards the main hallway.

Suddenly, Darian speaks. "What about the play?"

Gwen stops in her tracks. "What play?"

"What play?" he says. "The one-woman play you wrote? Remember? I'd like to hear it."

She folds her arms, as her brow lifts to his smiling eyes.

"Like you really want to hear it. You're just flattering me now, aren't you?"

"No, I'm dead serious. Tonight, in the playhouse. You know I have a playhouse up the path," he points. "Come on, perform for me Gwen. I dare you to."

"Oh you *dare me*?" she breaks a tiny smirk.

"Yeah, I dare you." He adds one.

"Okay, but under one condition."

"*Shoot.*"

"The one condition, that you make the appropriate arrangements for my getaway tomorrow when I awake."

"Getaway?" he looks confused. "Sure, it's a deal, and hell, who knows," he fires up a smoke, "if you really blow me away, maybe you can stay here while I'm gone for... however long."

His words flinch zero hope to her. Any more of *his promises* will mean an emergency call to a groundskeeper equipped with a wheelbarrow and shovel, to dig him out from his bullshit that's now knee-high.

"Oh yeah, sure, I bet Santos and your bitch publicist would just *love me around,*" Gwen tests.

Darian doesn't defend Sheila or acknowledge her bet of wishful thinking. She's bothered once again by his aversion, but he redeems by again inviting her to spend the entire day with him. But she mind-fucks him back.

"Hmm, let's see now. If I've got a one-time showcase for the *greatest ever* tonight, I think I'd better be prepared. That means I go into town for the small props I need. Now wouldn't you agree?" she smirks.

"Well, I've always counted on just a stage," he teases, "but if it means that much to you, go right ahead. The day is yours."

"Really? Whatever I wish?" She extends her needy palm and arches her brow.

Darian knows that womanly twist all too well. She'd like a tiny budget of expense money from the executive producer of *Shake-speare's Cub.*

He heads over to a cupboard drawer below where a phone rests and pulls a platinum credit card from it. He hands it over to her, like the silver spoon she never did find for the sugar she never did miss. He tells her to buy "whatever she needs" for her performance tonight. He doesn't give her a limit, nor does he worry even the slightest. Gwen's eyes almost pop. Not over his lack of concern for her spending limit, but at the inscription of the cardholder's identity that reads, "*Mr. David Faulkner.*"

"Who's David Faulkner?" she asks.

He flips his bangs for a thought. "Come on, Gwen, you don't think I was born with the last name of *Fable,* now do you? I mean everyone in Hollywood changes their name to protect their true identity."

"Oh, really? And just what do *you* have to protect yourself from?"

"Psychos like you."

She is a second from being offended. But in perfect timing he smiles.

"Now go on and take care of your business, I have a few things to discuss with my A-1 security *clowns* out there."

He exits to the yard, while Gwen scratches her fingernail over the inscription of "Mr. David Faulkner."

Psychos like you.

CHAPTER 61

WHILE GWEN'S IN TOWN ROUNDING UP PROPS for her playhouse debut, Darian is lounging in faded Levi's and a white T-shirt big enough to make Santos look thin. His calloused bare feet are tucked back in those blister-causing loafers that hang aloft the sofa's arm. There, he plops in his customary position to begin another daily ritual of the maximum tidbits, in day 93 of what the press has now dubbed *"The Shrouded Butcher of Beverly Hills."* Darian balks to carry on with his Bloody Mary feeding into the late afternoon, opting for Gatorade, to win a pre-game jump on his newfound sobriety that supposedly begins in less than 24 hours some 3,000 miles away. He must keep his head on straight, be courteous, and extra attentive tonight for his playwright "friend," who just may turn out with her driving ambition to be what they call in the biz "a diamond in the rough."

He has a hint of optimism today on the murder investigation, as he puts his operators on full alert to forward through any significant calls to him during this day. When the phone finally does ring around 5:30, it's from his lost friend of three weeks, Mary. Sensing the frustration of her tone after his guilty opening, Darian greenlights her to pack up and return to her neglected garden. Anytime *after* Monday morning. And with those few magic words, Mary cuts him short, before he reneges again on his given word. A second call follows shortly after from his other buddy, Detective Murray. Darian readies himself for full assault on "this drunk who staggers his wife's murder investigation."

"Oh, Darian, my boy!" greets the exalted Murray, "I've got some breaking news on my end here!"

"Shoot!" blasts his boy with a lost patience.

"Easy, Darian, you're going to like this. Alrighty then! We've finally found a match on a print from the Testa crime scene."

The Testa crime scene? Darian baffles a look to the receiver. *Who gives a shit about the pig's murder? What's this to do with my fine and decent dead wife?* There'd better be more. The cold silence on the other end bullies the Irish wise man to unwrap the secret gift he bares.

"Now before you jump on me, I must tell you, Darian, this is *very* much a tie into Faith's death. We found a print. It's a white female. It appears to be a match on a suspect with quite a twisted history, one that we believe ties into *both* murders."

"How?" Darian softens.

"Well, we're not sure about all the specifics yet, but she's on record with a rap sheet from prostitution to grand theft auto, right on into the possession of controlled substances. But more important, and somewhat bizarre you might say, we're leaning toward a normal woman in the higher class of society." Darian now wishes he were four or five Bloody ones into sipping. He'd like to have Murray repeat his confusing and blustered theory in simple layman terms, but he'd probably have to hit pause and rewind the *Sherlock Holmes mystery* he stole it from. Murray goes on.

"You see according to various sources, she's well known quietly in the inner circle of the *sleazy* upper elite. But she also has had ... ahh ... let's see here," he flips pages.

"Come on now, Detective, I haven't got all day."

"Alrighty then, listen! *One!* She's had quite a few visits in and out of several psychiatric wards in the Los Angeles area. *Two!* She's a pro conwoman. Now here's the kicker, *three*. We have her identity confirmed on video. She showed up on Seymore's arm at the Academy Awards and hasn't been seen since his murder. She appears to be normal and sane, but is dangerously not all there, causing myself to believe she's a very dangerous suspect on the loose."

"Well, with all due respect, Detective, it sounds like a hunch on your part. What's the bottom line? Is she going to be found or what?"

"Well, my dear *boy*, that's a small problem right now. You see, although we have a nationwide alert for her, and just released her photo to the press an hour ago, it feels like she may be in flight well out of L.A. and perhaps out of the country. But we do have reason to believe she may just well be in the New York metropolitan area."

"New York? Why would she come to New York?" Darian plays stupid.

"Well, why not, my boy! I mean if all is true, she most likely would like to get her claws into you next! That's why I'm warning you not to panic and just stay put, 'cause I think we may have a good handle on this one."

Darian has an instinct on who this suspect could be, but he wants Murray to hammer down the intuitive gift the actor was *cursed* with.

"Can you give me more specifics on this suspect, Detective, such as a name?"

"Well, the physical ID on her so far is, she's 5'8", early twenties, very attractive, and goes by every alias in the book, from Betty to Tabitha."

"Yeah, but you *do* have a *last name* on Betty or Tabitha, don't you, Detective?"

"Oh no, it's much too soon to let that cat out of *my* bag, lad. You know I'm not able to reveal any more information publicly until further notice; you understand now, don't you?"

The silence on the other end leaves Murray unsure. After all, what's the man who's given so much to a world with his acting and philanthropy going to leak from his castle that could jeopardize the capture of his wife's murderer? Not to mention, Darian's held his faith on Murray's capability after many months of clueless investigation. Surely just a tad of info won't hurt, and is nothing more than just hearsay between *him* and his *boy*.

"Alrighty, now listen," Murray whispers and bends the rules, "between you and me, and the valued extra protection I'm seeking for you, I'll go ahead. She goes by a dozen aliases on her first name, but here's the kicker. We have proof her legal last name is...*Faulkner*."

"Faulkner?" Darian mumbles into the line.

There's a long pause as Murray hones in for more response.

"*Sound familiar?*" Murray thunders.

"No, it doesn't, I mean, Faulkner, could be anyone. I don't have a clue on this one," Darian replies.

"Didn't think so, my boy! Well look then, I'll be arriving in New York early morning, so maybe I'll pay just a friendly visit tomorrow to check on you. Does that sound like a good idea now, Darian?"

"It sounds good, Detective. And hey, one more thing?"

"Go ahead, my boy."

"Thanks for staying on the case. It means a lot to me, *Jonathan*."

"My pleasure, *Darian*," Murray double strokes him back. "Hell, people like you don't have it so normal as most would like to think," he defends his *pride and joy*.

"Well, I'm glad you understand, Jonathan. Now, like they say in Hollywood, sir, you have a nice day."

Betty, Tabitha, drugs, California, and early twenties; Darian stares in a blank trance to the television. He grabs the remote control in his hand and is about to shut off the tube, but something in the *air* forces him not to. From the balcony he views his illustrious grounds and peers at a tip of Shakespeare's Cub, which sits in a distance.

"Faulkner" replays in his brain like a loop. Who is this woman who dares to share an uncommon last name as the greatest? Surely, she's not a close relation, but may possibly be a distant relative or *another* cousin. If his mother bore another, she would have never blessed it with the *bastard's* name she fled from.

The setup.

The dark cloud.

The turning point, and now his natural instinct.

The final resolution of his double-troubled life is all about to come to a closing run tonight. For tonight, he will face the greatest demon that has been locked, stocked, and buried in his unpurified soul since birth.

The performance of a lifetime will now be at another's expense, on *his* home turf. It's showdown between him and that *dark cloud* that's haunted him secretly. The lingering mist that floats to intoxicate any hope of brighter days he's been denied. Despite all the good that's blessed his soul, *evil* that waits to destroy him.

Darian looks to the TV show that's interrupted by a special report. The photo in the upper right-hand corner reiterates what he knew all along, the moment he set his baited trap.

He now confirms that evil *is* alive and roaming the walls of the only living god's kingdom. Darian Fable's kingdom. *The one and fucking only*, according to his bombastic and mulish vanity. Little David Faulkner has now made up his mind.

Tonight, the devil shall speaketh, and the taker shall taketh.

CHAPTER 62

A T 8:38 P.M. THE SUN IS ABSENT, the clouds are restless, and veins of lightning are silently teasing the grayish sky above. A peculiar humidity boldly seeps and swarms about the dusky air.

Gwen blasts the kitchen entrance, determined to sprint through the hallway to her room, but is cut off when face to face with *he* himself, who unexpectedly steps from the study.

"Well, hello there." Darian looks to his watch. "How was your day?"

"It was great," she says. "I just need a little more time to set up in the playhouse. Can you give me an hour?" She looks to her watch.

"Surely. Whatever you need, my dear."

"Good! How do I unload and … where do I go?"

"Just grab a golf cart, load it up. Santos will show you the way. He's already been briefed."

Darian then caresses her cheekbones softly. "You look good today, well rested."

Gwen feels awkward and terribly suspicious. She dissects his expression to a combination of numb and more than a little spacey.

"Are you feeling okay?" she asks.

"I'm fine. I'm looking forward to your performance tonight."

"Good, so am I!" She hopes to win a smile. "I think you'll be impressed."

"I already am." His touch leaves her cheekbones, *and the room*.

She watches his slow walk down the long hall. Time is short. Production is big.

She hurries to unload her Rover of props, to set up for her big *one-night run*.

• • •

A LITTLE OVER AN HOUR LATER, Gwen exits her quarters and scurries a floor down to personally escort her *royal* critic to the playhouse. As she taps softly to his heavy oak door, she is stunned over Darian's kingly attire upon answering. There he stands, boldly, in the infamous crushed-velvet smoking jacket he wore in fear as a boy. It fits to an almost tailored perfection and stuns brightly with the colored coordinates of his black, silky lounge pants. He sports black leather house slippers (minus socks of course), a white ruffled tuxedo shirt (the top button is popped), and a black chiffon silk scarf, which is tied around his neck, like an English pop star in the seventies. The only thing missing from Gwen's quick summary of him is a pipe, a cup of tea, and a mansion filled with Playboy playmates.

The beard on his face has vanished, leaving his complexion to glow smoother than the white satin hanky peeking from his jacket's upper left pocket. His hair is almost a mirrored shine. His mental state is surprisingly sharp, for a man who appeared an hour ago to be minutes away from dreamland.

It's now clear to Gwen (in black, white, and red velvet) what millions of men, women, and *more women* craved, rightfully so—for so many years. For he is, and has the glow, persona, and looks of nothing shy of the legendary superstar he rightfully *was*.

Gwen is overthrown and intimidated by his presence, as he makes a sly, last-minute effort to tighten up to the mirror he blatantly admires himself in.

"Are you ready?" Her eyes meet him in the mirror.

"The question is," he says, turning, "are you?"

He then cordially offers his arm and she accepts. To the downstairs and out the back door to the motored cart, they putt through the forests of flourishing green gardens, over a small, arched wooden bridge, and onto the old barn playhouse that lies a residential block away from the main quarters.

The once silent veins of lightning are now in a fidgety uproar. *Rumble* and *roll* is the theme in the sky but, as luck *should have it,* the downpour that begins without warning pelts in just as they reach the playhouse's creaky entrance.

"Shakespeare's Cub, how ironic," Gwen comments.

"Really? Why?"

"You'll see," she smiles.

• • •

DARIAN IS STUNNED OVER GWEN'S TASTE in art direction. His eyes awe, but they awe in fear, the glowing shrine of candles that burn the scents of apple and licorice, as the flames flicker dangerously close to the thick black-velvet curtain that warms the cold brick walls beyond the stage. At least three dozen of every size candleholders in a circular formation suggests a satanic ritual is about to take place in a town Steven King once called Salem. The owner of the playhouse now has an urge of caution, as he approaches center stage to role-play as fire marshall. He feels greatly concerned over this vigil burning of doom that kindles in the king's precious playhouse. He holds his critique silent, in fear of insulting Gwen's *vision* of *creativity*.

"What's with the candles?" he pleasantly asks.

Gwen's eyes pop at his sarcastic, *fucking nerve.*

"It's part of the concept; don't worry about them; I'm not going to burn your little playhouse down."

"Please," she politely directs, "be seated so *I* may begin."

Obliging to her request, he takes his seat, but she motions him to sit in the throne that controls the screen and movie projector. He doesn't like that seat. It reminds him of something out of that silly movie, *Star Wars,* with all those gadgets and buttons he's *still* not sure how to use.

"So you have film?" he asks.

"Of course! And I have it all set, cued, and ready to roll; thanks to your *boy,* Santos."

Darian looks over Gwen's costume head to toe. Too consumed with his own image, he didn't have time to observe the fashion getup she's flagged in. The long black-silk robe is uninviting to any sultry vision. She's wrapped it well over her shoulders concealing nearly every part of flesh on her succulent front. He zooms into her bare toes, which are polished in black satin to match her long, porcelain fingernails. As she weaves in and out of the burning candles and pushes *that ridiculous recital podium* to center stage, the dark eyeliner under her eyes accentuates her geisha-powdered, pale face with the help of the restless candlelight.

Meanwhile, the downpour of rain has turned to pounding golf balls of hail that slam into the old roof in perfect time to create a rhythm of commotion and turbulence.

Gwen makes her way behind *that* podium and pulls a small bundle of papers. She opens with a calm, cold stare to Darian, in a way, almost *too seriously*.

"Hello, and thank you for coming. This is my one-woman play. It was written, performed, and, in the end, shall be delivered by me *and only me*. Let's call the first act, as they say in showbiz, *a setup*. Mr. *David Faulkner*, I now give you *The Devil of Shakespeare*."

CHAPTER 63

IT WAS A CHILDHOOD FROM HELL; a bitch I hated, and a bastard who burns alongside her in flames," she recites calmly from the podium. "My only memories are the heat from the desert sun in the mornings and scurrying through Broadway lights at night. Flipping my pillow in one motel to another, I would nap with one eye awake, until the stench of mildew suffocated me to sleep. There, I'd be forced to listen to the two of them, conjure up a plan for hours over smokes, to retrieve the losses that forced them into a *countdown of desperation*.

"Then, one September, aside the pool that floated film from the slut's tanning oil, they finally hit their jackpot. It was on my fourteenth birthday, and though *Mom's* claim to fame was over someone I never knew, suddenly I had transformed into a prosperous piece of meat. Not from the dues I had paid as a junior road warrior, picking through seniors' purses at the nickel slots, but how, in her eyes, I had *blossomed* into a jackpot of sexual desire. A desire that would pay big in the city of lust and perversion. I never had candles on a birthday cake or a wipe to my messy face, but now suddenly on this *special* day, all odds were counting on me. A gift for little *Wendy* was on its way. *Just for my little girl.* I remember her words 'as soon as *you fin-*

ish with our friend from Texas,' she snickered, as a cigarette dangled from her smoky grin.

"All I remember about that night was Earl's heavy gold ring that dug about the flesh of my pinned arms. Sweat housed in the flabby rolls of his neck and dripped to his hairy chest while he tossed and flipped me like a rag doll. All I could do was lie and hold on for sixty torturing minutes with the guidance of a wall clock, whose second hand ticked by the hour. Soon, they would recover their losses, and I would recover mine. But only after Earl had his way and I 'learned my fucking lesson,' would we flee to the Promised Land where I'd been told a *prosperous future* would begin.

"Six days later we did arrive in that land of free enterprise. And five days later the bitch that spit me out—croaked. I didn't shed a tear over the rat poison I laced her drink with. I was seasoned and could now beat down any monster that dared to violate my walking hell. The bastard she married soon stopped taking a nightly liking to me. Others in town would ridicule on how this Charlie guy was nothing in comparison to the slut who bore me.

"I wouldn't believe any of those gossipers who smeared my *family* shame on every public urinal of their sinful village. I needed proof of this rumor of shame. Where is this person who fled from me, while I lay fertilized in the womb of a town's whore? Then out of nowhere, a forgotten town *angel* reappeared. She'd left many years before, to escape the ugliness that contaminated every hypocritical home. This woman told me of a message from above that signaled her long-awaited return. She'd vanished without warning many years before regretting the flee from her only child at 2. She had planned to return when he was wise enough to forgive, but stalled her course when learning of her sister-in-law's own. I warned her of the town's hatred and public scorning of me, to which she replied, *no warning is necessary*. Then, it happened. I asked one day if it were true of what the dead bitch and her sickness had dealt me.

"If what were true?' This angel tried to avoid the inevitable.

"She then looked at me. It was a *look* I never again would see in anyone else's eyes since that fateful afternoon.

"She said, 'A mother knows beyond any cloud of darkness, or any time and distance, the eyes of her lost child.'

"Then she bravely admitted. 'Yes, the eyes of my child are sadly living within your soul.'

"And with those haunting words, I couldn't tame my lifelong pursuit. The pursuit to hunt the other half, who, townspeople claimed, *justifiably fled many years ago*. But when I did finally escape westbound to search and destroy my rumor of horror, it was much too late. For he was now untouchable, unavailable, and about as close within my reach as the sky's distance from the bottom of the ocean.

"But I!" Gwen's eyes glow, "*I had a plan*. Then suddenly, on a rainy and fateful morning, this *person* changed course on me, the world, and fled eastbound. His cold and bold move only fueled my determination. And though I was never one to seek revenge, *someone* had to pay. *Anyone*. So I took it out on whomever I believed controlled my search, and his fortune of success. She was a 'good wife,' he would tell, and he was the 'perfect man,' she would sell. So now, if I may, I would like to show a little clip I like to call '*his fine decent wife*.' It's about the wife who dared to separate her perfect man's past from his imperfect half."

Gwen fastens her papers to the podium and steps to center stage. She can sense the hold she has on Darian.

By the balls, as they say, *by the balls*, she now controls the legend in the sweat of her sticky palm.

"Would you please roll tape?" she requests to him. Tears run down his cheeks as he slumps in shock in his chair. He flips any switch from the panel aside his arm. The screen buzzes down and settles just feet above the shrine of burning flames. A projector light shoots from the back wall.

Darian doesn't dare not obey. He just stares straight into Gwen's eyes while fighting back tears from his own.

CHAPTER 64

THROUGH THE ECHO CHAMBER OF THE PLAYHOUSE blare slaps and moans, as the screen focuses to an image of a man and a woman.

The camera, high above in a hidden corner makes it obvious the two subjects involved are in more than just a playful moment in this invasion of privacy.

Darian reaches to his robe for those eye specs. *Interesting,* he sights, it's an *Auntie Judy* production. No dialog, just "oohs," "ohs," and "oh yeahs!" This man's punishing this woman, and she's *loving* it. So what's the point in all this? he wonders.

The camera now zooms to a detailed close-up from its secret shooting angle. The flesh is still slamming away. It appears to be a shapely woman, by her wrapped thighs and panting rib cage. Her toes aim high over the man's brawny shoulders and immense frame.

The male subject still has his shirt on, while the woman, who once sported an evening dress, has it rolled above her waistline just below the mouthful of breasts his lips pin her down with.

The camera now pans from the party's neck, *up.* The lighting suddenly brightens and verifies the identity of the two performers.

Darian whips his bifocals off. His sudden jolt flares a glare from Gwen. "Just hold on!" she warns, "it's almost over."

He stays put like a good *disciple*, as the woman depicted on his movie screen moans in a mountain of ecstasy and groans in a drop or two of remorse.

One day you'll thank me for those movies, one day you'll thank me, Auntie Judy's prediction haunts over and over in Darian's mind.

He now eats his words from childhood. He was dead wrong. *This* acting is more than superb. It's realistic, natural, believable, and to the surprise of this critic, a 10 in performance. The Golden Globe, Blockbuster, People's Choice, and Academy Award belong to Miss Faith Barsolla, for *A Night at Swifty's*. For best performance by a male in a drama, it's none other than Mr. Seymore Testa of Summerville Studios. Gwen howls the loudest belt of laughter. Darian painfully stares on.

"Look at that, Darian Fable!" she says, her eyes lit brighter than any flame in the room. "Your loving wife, getting banged by the king of sleaze! Do you like it?!"

Darian stares at Gwen with hate, and threatens to slip out a side door from her performance.

"Sit down, you fucker!" she screams, reaching to her robe to draw her shiny designer *toy*.

Darian freezes all movement. "Just hold on now, there's no need to use that *gun*, Gwen."

"Get it right! It's *Wendy* you fucker!"

He slowly settles back to his seat.

The clip fades out as the flopping of looped tape snaps the silence of the room. The rain and hail have subsided, but now a fury of tension stampedes the chilly playhouse.

"Don't you fucking move!" she warns with her silver pistol drawn. "You and I have a little something to clear up, *Daddy*."

Darian doesn't blink an eye. Gwen trembles, clutching the pearl handle tightly, and softens her touch to the sensitive trigger.

"Remember the choice you made years ago!" she speaks.

His tongue freezes.

"Answer me!" she cocks the trigger.

His body follows.

"You carved your own fate when you fucked your whore aunt and knocked up my slut mother! All the time you were making movies and winning over your *fucking fans* with your *bitch wife*, I was getting tortured, getting raped, and getting trapped in a world of fucking hell! And now you're gonna pay, you evil *fucking* bastard. Just like your *bitch wife* paid the night I gave her a good lesson on the canyon! And just like that slob paid," she points to the screen, "after the *best* and *last fuck* he ever had!"

Darian remains calm, and rightfully so.

"I don't believe you could have done such a thing," he lies to her.

"What, suck your dick or killed your bitch wife?" Tears trickle down her cheeks. "Well, welcome to Hollywood, Mr. Fable, 'cause I'm here to prove you wrong. There's a lot of catching up you and I should probably do before you suffer and burn, but I don't think I have *the time!*"

Suddenly, she simmers down and begins to smile. The verge of her breaking down completely is moments away and Darian senses it. Now, he should speak. It will keep her distracted and buy him more bargaining time. *Santos, where the fuck are you?* he prays.

"Before I blow your fucking head off, would you like to see under my robe, *Daddy?*" She unties and disrobes to the floor. Stark naked, his eyes lose the barrel of the gun and shoot to the glow of her neck. It's the silver glow that he recognizes well. The missing locket from his dead and *unfaithful* wife. His "picture-perfect face" now suffocates with evil between Gwen's perfect nipples, erect from the damp air and adrenaline.

"Remember your little retirement speech, Daddy? Remember the sad and needy poor child dressed in white, hovering in the pouring rain, under the *sad* oak tree? Well, that was me!" she brags.

He attempts to speak, but she stiffens up her aim.

"Shut the fuck up!" she screams, to which he seals his lips. "It gets better, because once a whore, Daddy, *always* a whore."

She puts her robe back on and moves along the front of the stage, never leaving her sight from him, or her aim.

"You know the old saying, 'looks get you everywhere in Hollywood'... Well guess what? Mine got me anywhere by fucking that *fat pig*. I was able to keep on your trail and follow your every move, while the whole world wondered, 'Where's the *great Darian Fable* today?' I knew you *and* your bitch's *every* move. So let me ask you something, Daddy. Who's the *real* actor in this fucking family?"

"Are you finished yet?" he speaks.

"Shut the fuck up!" she screams.

Santos, he prays.

"Don't give your real name, *Darian!* It might reveal your true identity to some *psycho* like me. Some psycho who'll come back and haunt you. Some psycho, who'll cut your bitch wife into pieces! Some psycho, like your own fucking daughter that sucked you *so good* you little sick fucker! What's the matter; don't you answer your fan mail, Mr. Perfect? Cards, pictures, letters, more fucking letters! Is that any way to treat a fan, *Daddy?*" Tears stream down her cheeks. "Why didn't you come for me you bastard? Why didn't you!" Her feet stamp the stage.

Finally, she breaks down and ignores the direction of her aim, as she sobs to the floor. Darian refuses to storm the stage. Instead, he uses the moment in a peaceful manner.

"I wanted to come and rescue you. In fact, all I ever wanted was to make enough money to raise a family. *A normal family,* like the one *we* never had. But then fame happened, and it happened quickly. My mind and thinking started to *twist.*"

"What do you mean your *mind* started to twist?" she redirects her aim.

"Fame took over my soul. It froze any feelings towards others. I had to give something back to cover for the guilty suffering I endured on my run. But it was all a front. I was too angry inside, so to release the anger, I turned it into a little game. A game to fool the world into thinking I was somebody else. To outact everybody. I wanted to buy everyone into thinking I was on a much higher plane than a common man with a fortunate plan. And guess what? *It worked.* I knew you were out there, *Wendy.* I *saw* you under the oak tree, and I *saw* you in the pouring rain of traffic that morning. I had faith you'd come back to find me. And I kept the faith that once you did, you'd do my dirty work for me. Just like your mother promised before she *rudely* split on me. Just like so many others did ... so many others, like my demanding bitch wife."

Gwen drops her aim and relaxes her grip. "Are you saying you wanted her dead?"

"I'm saying I knew only you, Wendy, could give me the air I needed to breathe; and only you, Wendy, could finally take care of that bitch I married. I never wanted this much fame, but she and the others bullied me into it. Now, I have a little surprise for you."

CHAPTER 65

HE PULLS A BUNDLE OF ENVELOPES from his robe's pocket and tosses it to her feet.

"Open it," he commands.

Unraveling the rubber bands, Gwen holds in her shaky hand a stack of the opened envelopes stuffed with her potent writings. She looks them over and verifies her scriptured pleas of many years. Tightly fastened, in yearly numerical order, they're signed, "love Wendy," "your cousin Wendy," "a friend of Wendy," "Wendy from Pleasant Park," "love, a bitch," and last but not least, "love, your daughter, The Bitch."

The postmarks are even blatantly fresh on a few. Pomona, CA, Pleasant Park, IL, and one, for the record, that reads Inglewood, CA.

Gwen's stunned. "Where did you get these?"

"That's *my* secret. You see Wendy, I not only knew and thought about you for some years, I knew of your presence the minute I set eyes on you."

"What are you saying?"

"I'm saying when we met down the road last night, I knew I had to make up for all our lost time, all the love I had for you, all those years

252

missed from my selfish ambition, were for only you, *my little girl.*"

She clutches her gun, but now ignores any pressure to the sensitive trigger.

"Like I told you last night, *darling*... love is like an apple, that's oh so bittersweet, and guess what? Tonight you've bitten the apple," he begins to laugh. Gwen panics and aims the barrel straight on to him.

Darian senses it's time to perform. *How about Jack? Yeah, that's a good one,* he approaches center stage.

"You see, Gwen, *Wendy*, or whatever the *fuck* you are this week, it doesn't take a normal mind to make it through this little spooky world, it takes a monster's mind to spook this *big* crazy world. Welcome to the family, honey!" he extends his arms.

Her straight and narrow aim, suddenly waivers from fright.

Darian slowly but deliberately makes his way towards her.

Gwen inches little steps further back, and is now surrounded in the circular shrine of flames.

He wiggles his tongue and begs, "Please let me taste you again sweetheart," he licks his lips.

"Get back!" she yells.

He ignores.

"Use the knife, Wendy!" he cheers on, "use the knife, like you used on the *bitch* and Seymore the man! Come on, Wendy, Wenndee!" *He's got Jack down.*

Suddenly, he stops just before his last step boards the stage.

"You're not going to use that gun on *me*—are you, *daughter*?" He holds his hand out.

Gwen calmly whispers, "You're a sick fuck."

Darian spins his body and looks high above to the wooden rafters. He then snaps a look to the rows of burning candles. He bows his head, then pledges it high *beyond* the sky above. He wails in the loudest tone ever known to man, "Do unto others as they have done unto you!" Steam shoots from his windpipes, "Do you know who I am, you little fucking bitch? I'm the greatest of them all, and not even *poor little you* can stop me," he grins.

"Oh, yes I can."

She smiles and blasts five rounds, echoing louder than a cannon's boom on the fourth day of July.

Darian's body flies backwards, and crashes into the gallery of seats beyond the first row. He tries to rise, twitches, then slumps, and comes to a rest. Suddenly alarms fire off to reflections of flashing red lights, passing the glass-paned windows like *ghostly* shadows.

Gwen slips into shock and her body collapses to the stage. She shimmers in tears, while her gun, now rested on the floor, still points conveniently in Darian's direction. Even as he lies lifeless some thirty feet away, she must still beware.

Tears stream her pasty face. She has a moment of regret that passes quicker than those *ghostly* shadows.

Then, Darian's body slowly begins to rise. *Horror* now *rules* reality. He is not yet dead, but why? There's blood everywhere; on his face, robe, hands, and white ruffled shirt.

Gwen jumps to her feet, and *once more*, stiffens her aim. This time for certain, she'll hit him *dead on*.

Darian speaks.

"By the way, if you really *were* my number one fan, you'd know I hate guns, and that toy, my dear, is what we call in showbiz, a 'blank.' Quite a stunt, huh?" he laughs. "Now let me ask you something, honey, who's the real actor in this fucking family?"

And with those words, the playhouse doors kick open to a series of shotgun firing, which pellets Gwen's body backward into the burning candles and beyond. Chit chit, boom boom! Chit chit, boom boom! Load and explode, *reload* and *explode*. Shells, smoke, sparks, and fire, which takes its deepest breath into the velvet curtain—and *blows*.

Santos leads the nonstop massacre on Gwen that sprays from his shotgun. His *fully loaded* shotgun. Flame runs the entire curtain, burning faster than tissue paper. It plunges from its rod above and smothers Gwen's limp, bullet-holed corpse.

Santos and the dozen other guards then hasten the star from the burning barn, as Darian, with much sorrow and pain, sneaks in a last look to his most treasured asset—*Shakespeare's Cub* that now begins its decease.

Any evidence will now dissolve amongst the smoldering that clouds more of this already cloudy night. *Any* reminder of his wife's double life and daughter's lifetime fight will now be nothing more than a melted "dailie" of rumored evidence.

CHAPTER 66

SOME SIX HOURS LATER, FROM THE SKIES of a soggy and foggy morning, Detective Murray finally arrives to join the local investigating team already on the scene.

Darian must explain to him, and most likely the world, why he courageously took on the murderer of his *loving, innocent* wife and that "decent, okay" guy from Summerville. The hero must now act his way out from another circumstance of bizarre reality.

Murray halts the coroners before they load Gwen's crispy bones to the van. He pulls his flask, unpops the cap, and saturates the last few drops onto the plastic body bag.

"Detective," Darian walks quickly over, "what the hell are you doing throwing alcohol on the dead?"

"Alcohol?" Murray grins. "Relax, relax, my boy," he places his hand to Darian's shoulder, "it's holy water. I don't dare sip from these polluted bathings of society."

"Holy water?"

"That's right," Murray winks, "holy water, *David.*"

• • •

So, WHO REALLY IS THE DEVIL OF SHAKESPEARE? Was it his lost and distraught daughter whom he denounced for stardom and fame? Or was it his pushy, overdriven, and overprotective wife, who forced Darian to perform for the hungry masses?

Or was it, in fact, Mr. Fable himself, who fooled a world into believing he was somebody else? Somebody sent from above, on a specific mission for decency and heartfelt family values, in the ugly world of greed-perversion-violence-and-evil.

Or was it you, the reader, who by now we call the *disciple*?

You, who subscribed to the star's "fabled" life, in the picture-perfect flash-bulb world known to all as *celebrity*.

Whatever the case may be, remember the quote on life itself—from the little "nine to fiver" who sucked from his flask of optimism:

"Anything bizarre in this world is either a shocking reality or on its way to becoming another Hollywood script."

So goes the final bow in the life of another Hollywood immortal. The secret life of a man hailed by billions and despised by one. The man whose grim future is now back to normal, with endless sympathy, but false security, over the final capture of his tormented shadow.

They die in threes. The small, little three, who will quickly be forgotten.

But not he.

For he—commands the stage.

He—longs for your affection.

He—is ears for your applause.

For he—is a "Star."

Do you like Darian Fable?